THE ESTATE SALE MURDERS:

DEADMAN'S DIARY

BY

KEN HUDNALL

Omega Press
El Paso, Texas

Other Works by Ken Hudnall

FICTION

<u>Manhattan Conspiracy</u>
Blood On The Apple
Capital Crimes
Angel of Death

<u>The Darkness Series</u>
When Darkness Falls

<u>The Estate Sale Murders:</u>
Deadman's Diary

NON-FICTION

<u>The Occult Connection</u>
UFO's, Secret Societies and Ancient Gods
The Hidden Race

No Safe Haven: Homeland Insecurity

Northwood Conspiracy

<u>Spirits of the Border</u>
The History and Mystery of El Paso Del Norte
The History and Mystery of Fort Bliss, Texas
The History and Mystery of the Rio Grande
The History and Mystery of New Mexico
The History and Mystery of the Lone Star State
The History and Mystery of Arizona
The History and Mystery of Colorado
The History and Mystery of Tombstone, AZ
School Spirits
Military Ghosts
Restless Spirits
Echoes of the Past

The Veterans Practical Primer: Getting Your Benefits

Where No Car Has Gone Before

THE ESTATE SALE MURDERS: DEADMAN'S DIARY

All rights Reserved © 2012 By Ken Hudnall

No part of this books may be reproduced or transmitted in any form or by any means, graphic, electronic, or mechanical, including photocopying, recording, taping, or by any information storage retrieval system, without the written permission of the author.

OMEGA PRESS
An imprint of Omega Communications

For Information Address:

Omega Press
5823 N. Mesa, #839
El Paso, Texas 79912
Or
http://www.kenhudnall.com

FIRST EDITION

Printed in the United States of America

DEDICATION

As with all of my efforts, I must first give thanks to the greatest support any veteran, or writer, can have, my wife Sharon. She has encouraged me every step of the way.

I also wish to thank Georgia and Carl DeKoatz, the King and Queen of estate sales in El Paso, Texas. They gave me a very thorough, and somewhat expensive, education in the wonders of buying unbelievable treasures at Estate Sales and the secrets that can be exposed in the process.

CHAPTER ONE

Mesquite, New Mexico – July 23, 1961

The little sun-baked town of Mesquite, New Mexico was not much more than a wide spot in the road and never had been much of a gathering place. Long time residents used to say that nothing ever happened in Mesquite, except death and taxes and sometimes even the Grime Reaper couldn't find the town. Of course, the tax man never had any trouble.

During the unusually dry summer of 1951, Mesquite boasted a gas station (two pumps), a café, two feed stores, and a small general store. The sleepy little town was so far off the beaten path that the regulars seldom saw anyone new. So when the two attractive women in the fancy convertible stopped at the café, it was cause for a lot of talk and more than a few of the local men found a reason to go to the café to check out the impossibly long legs on the two new females.

Even old Marvin Dapple, the town drunk who always slept under the old wagon sitting behind the general store opened his rheumy eyes at the sound of the strange voices. For a long moment, he thought that one of them was the Virgin Mary that his mother had always told him about when he was a small boy. Both women were well beyond pretty, but one of them almost took his breath away. If the truth were known, it was thoughts of the younger of the two women that gave him wet dreams for several days after that one exciting glimpse of an angel. Another truth was that Marvin Dapple, later that same day from his somewhat hidden position also saw something that he was not supposed to see.

No one who had ever seen her could deny that the younger of the two women, 20-year-old Melanie Daniels, was drop dead gorgeous, with a wealth of dark brown hair framing a heart shaped face. She was tall; her long tanned legs displayed to the fullest by the short shorts and spike heels that she was wearing on this particular day. It was hardly the type of clothing best suited for touring the desert southwest, but Melanie Daniels liked to be the center of attention wherever she went and this outfit was calculated to achieve that goal. She had always used her body to get what she wanted, whether from man or woman.

Completing the picture that started with her well turned ankles her generous chest was barely constrained by the skimpy halter-top that she wore. She had the ends of her blouse fashionably tied beneath her breasts so that her flat stomach was also exposed to the viewing public. So skimpy was her outfit, that actually little, if any, of her physical assets were left to the imagination of the viewer. With the top of the new Rolls Royce Convertible down, she was working on her suntan as they drove. For the last hundred miles she had slept sprawled careless in the passenger seat of the convertible, which in turn was surrounded by long haul trucks. More than one trucker wished he was heading home to something like her. Unfortunately, what was not readily apparent to the casual observer was the fact that she was also spoiled, willful, less than a genius and spoke her mind, whether she knew what she was talking about nor not and sometimes she mouthed off at the wrong time.

The older woman, 39-year-old Dorothy Daniels, was platinum blonde, with a wealth of hair thick shining hair cascading down her shapely back and almost as beautiful as her daughter. It was also readily apparent to anyone who took the time to study the two that the older woman was as sweet and accommodating as her daughter was spoiled. While her own full breasts were somewhat smaller than her daughter's, one male Mesquite resident observed that they were of prime quality. Another commented on another of her physical attributes and it was true that the many years of tennis and horseback riding with her wealthy social set friends had given her a rear and legs that made most men's mouth water. To the men of Mesquite, New Mexico, they were a rare touch of class, something that they had read about or seen in the movies but never thought to see up close.

Just as evident as her physical beauty was the fact that Melanie Daniels was not a happy camper, not at all. More used to expensive restaurants and luxurious surroundings, than the dust and smells of the New Mexico countryside, she found the little café her mother had wanted to stop at to be utterly boring and very provincial. She adjusted her stylish sunglasses for the fifth time in less than ten minutes and glanced over at her mother in exasperation. Dorothy Daniels appeared to be having the time of her life associating with these people so clearly beneath her socially and showed no signs of being ready to get back on the road. She was totally engrossed in inspecting the genuine Indian souvenirs for sale along one wall of the quaint little café that had attracted her attention as they had driven past.

Like any properly brought up young lady of college age, with plenty of money, and doting parents, Melanie expected to always be the center of attention wherever she was and she demanded constant activity to keep her amused. When her mother had suggested that they drive back to New York from Los Angeles rather than fly, Melanie had jumped at the idea, picturing them going from 4 star hotel to 4 star hotel (only because there were no American 5 star hotels in her opinion) as they leisurely traveled across the country. Her idea of roughing it was not having a full time live in maid, so the situation in which she now found herself was totally foreign to her. When she had agreed to this trip, she had had no idea that her mother planned to see the sights so far off of the beaten path so to speak. So, as far as Melanie was concerned, the trip had degenerated into the Road Trip from Hell. Even the excitement of driving the new Rolls Royce convertible that her father had presented to her as a birthday present, with the wind blowing her long auburn hair, had worn off after the fifteenth stop along this dusty, dirty, sorry excuse for a road to look at the wonderful Indian jewelry that so fascinated her mother.

There are few things in this world that are perfect and Melanie, in spite of her beauty was far from perfect. As beautiful a picture as she presented to the world, Melanie was also what one friend had called a first class bitch. She was not used to having to abide by someone else's wishes and her mother's demand to stop at every wide spot in this godforsaken country was driving her up the proverbial wall. Unfortunately, Melanie had long ago learned that she didn't dare oppose her mother since the older woman had total control of her father's money. Making Dorothy mad could have very negative effects on Melanie's plans for the next school year.

At the best of times, her temper was mercurial and now, even though it was only one in the afternoon, Melanie was hot, tired and worst of all, sweaty. In spite of her liberal use of her special $200.00 per ounce perfume, she could actually smell herself, she thought in disgust, and everyone knew that a proper young lady, and especially a Vassar graduate, had the good taste not to sweat. To make matters even worse, the hole in the wall café that her mother had to enter was not even air conditioned, but rather cooled by two ceiling fans that seemed to accomplish little besides moving the heat around; she felt no cool air coming from any direction. She had no idea how her mother was able to appear so calm and cool when she was just dripping in this smothering heat.

Melanie took a deep breath and looked around the cafe, suddenly noticing that two dirty, unshaven men were sitting nearby staring directly at her partially exposed breasts. Normally she loved to be ogled, but only by the "best" people, not by such dirty, sweaty cretins. Why, she bet none of them had been to college, so as far as she was concerned, they were barely human. She frowned her displeasure at the two men as she self-consciously crossed her arms over her breasts and quickly walked over to pull at her mother's arm.

"Mother, please, can't we go?" she whined demandingly. "I am so hot and sweaty that I can't stand it. Can't we go now? I want to get to the hotel before dark."

Dorothy Daniels, looking cool and comfortable in the heat, her own sunglasses perched atop her blonde head, straightened from studying a beautifully hand worked silver and jade belt the silent Indian trader had laid out for her inspection and glanced at her daughter. Her somewhat annoyed, but resigned expression made it obvious that this was a common occurrence with her daughter and not one that Dorothy tolerated easily.

"We'll go in just a few minutes, my dear," she responded as calmly as she could to the agitation she clearly heard in her daughter's voice, "I want to get some of this unbelievable jewelry before we leave. My friends will just die of envy when I wear it."

"But mother," responded the girl between gritted teeth, trying not to pay any attention to the two dirty men that had moved closer to her. "I want to go now!"

Dorothy's normally placid features hardened into a look that Melanie knew well. She had finally pushed her mother too far and it was time to back off.

"If you want to go, my dear," Dorothy responded in a pleasant voice, though her hazel eyes were flashing little lights of anger, "then you can wait in the car while I finish dealing with this gentleman. But I am going to buy some of this jewelry and that is all there is too it!"

Realizing the futility of arguing with her mother, Melanie turned back toward the counter, where the manager was leaning on his brawny arms; his beady eyes never leaving her mother. Steeling herself for what she considered an ordeal, Melanie finally walked over to the counter and cleared her throat.

"Could I have a soda please, with lots of ice?" she asked as pleasantly as she could. She hated it when a man stared at her chest as she tried to talk to him, but the manager made no effort to hide the direction of his stares. She had no doubt that the lout was mentally undressing her. This was so degrading, she thought.

"Why sure thing, missy," the counterman responded, moving slowly to fill her request. His movements were slow and somewhat awkward since his eyes never left her well endowed chest the entire time he was filling her order.

Smiling her thanks, Melanie took the ice-cold soda bottle handed to her and the cup of ice. In spite of herself, as she carefully poured the contents of the bottle into the cup, Melanie shivered, feeling his leering eyes following her every movement. Though her clothing was certainly skimpy by anyone's standards, she felt positively naked under his intense state; it made her skin crawl. Even the sight of him, with his broken, discolored teeth and his unshaven face was repulsive to her.

She couldn't believe this place; it was like something out of a bad movie. There was even a faded poster on the wall behind the cash register urging support for the Ku Klux Klan, sporting the slogan "Native, White, Protestant, Supremacy". The Ku Klux Klan, she snorted to herself, please, it was 1951, not 1921. Everyone knew that really progressive people supported racial equality, as long as the lower classes didn't try to come to the clubs of the better people, she thought to herself. These people were not just the lower classes, they were positively Neanderthals, the type, she was sure, who wanted to club a woman and drag her to bed.

Though her parents didn't know it, Melanie was not a virgin; the Captain of the Duke University Football Team had claimed that honor after the homecoming dance. She was very much aware that every man in the place wanted to pull her down and have sex, but like most well bred young ladies of the era, she personally found sex dirty and sweaty, a chore that a woman performed in return for a life of luxury and ease with the right man. As for her, she planned to have the two required children to please her parents and then tell her husband hands off. She had no idea why sex was the topic on most men's minds, but from what she had seen here, who would want to sleep with any of the filthy inhabitants of this place? She could not imagine what type of women would marry such degenerate looking specimens.

Finally, she heard her mother's voice.

"All right, Melanie," Dorothy called from her place across the room. "If you are ready, I have finished my purchases, so we can go."

Leaving the half filled bottle of soda sitting on the spotted cheesecloth covering the worn table, Melanie crossed the room quickly to join her mother, her long tanned legs the object of every man's gaze. She would be so glad to get out of this one horse town with its filthy, smelly, leering men, she thought as she left the café to cross the dusty parking lot to slide behind the wheel of the new convertible. She was so intent on getting away from that place that she didn't notice it when her bare skin made contact with the sun warmed leather seat. Luckily the shade of a nearby sign had covered most of the driver's side of the car keeping it from being exposed to direct sunlight or she might have been burned by the contact of bare skin with very hot leather. Her mother carefully deposited her new purchases in the back seat before gingerly easing her bare legs onto the hot Cordovan leather of the front seat.

"Watch your speed," cautioned Dorothy as she pulled her sunglasses down over her lovely eyes, "these small town sheriffs like to give tickets to young girls in fancy cars."

"Oh, mother!" responded Melanie in exasperation as she started the engine and shifted into gear. "I am not a young girl, I am a woman and I wish you would stop treating me like a child."

Dorothy leaned her head back and closed her eyes behind her expensive sunglasses so that the sun bathed the smooth skin of her oval shaped face.

"Then quit acting like a spoiled child," she responded with a small smile, unaware that even as they spoke hidden eyes were observing their every move. "When I am shopping is not the time to try and pull me away from something I am interested in buying. I would have thought that by now you, of all people, would know that."

"Ugh," snorted Melanie checking her makeup in the rearview mirror before pulling out of the gravel covered parking lot, "but those filthy men, didn't you see them? They kept looking at me like I was a side of beef at a picnic of starving men; I expected one of them to reach out and try to grab my arm or some other part of my anatomy."

A peal of laughter erupted from Dorothy as her face split with that 1000-watt smile that Melanie's father loved so much about his wife. Melanie might be more physically attractive than her mother, but Dorothy had a spark that could turn men's heads and light up the darkest room like it was noon that Melanie sadly lacked.

"But dear, that's what we both spend all of that money on in beauty parlors and spas. We secretly want men to want to reach out and try to grab some part of our anatomy. It's called being sexy and desirable, my dear. When men quit wanting to reach out and grab some part of your anatomy then you may as well be dead. Enjoy it while you are young, because you will lose it soon enough."

Melanie shivered again; it was hard for her to think that she would one day be old.

"Well, those men back there were just plain revolting," she responded, her eyes back on the road, both hands on the wheel of the expensive machine. "I wouldn't want to have a conversation with one of them, much less hop into bed. Why, I saw the counterman pull a creature from his hair and squash it with his fingers as if it was the most common thing in the world. How gross! And the smell in that place was positively revolting."

At that moment, something struck her painfully behind her right ear. Her foot instinctively moved from gas pedal to the brake pedal as a steady pressure on the back of her heard forced her to lean her upper body forward.

"What is it, Melanie?" asked Dorothy in concern, raising her head to look at her daughter. "What's wrong?"

From the corner of her eye, Melanie could see that a look of shock and fear suddenly appeared on her mother's face. It took Melanie only a moment longer to realize that it had been the barrel of a pistol that had painfully struck her behind the right ear. Suddenly she pictured the back seat as she had seen it when she had jumped so quickly into the car. A Navajo blanket her mother had purchased only that morning had covered the passenger side of the backseat as well as the floorboard, but when they had entered the café, it had been folded neatly on one end of the seat. It was clear that someone had been hiding beneath that blanket when they had gotten back into the car. Now whoever held the pistol to her head applied more pressure, forcing her head further forward.

"Don't worry ladies, I'm just one of those smelly people, inviting you two pretty ladies to a little get together so us smelly people can get to know you better," sneered a rough voice from the back seat.

The voice was silent for a moment, but the pressure of the pistol against the back of Melanie's head never wavered. She was suddenly aware that the man in the back seat was no longer sitting directly behind her. She could smell his bad breath as he leaned forward so that he head was close to hers.

"Now both of you just sit still, drive where I tell you or I will kill this bitch right now!"

Neither woman answered, neither knowing what to say. Melanie trembled as a rough hand suddenly snaked between the seats to cup her right breast. She had the feeling that she would not enjoy what happened next.

CHAPTER TWO

EL PASO, TEXAS SHERIFF'S OFFICE – August 10, 1961

One had to only look at Wilbert Daniels and his three-piece Italian suit, his highly shined Italian shoes and his big gold Rolex Presidential watch to know that he was very wealthy and very used to having his own way. A rich powerful attorney in his own right and the only son of Conrad Daniels the man who either owned or controlled almost every major defense contractor in the country, Wilbert Daniels was not a man to be trifled with. Right now, he was demanding that the Sheriff of El Paso County mobilize every possible man in a search for his missing wife and daughter. Andrew J. Mosley, the current county sheriff was not a man used to being told what to do; in his own sphere he was just as powerful as Wilbert Daniels and the stolen and extorted money he had buried about the county made him also a very wealthy man, though he was not in Daniel's class by a long shot. However, what Daniels had that Mosley did not was national political clout and he was bringing some serious heat to bear on the county officials.

The sheriff was well aware that the Mayor of El Paso had already had a call from the Texas State Governor, personally, as well as both the State and Federal Attorneys General. The Sheriff knew about the calls because as soon as the mayor got off the phone with the Governor, he had called to raise hell with Mosley. To make matters worse, just before Daniels had burst unannounced into his office, the Sheriff himself had been badgered by that god-damn nigger loving J. fucking Edgar Hoover of the high and mighty FBI, demanding to know what was being done to find the Daniels women.

Mosley had assured Hoover, and now Mr. Daniels, that there was no cause for alarm, that the missing pair would most likely turn up and there would be no harm done. It was Mosley's very considered opinion that the two women were hidden away in some out of the way spot having their brains fucked out by some young studs they had met along the road. That's what happened when you have women too much money and a car, the Sheriff thought to himself.

Mosley was sure that he had halfway convinced the Mayor and maybe Hoover, that they were needlessly worried, however, Daniels was not so easily pacified and he was not some local husband that could be browbeaten into silence by Mosley and the power of his badge. Daniels was a very prominent man who demanded answers and had the power to get them.

For his part, Wilbert Daniels was beside himself with worry as he paced the hardwood floor of Sheriff Andy Mosley's office. Sheriff Mosley just sat quietly, puffing calmly on a big $3.00 cigar Daniels had given him earlier and watched his visitor pace. He figured that if he played his cards right, he could easily make himself a pot full of money out of this big northern lawyer to find his wayward wife and daughter. His thoughts were interrupted when Daniels finally stopped his angry pacing and came over to lean over Mosley's desk.

"Sheriff, I want to know what you plan to do to find my wife and my daughter!" the big man demanded. His normally ruddy features were bright red with anger and worry. "So far I have not seen much in the way of activity by your department! Maybe I should call in the Federal Bureau of Investigation if your department is not up to handling this situation. I know J. Edgar Hoover, personally and he'd get results, let me assure you!"

Mosley flushed and looked down to hide his growing anger. The last thing he wanted was for some outside federal people to get involved in this thing. He also knew that he could not afford to lose his temper with a man like Daniels and it grated on him to have to kowtow to mister high and mighty Yankee lawyer in his own office, but money was money and Daniels represented a lot of it. But by all that was holy, he would not have some high and mighty big shot come into his county and tell him what to do. No sir, he would make it clear that Sheriff Andrew J. Mosley was not a man to be trifled with.

"Now, Mr. Daniels," he began after clearing his throat and spitting into the brass spittoon sitting beside his desk. "We don't need no god damn ya---, I mean my department is perfectly capable of finding your women without outside interference. I want you to know that ever since I got your call, I have had both the Sheriff's Reserve and the Sheriff's Posse scouring the countryside looking for your womenfolk. I have also talked with the head of the New Mexico state police and been promised their full cooperation. While we are searching the Texas side of the border, they are also scouring the desert between here and the last place your wife and daughter were seen. All told, there are over 350 fulltime law enforcement personnel and a 150 volunteers looking underneath every rock and behind every cactus between here and Las Cruces, New Mexico. You can rest assured that we will find them."

Mosley paused to puff the cigar and then held it out to study the lit tip.

"Now we do have some progress," he continued. "We managed to find some people who saw that fancy car they were driving cross the state line into Texas and come into this very county. The two women appeared to be fine at that time and operating under their own power, so they were not kidnapped in New Mexico and taken into Texas, but rather, if they were kidnapped, it seems to have happened here in Texas. So, as I see it, that FBI feller has no legal right to get involved in what happens in my county unless it can be established that your wife and daughter were taken back into New Mexico or into Mexico, which we ain't been able to establish."

No siree, thought Mosley to himself, we don't want that Hoover feller involved in this. Hoover was a glory hog and would not let this thing go, especially when you post that big reward that you mentioned to the Governor, yesterday, thought Mosley to himself. He could almost feel that money burning a hole in his pocket right now. He just had to play this big fish like the skillful angler he was until that reward reached as high as it could go. This could be the big payoff that would get him that big ranch he had always wanted and a very satisfying retirement.

A SMALL ADOBE HOUSE OUTSIDE ANTHONY, TEXAS

The town of Anthony sits exactly on the line between the states of New Mexico and Texas. Therefore, there is an Anthony, New Mexico and an Anthony, Texas. Though neither community is very big, and both are far from the two closest major towns, Las Cruces in New Mexico and El Paso in Texas. Most of the families in the surround area are subsistence farmers. One such farm belongs to Cletus Brownlee.

On particular day, Cletus Brownlee was a man in the throes of the most exciting event that had ever happened to him. Cletus was not an overly intelligent man and he was not much bigger than most fifteen year olds in the county, though he was in his mid thirties. He had always barely subsisted, making do on the wages he earned from odd jobs at the various neighboring farms around the county and what little he could grow on the worn out land left him by his father.

In fact, no matter how hard he tried, about all the farm left to him by his daddy was able to grow was an annual crop of tumbleweeds. Now he had a once in a lifetime chance to make some real money. All he had to do was wait and make sure that those two fancy women did not get away from him. He knew that his friend would handle the hard part for him, getting all of that beautiful money.

On this day, Cletus was sitting at his kitchen table, staring out at the desert, though he was actually reliving the last few hours. Finally, unable to contain his excitement, Cletus got to his feet and walked through the house to the trap door that concealed the entrance to the root cellar located on the screened back porch of his home. Moving the big water barrel that he kept sitting on top of the trap door, Cletus carefully descended the steps into a dark, dank hole in the ground perhaps fifteen feet long and a dozen or so feet wide. Normally a place for the storing of junk and those perishables that needed to be kept somewhat cool, the pit was now cleaned out and furnished with two iron beds.

Over the years he, and his daddy before him, had used the cellar for a number of uses, some legal and many illegal. It had been a family tradition to keep the very existence of that cellar a secret from everyone else. While he had never questioned his daddy's rule, he could see how, especially now, important secrets could be, thought Cletus to himself, since tied spread-eagled on each of the rickety beds was a blindfolded, gagged, naked female. He had been the one hiding in the back of that fancy car and he was the one that now held the two Daniels women prisoner. Melanie Daniels never had gotten to that four star hotel where she had been planning to spend the night almost two weeks before.

Most people thought that Cletus was not smart enough to do anything complicated, but he had shown them. He kept replaying in his mind, over and over how he had climbed into the back seat of that fancy car of theirs and hidden himself beneath that scratchy old Indian rug on the back seat while they were in the cafe. With his small size, it had not been hard for him to conceal himself behind the front seats. He had been afraid that one of them would spot him hiding under that rug, but other than throwing their new purchases onto the seat, neither of them had paid any attention to the rear of the car.

It hadn't been his idea to kidnap the two women, of course, for Cletus had rarely had an original idea in his life. It had been his new friend who had suggested the plan, but once it had been suggested, he had thought it was a great idea. Though Cletus never had known how his new friend had known that the two women would be coming along when they did, the time schedule that had been furnished to Cletus had not been more than an hour off on the estimate of the time the two women would be at the café. Then later, as his friend had told him would happen, when he had stuck the gun in the back of the girl's head and threatened to blow her head off, he had gotten total cooperation from both women.

All his life, women had shunned Cletus due to his odd appearance and his small stature, so it was a great boost to his ego to have two such beautiful women obeying his every command. The fact they were obeying him only due to their fear of the gun he held in one grubby paw made it no less a turn on to a man who had very little experience with women. He trembled at the thoughts of the things he planned to do to them.

With the blindfolds and the gags, he couldn't tell at first if they were awake or asleep when he lit the lantern hanging from the ceiling. Actually, he really didn't care what their condition was, he just liked to stand over them and look at their naked bodies; he found just looking at their bound bodies to be so exciting that he had even come in his pants once or twice. At first they had struggled when they had heard him moving around the cellar, but now they just lay quietly.

On this visit, he finally got up the nerve to gingerly sit on the edge of the younger woman's bed and timidly run one hand up her smooth, tanned belly to cup one of her full breasts, the nipple already turgid in the slightly cool air of the cellar. She reacted as she did in the car, by making muffled protests and trying to pull away from him. However, she was tied so tightly to the old bed that she could barely move. Cletus just squeezed that full breast until she finally subsided with painful moans.

Knowing that there was nothing she could do to stop him, Cletus then tightened his grip in the breast, leaned forward, and gently licked the nipple with his tongue. She stiffened as if he had stuck her with a needle and made muffled sounds into her gag as she tried to pull away from him attentions. Finally, he closed his lips around the nipple and began to suckle like a baby. He was lost in bliss. He had always dreamed of doing this to a real live woman and now he had one that couldn't say no.

The young one, Melanie he had heard her called, was the one that had made the most fuss when he had first gotten them into the cellar and ordered the two women to strip naked. There was some argument, but finally, after he had been forced to slap the younger one, both of them had finally undressed. For a long time he had forced them to just stand in the lantern light so that he could look at them. Both had tried to keep one arm covering their breasts from his eyes while the other hand covered their privates. He finally made them put there hands behind their heads so that he could get a good look at their titties.

He had been somewhat concerned about being able to tie the two of them up at the same time. He had been afraid that one would try to run while his attention was on the other. He had finally solved this problem by having the younger one tie up the older woman. Then, when she least suspected it, he had shoved a rag soaked with ether over the mouth and nose of the younger one. She had struggled like a wildcat, before finally sagging against him.

It took some doing, but he had finally gotten the unconscious woman onto the bed and tied spread eagled to the frame. Partially to be on the safe side and partially because it turned him on, he then used the ether soaked rag to subdue the older woman. It only took him a minute to tie the older woman flat on her back like her daughter. However, just touching their skin had so excited him that Cletus decided that he had to have one of them.

He decided to take the young one first. Untying her, Cletus pulled the unresisting young woman back to her feet and manhandled her over to the wooden table by the stairs. After years of sexual fantasies that he could never hope to realize, he now had to chance to do everything he had ever dreamed to a woman. Though she was very groggy from the ether, Melanie had made angry sounds when he had first grabbed her, but then she had gone into hysterics when he had pushed her face down over the table and penetrated her from the rear that first time. Dominating such a beautiful woman had taken him to heights of passion that he had never reached or even dreamed of before.

Yeah, he thought, the young one was not cooperative at all, not like the older one; that one had taken everything he had done to her in stride, even cooperating with him fully. After he satisfied himself with the younger woman's anus, he had cuffed her up side of her head twice for struggling before pulling her back to the bed and tying her tightly on her back. Then he untied the older one and pulled her unresisting body over to the table. To his surprise, she had bent over the table without being asked. She also did not resist when he slid into her rear. To his surprise, it was even better with her than it had been with the young one.

He had a hard time understanding the young one, though he was himself almost a virgin, he was certain that he had done everything right, but for some reason she had not liked it when he had taken her, he wasn't really sure why. Cletus had little actual experience with woman and from what he had heard at the local beer joint and read in those magazines that most stores keep under the counter, he thought all women liked sex all of the time. He was also sure that he was a great lover, at least that's what Mesquite's only prostitute had told him on the few times he had the money and the nerve to go see her. With so little experience with females, he was about to believe that he really didn't understand them at all.

Cletus enjoyed his newfound feeling of power over these beautiful, rich women. He knew that if he had had the nerve to do something like what he had done to them last night to a woman of their quality outside the cellar, she would have had him horsewhipped. Even as inexperienced with women as he was, he knew that if he grabbed a woman's titty on the street the least she would have done is slapped him silly for daring to even touch her. But here, the haughty young woman's tightly bound wrists made resistance impossible. In this cellar, he was the king. He could quite literally do anything he wanted to do to either of these women, he thought, as his eyes drank in Melanie's naked beauty as a thirsty man drank water.

Gaining a little courage, but still keeping the one breast with its damp nipple cupped tightly in his right hand, he slowly ran his left hand down her belly to the full bush of auburn hair between her wide spread legs. One of his questing fingers unexpectedly found a furrow beneath the tangled hair and his dirty fingertip slid slowly into a very moist area. He was totally shocked when the girl gave out a low sensual moan, her legs went rigid and her stomach muscles tightened. He couldn't tell if he had hurt her or she liked it, so he kept his finger in the moist spot and began to slowly move it in and out. To his surprise and pleasure, after a few moments, the bound young woman began to move her hips up and down, slowly, in time to his finger movements and her breathing rhythm changed sharply. He felt that he had made a major discovery. When he had first fucked her after making them strip, she had not acted this way at all. He was puzzled about the change.

What other discoveries Cletus might have made that afternoon were brought to a sudden stop when he heard a sharp whistle from outside the cellar entrance. Someone had entered his house and it just would not do for that someone to find him here with these two women. Regretfully removing his finger from between Melanie's widely separated thighs, his withdrawal eliciting a protesting moan from the bound young woman. Cletus wiped his hands on his pants, glanced at the older woman to make sure that she was not getting loose and quickly went up the steps to the house. Silently, he eased the trap door leading to the cellar back into place and moved the water barrel back to its original place.

As he came cautiously into the small living room, he relaxed when he saw that his visitor was his new friend. He had hoped that his friend would come by so that he could brag about how successful he had been in kidnapping the two women. Once people knew that he, Cletus Brownlee had pulled off what the papers was calling the kidnapping of the decade, people would quit thinking he was stupid and fit only for the lowest paying jobs. Cletus knew that he was smart and wanted others to know it.

"I'm glad you came by," he burst out before his friend could say anything. "I got them, just like we talked about, I got both of them. They is gorgeous; I stripped both of them stark naked just like we said I could. I made love to both of them, more than once. God, it was just wonderful!"

His friend nodded and favored Cletus with a small smile.

"Any problems?" his friend asked softly, as if afraid someone would overhear them. "Did anyone see you kidnap them?"

"None," answered Cletus, who then paused, as a thought struck him. His hesitation was only momentary, but his friend immediately picked up on it. Cletus had been certain that his friend was smart enough to know that he had encountered a small problem. It was really nothing to worry about, but it was still unexpected.

"Tell me Cletus," his friend urged quietly. "Tell me what the problem was that you ran into."

"Well," Cletus finally said, reluctantly, "I think that someone may have seen me get into the back of their car. I'm not sure, but it is possible."

"Who?" demanded his friend, anger tinting the soft voice for the first time, "We had everything perfectly planned; so who was it, Cletus?"

"Uh, well, I looked all around just like you told me to, but I couldn't see him under that damn wagon. No one could have seen him," defended Cletus, not wanting his friend to get angry. "It was just an accident and I really ain't sure that he saw anything, but he could have."

"Cletus," warned his friend, taking a step forward. "I won't ask again, who do you think saw you hide in the back of the car?"

"It was old Marvin Dapple, I think he may have seen me," finally confessed Cletus shamefacedly, his head down, knowing he had disappointed his new friend. "That old drunk was sleeping under the wagon across the road from the café. I think I saw him rise up and look straight at me as I slipped into the back of that fancy car, but I ain't sure."

Cletus fell silent for a moment, but he wanted his friend to understand that there had been nothing he could have done about it.

"I would of taken care of that old drunk right then and there, but I heard them two coming afore I could get back out and take care of that old man," he explained hurriedly. "And I didn't know how to get in touch with you, so I waited to see if you thought we should do something about Dapple or just let it go."

His friend realized that Cletus was upset by the thought that he might have made a mistake and hastened to make amends. The last thing needed now was for Cletus to get cold feet about their little venture or to have a temper fit and either let the two captives go or tell someone what he had done. Laying a gloved hand on Cletus's skinny shoulder made the chastened man wiggle something like a puppy wanting attention. Cletus had few friends in this world and didn't want to make one mad, especially this one.

"No, there's no reason for you to worry about one old drunk. You did very well, Cletus," responded his friend, releasing the shoulder and laying a comradely arm across Cletus's narrow shoulders. "Don't worry! I'll deal with Old Dapple. You just think about enjoying your two pretty guests and all of that money we'll get from old man Daniels for their safe return. Think of all of the things that you can do with all of that money."

"Man, I can't wait," moaned Cletus, rubbing his hands together in excitement, almost sexually excited at the thought of having more money than he could spending a life time. "We'll have a new life before you know it. A new life far from this godforsaken border town, I can't wait. Jesus, I can't wait."

"Where did you put their car?" asked his friend casually. "Did you put it where no one would find it?"

"I hid it up at the old cave on Mount Franklin where my day used to make his bootleg likker," responded Cletus proudly. "Don't nobody ever go up there any more, so I drove that fancy car right into the cave and then covered up the entrance. Ain't nobody gonna find that car until it rusts into dust."

"Anyone see you driving that car?" demanded his friend with narrowed eyes. "If anyone did, that could really cause a problem."

Cletus emphatically shook his shaggy head. "No sirree, I made damn sure no one saw me. I took only back roads until I got them two here and I drove up to the cave in the middle of the night with my old bicycle in the back seat. Then after I covered the cave, I peddled my way back here. I am positive no one saw me hide that car."

"Did you bring the things from the car that I told you to bring?"

Cletus nodded so emphatically that his friend thought his head would fall off.

"I sure did, just like you told me," gushed Cletus, glad to be able to talk about something he had done just as he had been told to do.

"The car keys, the registration card, their suitcases and some fancy Indian jewelry the older woman bought at the café in Mesquite are on the table at the bottom of the cellar steps."

Slowly, his friend led him toward the back door of the little house.

"Tell me about this cellar of your, Cletus," asked his friend curiously. "I know that you told me that it was a secret, but how can you be sure that the search parties won't find it and let those two women out? You do know that what you did was against the law and that if they get out and tell anyone that you would be arrested and sent to prison before we got the money. Then we would not be able to start that new life."

This was solid ground to Cletus and he hastened to reassure his friend.

"Don't nobody know about this cellar but you and me," he said enthusiastically, leading the way toward the porch. "My daddy dug it all by hisself about thirty years ago when he started to smuggle illegal likker and wetbacks across the border. He would hide both the likker and the wetbacks here until he could take them north. This place was never found by the law or anyone else for that matter. Now that he's dead and buried, nobody knows this old cellar even exists but you and me."

Reaching the sheltered porch, Cletus led to way over to the barrel and manhandled it aside. He pulled the trap door open and descended the rough hewed steps. At the bottom, he relit the lantern and turned toward his friend who had stopped on the bottom step. His mouth fell open and his eyes bugged out to see that his friend held a pistol like soldiers used in one gloved hand. Cletus opened his mouth to asked why his friend was holding the pistol, since they had agreed that the two women couldn't be hurt if they were going to collect any ransom for the two, but before he could utter a word his friend assumed a two hand stance and pulled the trigger twice, both bullets hit Cletus in his chest.

The shock and pain of the .45 caliber slugs hitting him was so great that he never heard the boom the big gun made. The force of the bullets hitting actually knocked the little man several feet backward, but he stayed on his feet. Slowly, like an inflatable doll with an air leak, the little man slowly folded to his knees and then fell face down on the dirt floor of the cellar. The hydrostatic shock of the bullets hitting his body had ensured that Brownlee was dead, but for him to stay on his feet was enough to momentary spook the killer, nonetheless.

The sound of the large caliber weapon being fired in such a confined space sounded like a cannon had gone off in that cellar. Unable to see what had happened and already terrified after having been kidnapped and raped repeatedly, the two women went into muffled hysterics while the killer reacted as if hit in the head. The killer had not anticipated the pain to the ears caused by firing a large caliber gun in that small cellar. Clapping both hands over ringing ears, the killer staggered back up the rough wooden steps to the fresh air above. It was several minutes before the after effects the two gun shots had lessened enough for any of the three people that had been in the cellar to able to hear anything. The first thing the killer was able to hear were both of the women sobbing in fear from the cellar below.

Ignoring the prisoners for a moment, the killer walked off the back porch and around the house to stare at the distant road to make sure that no one had heard the two shots and decided to investigate. Luckily, random gunshots, if anyone outside the enclosed cellar had even heard them, were relatively common on the Texas prairie. Someone was always either having a little target practice or shooting at coyotes. The killer waited several long minutes before being reassured that no one had paid the slightest attention to the sounds.

Once assured that no one outside had heard the shots, the good friend of the late Cletus Brownlee pulled the trap door shut and descended the steps once more. Stopping at the table, the killer pocketed the smaller of the items Brownlee had mentioned bringing back to the cellar. They would be important to the overall plan, the killer thought.

Walking over to stand over the two women, who were straining to escape from their bonds, the silent figure studied them for some time. Naturally, having heard the shots and the sound of a body falling on the packed earth floor each thought that the other had been injured. Their panicked struggles to free themselves were so violent that they actually moved the iron bed frames, to which they were tightly tied, several inches from the original position, but Cletus had tied them too tightly; they were helpless to actually escape.

Finally the killer removed the long topcoat and tossed it carelessly aside, the .45 followed a few seconds later, but the gloves were retained. There was always the possibility that if they were found, authorities could get fingerprints from something that the killer carelessly touched. It would ruin everything if the identity of the killer were discovered, so even though the need to wear the gloves limited the planned activities, the killer was forced to continue to wear the tight leather driving gloves.

Leaning over Dorothy Daniels' helpless body, the killer threw one leg over her spread-eagled form and sat down on her pelvis. The killer felt the woman tense, clearly expecting more sexual abuse. Sex had been the last thing on the killer's mind and was very much surprised to find that the just as Cletus had indicated, the sight of the helpless women was a massive sexual turn on. In fact, the sight of the two helpless women recalled to the killer's mind those nights watching the two walking around their home in filmy nightgowns, their charms exposed as if they had been naked. Unfortunately, at that time, the Daniels women had the upper hand, so taking them was impossible, but now, it was almost expected.

Anyone watching would have understood that the flaring nostrils, rapid breathing, and continual moistening of lips were clear signs that the killer was in a highly excited state. Leaning forward the killer began to rub the gloved hands over Dorothy's taunt belly slowly and sensually, working up toward the prisoner's proud breasts. Believing that it was still that disgusting little man touching her, Dorothy was determined not to let her tormentor know how disgusting she found what was being done to her. She had cooperated with the little man, but only in the hopes that he would not hurt them and that they could eventually get free. She continued to endure everything silently.

Finally, the killer reached out with both gloved hands and suddenly grabbed Dorothy's full left breast, squeezing it tightly until the nipple, already turgid in the cool air of the cellar stood up proud and tall. Leaning forward, the killer took the firm nipple between strong white teeth and began to nurse like a baby at a bottle. Dorothy instinctively tried to pull away, but knew that it was hopeless to struggle; she was tied so tightly that she was barely able to move a muscle. She finally went limp and let her attacker ravish her helpless body; only her soft muffled sobs gave any indication of her state of mind. Finally, the killer finished enjoying Dorothy and rolled off of her helpless, naked body to stand swaying beside the bed.

If there was only more time, the killer thought with regret, this woman was a keeper, she was so highly sexed that her body responded almost of its own accord. Of course, from a practical standpoint, if Dorothy were ever found, she would be returned to old man Daniels, which was out of the question. There was the possibility that this one could be beaten into submission and she would become very obedient; the killer could think of many things that could be done with and to a woman so submissive. But the killer knew that sadly, it was only a dream; certainly there was no way that the killer could allow her to live.

With a sigh of regret, the killer turned from Dorothy and walked slowly over to the discarded coat. Leaning down, the killer pulled a long thick object wrapped in a cloth from the right pocket of the discarded topcoat. Slowly unwrapping and examining the object closely, the killer walked back to stand directly under the hissing lantern to confirm how to use the object held up to the light. The greasy coating of Vaseline covering the object glistened in the dim light. Just holding the cigar shaped item caused a thrill of sexual desire to run through the killer. From past experience, understanding how to use the item, the killer leaned back over Dorothy's helpless body and slowly ran the device up and down the soft skin of her belly.

"I wouldn't want you to get bored while you daughter and I past the time renewing our acquaintance," rasped the killer in a low throaty whisper, "so I brought you a present that I understand that you rich bitches like to use. In this part of the country, it was very hard to find something like this, but nothing but the best for you, heh, bitch. This should keep you occupied and out of the way while your daughter and I have some fun."

While talking the killer had continued to run the device gently up and down Dorothy's taut stomach, but suddenly, with a single twisting thrust, the killer thrust the thick, Vaseline covered, dildo deeply into Dorothy's unprotected and somewhat moist vagina. Seeing the state of her sexual organ, the killer mused that Dorothy was a little excited in spite of herself. Stunned by the unexpected penetration of her most sensitive area by something as thick and hard as the unyielding dildo, Dorothy reacted as if she had received an electric shock. In reaction, every muscle in her delectable body went taut, actually lifting her entire body slightly off the dingy bed as she tried with all of her might to force the foreign object out of her with her superb muscle control.

Unfortunately for Dorothy, the killer had prepared for this possibility; attached to the dildo was a slim leather harness that was quickly, though somewhat clumsily, pulled up and fastened around the slim waist of Dorothy Daniels, keeping the dildo firmly in place. Assured that the captive would not be able to expel the device, the killer pressed a button on the top of the device and a low intense hum that filled the little room. The thick dildo was also a powerful little vibrator.

When the rapid vibration begin Dorothy went wild, raising her rear completely off of the bed and violently bucking her hips to expel the device that was thoroughly violating her until she finally realized that it was a futile effort. By that time, the effect on her sexual organs of the vibrating artificial length that filled her like her husband never had, was forcing her closer and closer to an earth shattering orgasm she definitely did not want to have. Finally, wildly turning her head, the only part of her body not tied in such as way as to be motionless, Dorothy could contain herself no longer and with a scream that even the gag between her puffy red lips could not muffle, she gave into a sexual orgasm that lasted for several minutes before she went completely limp and actually passed out.

Laughing loudly at the woman's antics, the killer reached down between Dorothy's widely spread, sweat coated legs and turned the humming vibrator to an even higher speed. The only reaction from the unconscious woman was a low moan and a slow movement of her slim hips. Even unconscious, her sex drive had a mind of its own. Satisfied that Dorothy would not pay any attention to anything else, the killer now stepped over to the daughter's bed.

"How does it feel, Melanie to know that your mother likes to take it from an electric dildo? Did you hear the scream, my dear, as she got off on her new toy? Is she that big a slut that she gets off on even an electric dildo? I know that you both have one at home and the one your mother is enjoying is just like the one she has in her bedside table. Is that what you rich bitches are taught?" the killer mocked the younger woman without taking two deep blue eyes off of Dorothy's slowly writhing body. "Do you like a dildo better than a man's penis?"

Even as the killer watched, the slow movement of the bound woman's hips was quickening as the vibrator brought her unconscious body closer and closer to another massive orgasm. Leaning down, the killer's pink tongue began to gently lick one of Melanie's delicate ears.

Melanie struggled to pull her head away, but the killer ended this resistance by tightly grabbing one of the young woman's full breasts and twisting.

"Is it true that everything is better with electricity? Has technology replaced the need for a man?" The killer paused to taut the captive again. "I guess like mother like daughter, huh, Melanie. You are a slut daughter of an even bigger slut mother!"

Even in the dim light of the lantern, the killer's hate filled eyes could see that Dorothy's slim, muscular, tanned thighs were covered with a glistening sheen of both sweat and her own juices. The first orgasm must have been tremendous, thought the killer enviously, to knock her out like that. This would have to be the ultimate degradation for a rich powerful woman such as Dorothy Daniels, thought the killer viciously, to have absolutely no control over even her own body and to be forced to come at the whim of another. Many afternoons at the tennis court, the killer had watched Dorothy flounce around in her revealing tennis outfit, dreaming about getting between those shapely legs. Now the dream had become a reality.

Now to complete the revenge, thought the killer gleefully, by dealing with the real culprit: the arrogant daughter, the whore who had had the nerve to humiliate and reject the killer's advances.

Chuckling, the killer walked over to the discarded coat to retrieve another wrapped dildo before returning to sit down on the edge of Melanie's bed. Slowly, the killer ran one gloved hand over the helpless woman's trembling body. Being blindfolded, Melanie was unable to see what had happened to her mother, but whatever it was, she was afraid she was in for even worse. There was no doubt that someone had just been shot, maybe she would be next. Being unable to see was the worst torture of all, Melanie thought to herself. If she could see, she could prepare herself for whatever was to come.

"If you hadn't been such a spoiled bitch, I could have given you pleasures every night, just like your mother is enjoying," soothed the killer in a low melodious voice. "But no, you rejected my advances, you had to be a vicious, spoiled bitch and reject me, humiliate me, and ruin everything. I had everything planned, we would have been happy together, but you had to be a snot nosed bitch. Now you will pay."

Melanie froze at the killer's words; suddenly it was all clear to her. They person that they had been kidnapped by was someone she knew. Her mind raced as she tried to place the voice. There was only one person she knew that lived in this part of the country but surely he wouldn't ----- but, she suddenly remembered what she had done, he had asked her to marry him and she had in fact rejected him, publicly. In fact, she had taken great enjoyment out of embarrassing him in front of his friends and she knew that he was a proud young man from a very wealthy family.

At first, she had been thrilled when he had asked her to marry him, but her friends had pointed out that he was from a backward part of the country and just didn't fit in with the right people. In spite of a certain animal attraction she felt for the man and being somewhat insecure, she didn't want anyone in her social circle to think badly of her so she loudly rejected him in the most insulting terms she could think of, in front of her entire social circle. They had all laughed at him until he had left, his face flushed with embarrassment and anger. She had certainly been a first class bitch, she thought to herself, but she had never dreamed he would take his anger out at her in this fashion.

Straining against the wad of cloth filling her generous mouth, Melanie tried to speak, to tell the killer that she was sorry. To tell him that if he would let her go that she would be good to him, she would change her mind and marry him. But he was paying no attention to her efforts to talk. The situation had gone far beyond a simple I am sorry, she realized. The situation had, in fact, turned murderous.

"There, there my dear," the killer's soft voice came from only inches from her ear, so close the breath whistled in her ear. Melanie's mind was racing, something was wrong, the voice sounded familiar, but it did not fit the voice that she remembered from her rejected suitor.

"Don't fret, because there is nothing you can do to make it up to me," whispered the killer hoarsely. "You rejected me, publicly humiliated me, but you should have known that no one rejects me. You thought you were better than me and my family didn't you. But now who has the upper hand?"

Melanie was distracted by the feeling of something slick and slimy sliding beneath her ass. Again she tried to pull away, her anus still sore from were the kidnapper had penetrated her earlier. She tightened her buttocks in response to the probing, but in spite of her best efforts, she felt the slimy thing slide slowly into her already irritated anus. Realizing that she would not be able to stop whatever her captor planned, Melanie finally relaxed and laid back. She was hardly surprised when whatever filled her began to vibrate.

At that moment, Dorothy Daniels gave out with a loud moan and began to rapidly move her hips once again, her sex drive kicked into overdrive in response to the maddening vibrator. The thought of the haughty Dorothy Daniels being serviced by a battery operated vibrator sent the killer into peals of delighted laughter. It was absolutely amazing, but even semi-conscious, the older woman was responding to the power of the vibrator in such a fashion. For a moment, the killer paused to wonder which would give out first, the woman or the batteries. It was a pity that question would never be answered.

"Can you move your hips like your mamma's, my dear?" asked the killer mockingly, beginning to move the vibrating dildo slowly in and out of Melanie's anus while tightening one hand on a full breast and squeezing until Melanie moaned in a combination of pleasure and pain. Unable to resist the temptation, the killer leaned forward and the caught the captured nipple between two rows of strong white teeth and bit gently, causing Melanie to scream in pain. At the same time the killer pushed the vibrator completely into the now slick rear entrance of the beautiful young woman.

"Hell, girl, she moves that rear of hers like the swinging doors of a saloon on payday. I bet you could do the same thing; that is if you wanted to. You know I always liked to watch you walk. The way you move your hips is enough to turn on anybody. And your peach shaped ass is just waiting for someone to slide into it."

Rising from the bed, the killer began to undress slowly, letting each piece of discarded clothing drop slowly to the floor beside the bed. Finally, the killer stood naked, except for the gloves, looking down at the captive girl tied spread eagled to the bed and now writhing in the throes of sexual excitement caused by the vibrator buried in her. The killer's sexual excitement was so intense it was hard to breath; for a moment, the killer feared having a heart attack as a result of too much excitement.

"Why don't we find out how well you can move those hips of yours, bitch," growled the killer dropping down on the helpless girl's bound body and shoving between the captive's widely spread legs. "Let's see how you like this big boy!"

Melanie was unable to resist, having finally given in to the ravishing of her anus while at the same time she was afraid to do anything that might anger her captor. In the part of her mine that was not being driven insane by sexual excitement, Melanie was sure that there was some kind of mental problem at the back of the murderer's actions. She had decided to go along with anything demanded of her; that is until she felt the impossible size of the member that penetrated her vagina. With her legs stretched so widely apart, one tied to each of the legs at the foot of the bed, and her anus full of a vibrating dildo, she was unable to keep from taking the penetration so deep that she was overwhelmed with stabbing pain.

Her muffled screams of agony, inner mixed with moans of sexual excitement brought on by the intense vibration in her rear, were met with peals of delighted laughter from her ravisher. Knowing that she was in terrible pain only led her out of control attacker to continue with more assaults of the same kind until Melanie finally passed out from the sheer pain. Her respite was brief; for Melanie was revived by the killer pouring cold water on her tear stained face.

"None of that my dear," snapped the killer. "I need you completely awake to enjoy every minute of the treats that I have in store for you, because we have a long afternoon ahead. It has been a while since we have been together like this, so we need to get reacquainted and I want you to enjoy every minute of it. After all, I put a lot of planning into arranging our little reunion."

The killer's words were accompanied by a renewal of the sexual assault that brought shrieks of agony from Melanie that even the gag stuffed into her mouth was unable to muffle. Again and again, the killer penetrated the helpless young woman, enjoying the sounds of pain each shove elicited. The killer's response to Melanie's agonized moans was only more peals of delighted, perverted laughter.

Not really aware of what was happening to her daughter only a few feet away, Dorothy's only contribution to the noise level in the cellar was a high pitched moan of sexual pleasure and the creaking of the rusty springs of the old bed in response to Dorothy's wildly bouncing rear as the vibrating dildo brought her to yet another shattering orgasm.

CHAPTER THREE

THE OFFICE OF SHERIFF ANDREW J. MOSLEY

Sheriff Mosley was a deeply satisfied man; he was the happiest when a plan came together and this time he felt that he had hit the mother lode. Only that morning, Wilbert Daniels had agreed to post a reward for information leading to the return of his wife and daughter that represented more money than even a county Sheriff was likely to see in an entire lifetime. Wilbert Daniels had posted a reward of over $250,000.00 dollars to be paid to anyone who could furnish information that would lead to the finding of his family. God, Mosley got the shakes every time he thought about that much money, whatever he had to do, that $250,000.00 was going to be his.

Making it even better, mister big shot, ordering everyone around, Daniels himself had left that morning on the train for Austin to meet with the Governor regarding arranging a statewide search for his wife and daughter, so he was out of Mosley's hair. Now that the fancy bastard was out of the way, the sheriff could really get working and find out what had happened to those women. Whoever had snatched them, for in spite of what he had been telling everyone, Mosley knew that there was no doubt it had been a kidnapping. He was positive that someone had snatched the snatch, so to speak, even though no ransom note had been received. Even worse, this crime had been committed in his county which was a personal affront to the dignity of his office and to him in general. Whoever that bastard had been that had kidnapped these two women, thought Mosley, he was going to be one sorry bastard when the sheriff found him.

Mosley had been in office for over ten years and before that he had been chief deputy to the former sheriff for eight years. During that time, he had arranged a series of informants that was so wide spread that nothing happened in southwest Texas and southeastern New Mexico that he could not find out about. Deciding it was time to pull out all of the stops, he reached for the phone, his hand freezing when his office door flew open to admit a giant of a man. From the top of his black Stetson to the tips of his handmade boots, Texas Ranger Captain Ezra Hughes, at 6'4" and 260 pounds of muscle, rawhide, and gristle, was one of the most feared lawmen in the state.

What few people knew, however, was that the Ranger also had his finger in half of the smuggling and graft from the Mexican Border to the Oklahoma State Line. From the swagger in his walk and sight of the low riding, well used, ivory handled .44 Magnum on his right hip, it was clear to Sheriff Mosley that Ranger Hughes had come to conduct business. That attitude on the part of Hughes did not bode well for whoever he had set his sights on and Mosley had the sinking feeling that those sights were set on him.

"Andy, we's got to talk!" the Ranger growled as he dropped into the visitor's chair across the desk from Mosley and dropped his sweat stained Stetson onto the floor. The stoutly built chair groaned loudly at the suddenly onslaught of the Ranger's 260 pounds. "What kind of shit are you trying to peddle to this Yankee lawyer?"

Something inside Mosley just withered up and died as he contemplated the end of his plans for getting some fast money out of that Yankee lawyer. He removed his hand from the phone, leaned back in his chair, and stared at the ceiling. Shit and it had been such a good day, he thought to himself.

"Well, I'm waitin! Has the cat got your tongue?" growled Hughes, crossing his right foot over his left knee and pulling a big cigar from his inside jacket pocket. Striking a big kitchen match on the arm of the chair, he applied the flame to the end of the cigar puffed it to life.

"Why Ranger Hughes, I have no idea what you are talking about," sputtered Mosley, putting on an injured air. "I'm just doing my job as Sheriff of this county. I've got to find his wife and daughter."

Hughes blew out a big smoke ring and watched it float toward the ceiling.

"Bull shit!" he snapped, suddenly pinning the sheriff with two cold steel gray eyes that had put the fear of God into more than one law breaker in the Great State of Texas. "Andy Mosley, I have known you for over twenty years and I have seen you pull some real shady deals. You know as well as I do that you always have an angle going. Now what are you cooking up with this Yankee Lawyer?"

Mosley was in a quandary, he knew that though Hughes might talk like a hick, but it was only an act that had taken him to the top of the Texas Ranger organization. Though he was only thirty- nine, more than one Governor had tried to put him out to pasture due to his rigid moral code that abhorred graft, unless he was getting a piece of it, but Hughes was just too smart for them. Mosley thought about lying through his teeth, but he knew that he's never get away with what he planned with Ranger Captain Hughes prowling around. Finally, he decided to come clean.

"Well, hell, Ezra, this Yankee has got more money than God and he's willing to spend whatever it will take to find his wife and daughter," Mosley finally admitted. "I'm just helping him spend the money where it will do the best."

"And most of it goes into your pocket, I suppose!" snapped Hughes, taking another puff off of his cigar, his eyes now contemplating the rough-hewn ceiling of the office.

"Hell, man!" snapped Mosley pointing his right forefinger at the Ranger, irritated more at Hughes being correct in his guess than at the Ranger's subtle accusation that he was fleecing the distraught husband and father. "This dastardly deed happened in my county, so we're going to find both of them females as well as the bastards that grabbed them, but there's no reason that I can't make something on the side is there? You know as well as I do that this job don't pay a hell of a lot and I've got to think of my future. I don't plan to spend my retirement years counting pennies or working for some rancher.

"That Yankee will get everything he's paid for and then some. There's no one that knows this county like me and I aim to spend every waking minute searching for them two females. So I ain't ashamed of anything that I have said or done with that Daniels feller."

Hughes flicked his cigar ashes on the genuine mahogany floor of the Sheriff's office and settled back into his chair more comfortably.

"Now Andy, don't go and get your dander up," rumbled Hughes more softly. "I ain't here to rile you up or to interfere with your plans, but to offer my help."

The unexpected offer caught Mosley off guard and he forgot what he was saying, his mouth just hanging open in a comical fashion. The last thing he had expected was for Hughes to offer to help him with his plans. Normally anytime Hughes got involved, any rewards went to him and the Rangers, which meant most of it, went into Hughes' pocket.

"You keep your mouth open like that and you'll catch flies," observed Hughes, taking another puff off of his big cigar.

Suddenly realizing his mouth was still hanging open, Mosley shut it and leaned forward intently, resting both arms on the top of his desk.

"You'll help me?" he asked slowly. This was a side of Hughes that he had never seen before. "You, Mr. Straight laced Texas Ranger will help me, flee—I mean assist Mr. Daniels?"

Hughes suddenly grinned at the confusion evident on Mosley's face.

"Sure, for $250,000.00 of the money you stand to make on this deal," answered Hughes calmly, as he studied the end of his cigar as if fascinated with the burning ash. "I think it is time that I got a piece of the pie you keep carving up just for yourself."

Mosley was completely silent for a moment and then, as Hughes had anticipated Mosley erupted out of his chair and stormed around the desk. His face was red as a beet.

"Man you are insane!" Mosley snapped, stopping, his hands on his hips defiantly, to tower over the big Ranger. Hughes continued to sit calmly, contemplating the end of his cigar. "That's the entire reward amount. If I give you that, then there's nothing left for me. I do all of the work and you take all of the money, I won't do it!"

Hughes finally glanced up at the red faced Sheriff and grinned.

"Let's not forget the other half a million dollars Daniels' father-in-law offered you to find his only child," offered Hughes. "By my calculations, that makes about $750,000.00 you stand to make on this deal and I only want a third of that, not even half. I am sure that you can make a very nice retirement on $500,000.00 plus all the other money you have squeezed out of people over the last eighteen years. I figure that should come to about two million dollars or so."

Mosley suddenly deflated and backed up against his desk. He hadn't thought that anyone else knew about that arrangement or about the money he had been socking away over the years he had been in office.

"Uh, how?" he began as he backed around the desk to drop into his chair once again. His legs felt like jelly, unable to support him.

"How did I know about that offer her father made?" Hughes supplied, with a wide grin on his leathery face. "I could point to my brilliant detective instincts, but it is really very simple. I ran into Daniels at the train station and in the course of our conversations he told me about the reward that he had offered you and the money that Mrs. Daniel's father had offered to kick in. In fact he asked me about the wisdom of making such an offer to you. It seems that, for some obscure reason, you really didn't impress Mr. Daniels. But I told him I had the greatest of faith in your ability to find his daughter and that the offer was a wise move. So you see Andy, I actually earned my part of the money."

Mosley suddenly realized that he was trapped. If he agreed to let Hughes in on the money, all would go well and if he refused, Hughes was just ornery enough to queer the whole deal. Even worse, apparently Hughes knew about some of his other scams; he could get him in plenty of trouble.

"Well then Ranger, I guess we have a deal," Mosley finally sighed. As near as the Sheriff could figure, he really didn't have any options and, after all, half a loaf was better than no bread at all.

"Good," responded Hughes, taking another big puff from his cigar. "Then let's us go find them poor kidnapped women folk for Mr. Daniels and get us our money."

THE SMALL ADOBE HOUSE OUTSIDE ANTHONY, TEXAS

It was just approaching dusk when there was the creak of rusty hinges and the hidden trap door on the back porch of Cletus Brownlee's adobe house slowly raised. The killer, once again dressed in the concealing topcoat almost staggered up the steps to sit on the edge of the cellar opening, head thrown back, lungs filling with the cooler evening air. The searing heat of the west Texas afternoon was beginning to dissipate as night approached. The killer had abused the two women for over six hours before deciding it was time to end the game in the only way that it could be ended. The now cold body of Cletus Brownlee had lain forgotten at the bottom of the steps, a silent witness to the ravishing of the two society women.

It had taken more than two hours, but Melanie, between the vibrating dildo penetrating her rear end and the killer's sexual assault, had finally been brought to a major orgasm that left her limp and dazed. The killer had played every possible sex game with the two women that the killer had ever heard of and even made up a few new ones. All three of them also experienced several earth shattering sexual orgasms that left them almost unable to breath.

Then the killer had undertaken the preparations for the evening that had been long dreamed about. Slowly and carefully, using saving cream form Cletus' bathroom, the killer had shaved the public hair off of each of the captives. Melanie had struggled as usual, at the touch of the razor, but Dorothy had been shaved without removing the vibrator so she had barely noticed.

As the killer had hoped, the continual assault upon Dorothy's sexual organs had finally reduced the always highly sexed woman to a semi conscious automaton and she had offered no resistance when the killer had untied her long enough to move almost drag her unresisting body over and re-tie her face down over her daughter's bound body. This time, the two women had been tied so that each of them had their face in the other's freshly shaven crotch. It had taken some coaching and the administering of some pain, but finally, the killer had gotten each woman to bring the other to a final orgasm orally. In fact, the two captives had gotten so into this last game that they actually brought each other to several orgasms, several more than the killer had planned.

At this point, the killer had decided, with a great deal of regret that it was now time to end the show. However, no action was taken immediately, since it took several minutes for the killer to come down from the powerful sexual high brought about by the hours of torture and abuse inflicted on the helpless captives. In the aftermath of such powerful emotions, the killer was seized with an almost paralyzing lethargy; nothing seemed to matter but sleep. In fact, after having so many organisms that the count had been lost, the killer had actually fallen asleep sprawled on top of Dorothy Daniel's semi-conscious body, having gotten astride her back and ridden the bound woman like a horse as she and her daughter brought each other to their final orgasm.

Sitting on the edge of the entrance to the cellar, the killer dozed off again and when next the killer was aware of events, over an hour had passed. With a major effort of will, the killer pulled out of the blissful state that now had replaced the overpowering desire to kill. The first thing that the killer realized was that there was a bloody knife still clutched tightly in one gloved hand. With a shudder at the memory of the tortures that the knife had been used to inflict on the once gorgeous bodies of the two Daniels women, the incriminating weapon was quickly tossed back into the cellar, to lie in the dirt beside the dead body of Cletus Brownlee. The knife could be disposed of, but the memory of Melanie's eyes widening in shock and pain as the knife was rammed into her side for the final time would always remain in the killer's mind.

The killer had realized from the first that the bodies of all three of the victims needed to disappear, but how to do it still remained a puzzle. In the careful planning that had gone into the kidnapping, the important step of what to do with the bodies had been somehow overlooked. Certainly, leaving them sealed in the secret cellar beneath the old adobe house would work in the short run, but there was always the danger of someone stumbling on the hidden trap door and then there would be hell to pay.

Just as it appeared that the killer would have to trust to blind luck to hide the crime, a memory of Cletus bragging about his daddy's gold mine in the mountains resurfaced. If Cletus had been working the mine, then just possibly there was some dynamite lying around the property or in the old lean-to of a barn out back. Making sure not to be seen from the distant road, the killer quickly searched the sorry excuse for a house that had been the Brownlee homestead for three generations and then crossed the littered yard to the sod topped lean-to that had housed the three cows that the Brownlee's had once depended on for milk.

Turning on the flashlight that the killer had found on Brownlee's dresser, the dark barn was quickly but thoroughly searched. The only sign that there might have been explosives in the barn at one time were four relatively new looking blasting caps lying in a small box in an old chest of drawers that had been relegated to the barn at some time in the distant past.

Just as the killer was ready to give up and leave, in the last dingy stall that was entered, the killer's foot hit a box hidden beneath some moldy hay. Kneeling down, the hay was brushed aside so that a faded label proclaiming that the box held TNT came to light. The killer had hit the jackpot.

Carefully, the killer worked to pry up part of the lid to reveal that there were six sticks of the deadly explosive still lying in the box just as the sticks had been packed by the manufacturer. There was also no doubt that the dynamite had been in that barn for a long time as the killer noticed that the dynamite was so old that it was beginning to sweat, a sure sign that it was becoming unstable, all the better for the killer's plan.

Taking a long length of dirty fuse that was lying on top of the dynamite and gingerly picking up the four blasting caps from the chest of drawers on the way out of the barn, the killer returned to the house with all of the pieces needed to cover the crimes. With the addition of a large can of gasoline from the small generator building nearby, the killer began to make preparations.

There was no question in the killer's mind that an extraordinary bit of luck had been involved in the successful outcome of what had originally seemed a harebrained scheme. It was lucky that mutual friends had mentioned that the Daniels women would be driving this way and it was certainly lucky that the power lines were not yet all through the county and that Brownlee still got his electricity from a generator.

First the contents of the large gasoline can were spread liberally throughout the little adobe and the half full can was then thrown into the cellar. Then it was time for the hardest part of the plan. Carefully, the four unstable sticks of dynamite were tied together with a length of fuse and then the blasting cap was attached to the end that was inserted into the bundle. Then the homemade bomb was laid gently in the middle of the floor in the center of the adobe. Hopefully, the ensuing explosion would split the floor support and drop the house into the cellar, effectively covering the evidence of the crime. Since gas and oil exploration was part of the family business, the killer had watched explosives being used for several years, so preparing the dynamite for use was relatively simple. The killer estimated that the length of fuse available would allow twenty minutes for an escape, so there was no need to rush.

Finally, with the stage carefully set, the killer carefully lit the fuse and walked calmly to the car. Taking great pains not to do anything out of the ordinary that might call attention to the car, the killer was still several miles away when the night sky was lit up like the fourth of July by the explosion of the dynamite as the adobe was demolished. As the killer had hoped, the explosion and the ensuing raging fire that consumed the dried out wood of the support beams hid any sign that there was a secret cellar beneath the foundation of the house.

Laughing manically, the shrouded figure of the killer faded into the gathering darkness. Soon only the soft whisper of the desert wind was the only

MESQUITE, NEW MEXICO

That same night, two hours after the spectacular explosion at the Brownlee farm, and some miles away, Marvin Dapple, Mesquite's only official town drunk was staggering alongside Highway 28 toward the hovel he had called home for many years. Usually Marvin slept under the wagon across the street from the Mesquite café, but on this night, he didn't even have the price of a drink and had decided to go home, that is if his long-suffering wife would let him in the front door.

As much as his wife hated him, Marvin hated his wife even more. Unfortunately, tonight Marvin had little choice but to go home for a change, for on this day, the unthinkable had happened. Marvin had run out of both whiskey and money. So he was headed home to get one or the other from that harridan he had married. Hell, he thought, them damn kids he had whelped weren't much better.

As he staggered along Marvin tried to remember how long he had been married, but he just couldn't remember. The years and the alcohol fog were making him more forgetful every day. But suddenly in his befuddled mind was a picture of his wife as she had looked on their wedding day. She had been beautiful and their new life had been filled with hope. That is until he had fallen victim to the pressures of a growing family and the family curse, alcohol. He had tried not to repeat the mistakes of his daddy, but soon he had given in to the urge and fell into a living hell, living from bottle to bottle and crushing their dreams in the process. Now theirs was a love-hate relationship; she loved him then, but she hated him now. But he was still her husband and he had his rights, damn it! Hell, he giggled to himself, he might even bed the old heifer before going back to the peace and quiet of his wagon.

For a moment he thought he heard a car coming from behind him and turned to flag down a ride. To his surprise, he couldn't see the lights of a car, though it was overcast and no stars were shining, he should still be able to see car lights, he thought. Damn, he was drunker than he thought, he mumbled to himself, now he was hearing things. Still mumbling to himself, Marvin turned and continued to stagger down the side of the road toward home, steeling himself for the battle that he knew was to come if he wanted a roof, a drink and some money for more whiskey on this night.

Finally, after what seemed like an eternity, Marvin Dapple reached the home he had built with his own two hands for his new wife and himself all those long years ago. It didn't look like much now, but once it had been a beautiful place, filled with laughter and good smells. Once, he mumbled to himself as he staggered toward the porch. He could see that there were lights burning in the front window; so he knew that the woman he once called his wife was home.

Stumbling onto the porch, he pounded on the peeling front door for several minutes before the porch light was turned on and he heard a voice from the other side of the door.

"Who is it?" came a quavering voice from the other side of the door.

"It's me, my dear," answered Marvin in his most endearing tone as he straightened his wrinkled jacket and smoothed his mussed hair with his rough, dirty hands. "I've come to spend an evening with you, me darling, and the children. Open up, it's tired and thirsty I am."

"Go away, you bastard!" his long suffering wife yelled back through the door, anger replacing the fear that had been in her voice only a moment ago. "I have already told you that I never want to see you again."

"You can't keep me out, you heartless bitch. This is my home, I built this house with my own two hands, you heartless slag, and those are my children," he bellowed, resuming his pounding on the door. "Open up right now, you are my wife! I have my rights!"

Suddenly the door was pulled open and he stumbled forward, losing his balance as he swung once again at the door that was now open. Marvin started to push his way inside, but he hastily stepped back when he saw that his wife was holding his old double barrel shotgun tightly in her hands and pointing it directly at his face. Behind his wife he could see the white faces of his three daughters. They were all looking at him like he was some kind of creature from the fires of Hell come to harm them.

"Now see here, woman," Marvin began, his resolution to control his temper no matter what happened deserting him in the face of the shotgun.

Whatever else Marvin might have said would never be known for at that moment, there was the sound of a large caliber pistol firing from the direction of the roadway. A barely visible figure standing near the roadway fired three shots that all struck Marvin in the upper back, propelling him forward to die at his wife's feet.

Though thunderstruck at the sight of her dead husband, Mrs. Minerva Dapple had the presence of mind to step onto the porch and fire both barrels of the old scattergun in the general direction of the shooter. It was impossible to tell whether or not she hit anything, but the sound of a car racing away at high speed was quickly heard, though no lights were seen. The only visible evidence left of what had just transpired was the dead body of Marvin Dapple. A life snuffed out that would be little mourned.

THE HOME OF A KILLER

Arriving home, the killer parked the car beside the garage and sat quietly wanting to see if anyone noticed the somewhat late arrival. After a while, the killer got out of the car, closing the door softly and for a moment the killer paused and considered the spider webbing caused by the shotgun pellets that had hit the rear window. At least that crazy old woman had missed hitting anything else, thought the killer, stifling another fit of giggling. It wouldn't do to make any noise until everything was done. Noise at this stage could ruin everything.

Putting the matter out of mine, making sure to keep to the darkest areas of the yard, the killer entered the main house through the back door. Though voices could be heard in the dining room, no one noticed the killer take the back stairs to the second floor and quietly enter a room at the far end of the hall. Breathing a sigh of relief at reaching this sanctuary without notice, the killer stripped naked, piling the clothing that had been worn during the murder in the middle of the room and went to stand in front of a full-length mirror.

Though the killer had been too excited to either notice or care, there were several large streaks of blood on the killer's chest and both arms were streaked with the blood of Melanie Daniels' all the way to the shoulders. Stepping quickly to the bathroom, the killer started the shower, running the water full force and as hot as possible. Once the bathroom mirror was covered with steam and the shower stall was hot as a sauna, the killer stepped into the water stream and began to lather. Hair, body and beneath the fingernails were lathered and rinsed time and again until the killer was red as a lobster and there was absolutely no sign of blood. When finally the water going down the drain was clear and no longer reddish, the killer turned off the water and slowly dried off with a thick bath towel.

Returning to the bedroom, the killer quickly dressed in a pair of jeans and a Pendleton shirt before kneeling on the floor and removing the keys to the Daniels car, the car registration, and the several pieces of Indian jewelry from the pocket of the discarded coat. These items were laid aside for the moment. Then a large feed sack was pulled from beneath the bed and the discarded clothing, shoes, and several bloodstained, white towels were pushed into it. The sack and its contents were then rolled into a ball and tied tightly with a length of cord from the dresser. Only a few more steps to go and the plan would be complete, the killer thought, excitedly.

Taking the bundle under one arm, and dropping the jewelry and other items into a pocket, the killer eased upon the door to the hallway and listened intently. Only the sounds from the dining room below could be heard. Moving as silently as possible, the killer eased down the back stairs and exited the house through the kitchen. Running as quietly as possible and making sure to stay in the shadows once again, the killer ran across the large farm yard to a small house set well back from the main house.

Certain that no one was inside, the killer raised the welcome mat and picked up a key that opened the front door. Moving through the darkened home with a certainty that came with great familiarity, the killer entered the master bedroom and crossed to the closet. Opening the door, the killer stuffed the small bundle containing the bloodstained clothes and towels into the back of the closet. The .45 that had been used to kill Cletus Brownlee and Marvin Dapple was placed carefully into the drawer in the bedside table. The leather driving gloves, with the tell tale bloodstains, were placed neatly into the top drawer of the dresser with two other identical pair. Slowly sliding open the top drawer of the bedside table, the killer dropped the jewelry and the set of car keys into the drawer and slid it closed.

Having completed the plan, the killer left the small house quietly, replacing the door key beneath the mat and returning unseen to the main house. Using the back stairs to regain the second floor, the killer than calmly descended the main staircase, entered the dining room, and joined the family.

"What's for dinner? I'm starved!"

CHAPTER FOUR

THE BROWNLEE FARM, ANTHONY TEXAS

Sheriff Mosley and Ranger Captain Hughes stood at the edge of the destruction and carefully surveyed the jumble of burned timbers that had once been the Brownlee home. The explosion had obviously been tremendous, as a crater had been formed where the house had been and once the fire had burned through the house supports, the shattered remains of the structure had fallen into the hole then the walls of the crater had collapsed in on itself. It was clear that no one could have survived the fire.

The explosion and fire had been reported to the Sheriff's office last night, but word had not reached Mosley until this morning due to a late night drinking binge he had indulged in with Hughes. Though Hughes looked none the worse for wear in the light of day, Mosley had gone home and passed out. This morning he felt like shit and he had a vicious pounding headache; as a result he was very short tempered with everyone.

He turned to Rufus Jasper, head of the Anthony Volunteer Fire Department who stood nearby. As El Paso County Sheriff, Mosley had responsibility for policing Anthony as well as the rest of the county. He was prepared to answer the barrage of police questions that he knew would be coming his way any minute.

"Damn it, Rufus, you should have called me!" snapped Mosley, for the third time since arriving at the scene. It wouldn't do his reputation with the voters any good if word got around he had been passed out drunk when Cletus Brownlee's house had been blown sky high. He knew that Rufus Jasper had a big mouth and would tell everybody about not being able to find the Sheriff when the blast had happened. "This is a crime scene and you and your people have done contaminated it. You know that we have to preserve the scene and collect evidence."

"Now you see here, Sheriff," snapped Jasper, having had enough of Mosley trying to browbeat him in front of that silent Ranger. "Me and my people came all the way out here and put the fire out, that's all we did. Though by the time we got here the fire was too far gone for us to be able to put it out, anyways. We didn't none of us contam – uh, whatever you said we did. We just put out the damned fire. Then we looked for Cletus, but we never did find him."

The Volunteer Fire Captain stood glaring at Mosley for a moment, then spit a stream of tobacco juice on the ground, just missing Mosley's fancy, highly shined cowboy boots. Mosley could feel himself getting ready to lay into the arrogant prick; he wanted to hit him just one time right in the middle of his fat face.

"Sides, I sent my boy to the closest phone to call your office as soon as we got here and saw what the problem was. But no one could find you. It is strange that not even your deputy or anyone else had any idea where you had got off to," added Jasper, finally noticing Mosley's expression and wisely backing up a step.

Maybe spitting in the dirt so close to them fancy cowboy boots of the Sheriff's wasn't such a good idea, though Jasper. Mosley might be a blustering blow hard, but he was a tough man in a fight.

"So it ain't my fault you missed the whole thing. Hell man, your deputies should know where to reach you at all times."

Mosley's already short fuse was ready to explode when he was hailed by one of his Deputies.

"Sheriff, look what I found!" came the yell as Johnny Barton, one of his youngest deputies. Mosley turned around to snap at Barton, but paused as he saw Barton come out of what was left of the old barn lugging a dirty wooden box. Damn fool had no idea how dangerous it was for him to go poking around inside that old place, thought the Sheriff irritably. The force off the explosion that had destroyed the house had almost turned the old barn upside down. Hell, the place was older than dirt to start with and Cletus hadn't done a thing to repair with the house or the barn since his daddy had died ten years ago. It was miracle that the place hadn't fallen down a long time ago.

Mosley paused in the tirade he was ready to unleash on Rufus Jasper and started to tear into young Barton over needlessly exposing himself to danger when Deputy Barton dropped the box in the dirt at the Sheriff's feet, a big grin on his face. There still visible on the side of the box were the faded words 'DANGER: DYNAMITE HANDLE WITH CARE'.

"Aw hell," said the Sheriff looking at those standing around gawking at the box on the ground. "It ain't no wonder this whole place went up in a fourth of July type explosion. If I told him once, I told Cletus Brownlee a hundred times that he couldn't keep using that old dynamite his daddy had left over from working that old mine of his in the mountains. That stuff had to be at least fifteen years old and unstable as hell. There ain't no mystery about what caused this here blast."

The Sheriff pushed the box over slightly onto its side so that all of them could see the discoloration of the sides of the box. All of these men had grown up around miners and part time treasure hunters, so no one had to tell them what had caused the unusual stains inside the dynamite box.

"See them stains on the side of the box?" the Sheriff directed the question toward no one in particular. Being a man of a somewhat large ego, he never missed a chance to show everyone around him just how intelligent he was. He was aware that most of the men standing around knew the properties of dynamite as well as he did, but he was going to show off a little with his deductive reasoning.

"That is where the sticks of dynamite that were in this box sweated pure nitro right into the wood. Hell, when dynamite gets to sweating, a sneeze could have set them off. I bet that idiot had those sticks of dynamite in the house getting ready to go looking for that old lost gold mine his daddy is supposed to have found up in the Franklins and something set them off. Hell, I bet Cletus is scattered all over the county."

The Sheriff looked up and speared Jasper with an angry glare.

"You called Doc. Greenly?" he demanded suddenly. "You know that proper police procedure calls for the County Coroner to come pronounce the dead people dead."

Jasper suddenly looked uncomfortable and, suddenly realizing that everyone was looking at him, looked around the yard as if the county Coroner was going to appear by some miracle. In his haste to try and make the Sheriff look like a fool, he had forgotten to send for the Coroner.

"Uh, no, Sheriff," he finally admitted, grudgingly. "I guess in our haste to get the fire out and make sure that there were no bodies to be pulled out of the fire or living people to be rescued, we's plumb forgot to call for the Coroner. But like you said, there ain't no bodies here to be examined, so what good is the Coroner?"

"I'll just bet you did forget," snarled Mosley, spinning on the heel of one of his $400.00 Tony Lama boots and stomping toward his patrol car. "You amateurs should stay out of the business of us professional lawmen," he yelled over his shoulder as he stomped off. "Even if there ain't no bodies, we've got to have the Coroner."

Jasper took that chance to make himself scarce before the Sheriff let loose that well known temper of his. There would be other chances to let the voters see what a horse's ass Mosley really was before the next election where Jasper planned on running for Sheriff of El Paso County, himself.

Reaching into his car, Mosley grabbed the radio microphone and called dispatch. Marge Ferguson, the dispatcher answered almost immediately.

"This is dispatch. Sheriff, Judge Prestridge just called looking for you. He seemed pretty upset and said for you to get over to his place right now!"

That was certainly not good news. Judge Reginald Prestridge was from one of the oldest families in the state. His ancestor had died right alongside Davey Crockett at the Alamo, a distinction that had gotten him appointed U.S. Magistrate for the county. He always expected everyone to drop everything and take care of his problems, but at the same time he was a man that Mosley could not afford to antagonize, not with so much money on the table from that Daniels feller. Mosley raised the microphone to his mouth.

"OK, get old Doc Greenly out to Cletus Brownlee's place. It looks like Cletus has done blown himself to kingdom come and the coroner needs to be here if the body is found. Ranger Hughes and I will go see what's got Prestridge riled up."

"10-4 Sheriff, I'll send the Coroner right away."

Not bothering to answer, Mosley tossed the microphone onto the seat and looked over at Hughes who was standing with his arms folded across his massive chest staring intently into the still smoking crater.

"Ranger," he called out, "Judge Prestridge wants to see me; you want to ride along, or stay here with shit for brains?"

Turning from his study of the smoking crater, Hughes returned to join the Sheriff, circled the car and got into the passenger side.

"I reckon going along with you has got to be better than watching that shit burn," he growled, tipping the brim of his Stetson over his eyes and settling down in the seat. "That crater will be smoking for at least a week. If there was a body in that house, it fell into that crater when the house collapsed and by the time the fire is out there won't be nothing left of him but a few bones and some ash."

Hughes paused a moment, intrigued by a stray thought, but deciding to say nothing, yet. Instead he leaned back in the seat, pushed his hat over his eyes, and crossed his big arms.

"Since you are driving and I had such a late night, call me when we get there!"

With a snort, Mosley started the car and floored it, showering the Volunteer Firemen and his own deputies with a shower of dirt and small rocks. Though this flexing of his ego made him feel better, the Sheriff failed to see Jasper run a few yards after his cruiser shaking his fist at the Sheriff's school boyish prank of spinning his tires.

"Jackass!" bellowed the irate Chief of the Volunteer Fire Department, in his anger not caring who saw him lose his temper at the sheriff. In spite of his bluster, if the truth were known, the Sheriff intimidated him and that big silent Ranger absolutely terrified him. Now that Mosley was gone, he could strut and be a big shot in front of his subordinates. He was too angry to notice that even members of his own volunteer group were hiding smiles as they watched him have what amounted to a temper tantrum in the middle of what had been Cletus Brownlee's farm road. By dark, the entire county would know about it.

Such a display would surely have hurt his chances for election as Sheriff against a man as entrenched as Mosley if this had not been Mosley's last day to live.

THE PRESTRIDGE RANCH

Though it was unheard of, it was Judge Amos Prestridge, himself, that jerked opened the front door of his three story mansion before Mosley could even knock. So rather than just drop the hand that had been raised to knock on the ornate door, Mosley contented himself with removing his Stetson as if that had been his intention all along as he entered the richly appointed entry hall. Ranger Captain Hughes followed the Sheriff, but didn't bother to remove his hat. After all, he was a Texas Ranger and didn't have to answer to a mere magistrate, he only answered to the Governor.

"About damn time you got here!" snapped the Judge, his normally impeccable appearance and lofty demeanor both missing as he turned to storm back across the wide entry hall to the family room where his two sons, Neal 19 and Samuel, 21, and his wife, Angela McCardle Prestridge, waited, their faces pale. Something was clearly amiss, but neither Mosley nor Hughes had any idea what it might be.

"You called, Judge?" asked Mosley politely, nodding a greeting to Judge Mosley's wife, a rare occurrence on his part to be sure. He was known for ignoring a wife unless he had ulterior motives, so to speak. "Is there some kind of problem?"

"My baby!" suddenly wailed Mrs. Prestridge, a beautiful, well built former Miss Texas and runner up for Miss America some years ago, but who was now a cold-featured, blonde who had always appeared to everyone in town to have a lot in common with the Ice Queen. "Please find my baby!"

Judge Prestridge walked over to stand by his wife and awkwardly pat her back as she sobbed uncontrollably into a large kerchief she had clearly pulled from around her neck. "Don't cry, Angela, I am sure that the Sheriff can take care of this in short order. He'll find Eva for us."

Mosley finally couldn't help himself, hating to be out of the information loop, so to speak. He decided that it was time for him to take charge of this situation. Sheriff Mosley prided himself on being a take-charge type of guy. That's why he was such a good sheriff.

"Uh, Judge it would help if I knew what was wrong," Mosley finally said, but showing a great deal of tact and deference, he thought to himself.

Hughes glanced at Mosley and then back to the Judge. It was then that Hughes decided that Mosley was just a kiss ass. A man like him wouldn't last in the Rangers more than a day.

Prestridge took a deep breath, forcing himself to be calm, and ran one pudgy well-manicured hand through his thinning hair. For a man who had been called the Angel of Death for the many death sentences he had given out since first being elected to the Bench, Prestridge was clearly a very shaken man.

"It's our youngest, Eva," he finally said harshly, running his blunt fingers through his thinning hair. "She's been kidnapped by that Bertram Kennedy, the foreman here on my ranch. He's taking her somewhere to do God knows what to her!"

"Excuse me, Judge," interrupted Hughes in his rumbling voice. "I'm with the Texas Rangers, here assisting the sheriff in another matter. May I ask how you know that she was kidnapped?"

"Are you insinuating that our baby girl would run off with a man old enough to be her father?" screeched Angela Prestridge, her lovely, patrician features showing her outrage and grief as she pushed herself up from the couch and waved her arms angrily at the Ranger. "My God, she's an innocent child and he's a child molester, a criminal and you have to find him and get my baby back!"

Hughes crossed his arms across his wide chest and fixed the woman with a piercing glare. He had the feeling that there was a lot more that these folks could tell him, but surely would not.

"I'm sure that she is as pure as the driven snow, ma'am," soothed Mosley, stepping in front of Hughes while trying to calm the distraught wife and mother, but having little luck. "If you can just give us the facts, maybe we can find her."

"She's gone! Those are the facts," snapped the woman, dropping limply back onto the couch and covering her tear stained face with the kerchief. Whatever else the woman might have said was cut off as Judge Prestridge tired of her screeching.

"Angela, remember yourself!" Prestridge said in a warning voice. He looked over at his sons, "Take your mother to her bedroom, and help her lie down."

"I don't want to go lie down," protested the woman, "I want to find my baby. You all should be doing something, not standing here talking."

"Yelling at the Sheriff and the Ranger is not going to help find her," responded Prestridge tiredly. "Let the boys help you upstairs and I'll be up there in a few minutes."

There was no doubt that Angela Prestridge wanted to argue, but finally she dropped her shoulders resignedly and walked past the two lawmen toward the entry hall. The two boys followed along obediently.

Angela Prestridge might rant and rave, but there was no doubt that the Judge wore the pants in that family.

Once they were alone in the room, Judge Prestridge fixed himself a drink from the well stocked bar along the far wall, but he failed to offer the Sheriff or the Ranger anything to drink. Even in such straights, a man of Judge Prestridge's social position did not drink with the common people. Neither lawman said anything until the Judge had returned and dropped into an overstuffed leather chair with a tired sigh.

"Gentlemen, you have to forgive my wife," Prestridge began, holding his glass between both hands and rolling it slowly. "Our daughter being kidnapped has gotten her very distraught."

"Could you tell me about your daughter and why you think this foreman has abducted her?" asked Hughes, his dark eyes missing nothing of the Judge's demeanor or anything else in the room. Few people knew that Hughes had a photographic memory, which had served him well in his law enforcement career.

"What, oh, that's right, you don't know her, do you Ranger?" responded Prestridge, nodding to himself, not waiting for a response before he continued to talk. "Eva is very young, Ranger Hughes, she just turned 15 and is as beautiful as her mother. My little girl sure took after her mother in that regard."

"That's the God's honest truth, Ranger," interjected Mosley, nodding emphatically, never missing a chance to suck up to Prestridge. "That little girl is sure a looker."

Mosley was intent on getting in the conversation and missed the sharp look that Prestridge shot him. Like any father, anyone talking about his baby girl became someone to keep an eye on, especially when the girl in question was as lovely as Eva Prestridge.

Hughes, on the other hand, was well aware that Mosley's comments were disturbing the Judge, but he chose to completely ignore the Sheriff, intent on getting as much information out of the Judge as possible. He had long ago found that when a witness was upset or angry, that they tended to say more than they intended.

"Now who is this that you think kidnapped your daughter?" he asked suddenly.

Prestridge took a deep breath and then a long drink of his liquor to settle his nerves. "His name is Bertram Kennedy. He is, or was, the foreman here on the ranch. One of the boys had been into town and as he drove back, he saw Kennedy drive by him in my son's car with Eva about an hour ago. I sent men running after them as soon as I heard about it, but they had disappeared."

"Did your daughter appear to be trying to get away?" asked Hughes.

Prestridge fixed Hughes with a hard stare before dropping his eyes and sighing deeply. There were few people that could lock stares with Hughes and force him to look away.

"Ranger Hughes, do you know what you are insinuating about my daughter?" demanded Prestridge angrily, rising to his feet. "How dare you presume in this manner? I will have you know that my daughter is as sweet as she can be and absolutely a virgin!"

"Judge Prestridge," rumbled Hughes, his voice sounding like it had come from a great distance, "I am insinuating nothing about your daughter. I do not know her and have never even laid eyes on her. However, all of that aside, I am trying to gather information on a suspected kidnapping. You are the parent of the suspected kidnapped victim and I am asking you for information. That's all. Don't presume to assume that your suspicions are my own. When I am investigating a case, I do not presume but rather deal with facts and evidence."

Prestridge considered what Hughes had said before taking a deep breath and rubbing his face tiredly. Clearly this apparent kidnapping had taken a great deal out of him. Slowly he crossed to the window and looked out over his vast spread. He looked, but he was not really seeing anything, he was reviewing the life of his daughter. Hughes could clearly see that Judge Prestridge doted on his daughter. It would go hard on her kidnapper if Prestridge had any influence in his eventual sentencing, Hughes was sure.

"Eva is like any stunningly beautiful woman, Ranger," began Prestridge slowly, his voice flat and devoid of emotion. "She has been the center of attention of men since she was old enough to walk. I have seen the work crew watching her at the pool whenever they think I am not watching them. I know that they all want her, but they also know that I would kill any man that touched my daughter. But--."

"But what, Judge?" pressed Ranger Hughes.

"Well, I uh, ah, I am sure that it doesn't mean anything, but I have seen that Eva enjoys the men watching her far more than I really consider seemly," the Judge finally finished, trying to put a good face on his fears. "Come to think of it, she has been especially nice to Kennedy. But I am sure that she did not go with Kennedy of her own free will. There is no question in my mind that she was kidnapped."

"Where does this Kennedy stay?" questioned Ranger Hughes.

Judge Prestridge started suddenly and licked his lips nervously, symptoms of nervousness that did not escape Hughes' sharp eyes. The Ranger was certain that Prestridge knew far more than he was revealing to them.

"What?" he asked in some confusion.

Hughes narrowed his eyes and studied Prestridge carefully. Something did not ring true.

"Where does Kennedy live?" Hughes repeated his question.

"Oh, he has a small house near the bunkhouse, out back," responded Prestridge, a red flush appearing on his neck and lower jaw.

"Anyone else stay in that cottage besides Kennedy?" Hughes asked quickly.

Prestridge shook his head emphatically. "No, he's the foreman here and the foreman has his own private quarters here on the ranch. It was a tradition that my daddy started and I have continued."

Hughes turned toward the door, "Before we jump to conclusions, we need to search his house. Then maybe we can get some idea of where this jasper has gone with the young lady."

He had noticed that Prestridge's face had turned white as a sheet when he had mentioned searching Kennedy's quarters and that made him even more determined to get a look inside that little house. Without waiting for the Judge to guide him, Hughes left the main house and rounded the corner, heading for the bunkhouse and the small house near the barn. His nose told him that there was something there he needed to find. He neither knew nor cared if the Sheriff came with him.

THE COTTAGE OCCUPIED BY BERTRAM KENNEDY

Reaching the silent cottage sitting isolated to the rear of the bunkhouse, Hughes stepped gently up the three steps onto the small porch. As he reached for the doorknob, he heard a sound inside the house. The sound was heard only once, and could have been caused by anything, but Hughes' keen ears had identified the sound as being human in origin. Though the sound was faint, it was enough to let Ranger Hughes know that there was someone trying to move quietly about inside the little cottage. Someone, who clearly had no business being in there with the occupant away from home.

Cautiously, he pulled his Colt Single Action Army .45 and thumbed back the hammer, as he eased the door open. Concentrating, he could now clearly hear the sounds of someone moving about the cottage, while trying not to make any noise. Moving silently for so big a man, Hughes crossed the small living room and peered cautiously around the edge of the door leading into the larger of the two bedrooms of the little cottage. In the dimly lit room, the only light was coming from a gap in the curtains in the windows across the room Hughes could see a figure searching through the top drawer of the chest of drawers set against one wall. The breeze suddenly blew the stained curtains into the room, the open window leaving no doubt as to how the intruder had entered the cottage.

The open closet door and the rumpled appearance of the few items hanging inside the small closet also left no doubt as to the reason for the intruder being in the room. If the closet revealed nothing, then the chest of drawers was the next best spot to search. Apparently not finding what he, or she was searching for in the top drawer, the figure eased the drawer closed and opened the second drawer.

Hearing no other sounds in the cottage, Hughes decided that the intruder was probably alone. However, alone or not, Hughes was adamant that this one was not getting away before answering some questions. Seeing no visible weapon on the intruder, Hughes decided it was time to act. Raising his cocked weapon, which he had pointed toward the floor as he peered into the room, Hughes suddenly stepped into the center of the doorway, his .45 held in a two handed grip, the barrel centered on the middle of the figure's back.

"Freeze or die!" snapped Hughes, his trigger finger, whitened as it took up the slack. It would take only another ounce or two of pressure to fire the weapon. "I'm Captain Hughes of the Texas Rangers and I will not hesitate to drop you where you stand!"

CHAPTER FIVE

The unidentified searcher jerked as if to run for the open window, but finally took the wise course of action and froze at the sound of the Ranger's rough voice. The reputation of the Texas Rangers was highly respected as, no nonsense, law enforcement personnel. It was also well known that the Rangers did not play around. If one of them said he would drop a lawbreaker in his tracks, then that if just what he would do and it was a well-known fact. Hughes, himself, also had a growing reputation of being one who fired first and asked questions later. He had long been heard to say that if he made a mistake and shot the wrong person, it was better to be tried by twelve than carried by six.

"Raise your hands and they had better be empty!" ordered Hughes, his gun barrel never wavering from the center of the interloper's back.

Slowly, the intruder raised his gloved hands above his head. Prudently, he made no other movements.

"Now turn around, slowly!" snapped the Ranger.

The intruder turned to the right until Hughes was able to see that it was young Neal Prestridge that he had found rifling through the foreman's effects. A little puzzled, Hughes straightened up from his well-known shooting stance and lowered his weapon; through he did not ease the hammer down. It would only take a little effort to raise and fire the big .45 and from the scared look that Prestridge shot at the weapon, Hughes could see that Prestridge was well aware that he was not yet out of danger.

"Boy, suppose you tell me what you are doing here!" he demanded, taking a step forward toward his prisoner. "Do you know that I could have shot you as an intruder?"

At that moment, Hughes heard the sound of someone noisily entering the open front door. Prudently, Hughes stepped from the open doorway and backed up against the wall just inside the bedroom, where he could watch the doorway and keep an eye on young Prestridge. Knowing that it was entirely possible that Prestridge had an accomplice, Hughes glared at young Prestridge in warning as he raised his weapon, pointing it at the open bedroom doorway. He only lowered it when Sheriff Moseley came hustling into the bedroom to skid to a stop when he found himself looking down the barrel of Hughes' weapon.

"Jesus Christ, Ranger!" exclaimed Mosley, his eyes bugging out of his head like a tromped frog and his face turned white as a sheet at the sight of the big .45 pointed at his head. "What the hell are you doing?"

Hughes glared at Mosley for a long moment before he eased down the hammer of his weapon and slid it smoothly back into his holster.

"Being careful," Hughes responded laconically. "I came in here and found this young'un searching the place then heard someone come in the door. I learned long ago that you can't be too careful at a crime scene."

Mosley slumped back against the wall, his face covered with sweat. Hughes turned back toward young Prestridge while Mosley pulled himself together.

"Now suppose you tell me what you're doing here!" Hughes said firmly, his hands on his hips in a commanding stance.

Neal Prestridge tried to look tough, but quickly wilted under Hughes' stern stare. His stoic demeanor suddenly crumpled and he was a boy again. His shoulders slumped and the young man dropped onto the neatly made bed, his leather jacket zipped up, his arms tightly held close to his sides and his hands in his lap.

"I was hoping to find something that would tell me where Kennedy took Eva," he finally responded in a dull voice. "I wanted to keep her name out of the police records and the newspapers. I thought that if I could find where he took her, then I could go get her and bring her back here before anyone else knew about what had happened."

"That's a good thought, Neal," interjected the Sheriff, stepping between the Ranger and the defensive teenager. "Yes sir, us men have to look out for the little ladies. Did you find anything?"

He paused for a moment when there was no response of either young Prestridge or Ranger Hughes, before he continued to babble to no one in particular.

"I think that this young man acted in a perfectly understandable manner wanting to protect his sister and her reputation, Ranger," boomed

Mosley jovially, trying to regain control of situation while keeping a weather eye on the big brooding Texas Ranger. "Don't you think so, Ranger?"

Hughes only grunted in response as he walked over to glance at the items strewn across the bedspread. The small pile of Indian jewelry and the unusual looking set of keys tickled something in his memory. He was also aware that young Prestridge was holding out on them, he could sense it.

Suddenly, with the speed of a rattlesnake, Hughes grabbed the startled teenager by the collar of his jacket and twisted it tightly, jerking the young man roughly to his feet. As he had suspected, Prestridge grabbed at the arm holding his collar with both of his own hands. The bundle of papers and photographs that he had been hiding inside his jacket fell to his feet, scattering across the floor.

"No!" yelled Prestridge as he tried to drop to the floor and recover the papers.

He had forgotten that Hughes still had a firm grip on the collar of his jacket. Rather than release the young man, Hughes simply lifted him completely off of his feet as if he weighed only a few ounces and deposited him in the middle of the bed. Dropping to one knee, Hughes gathered the bundle of papers up on one big hand and stepped over to the window.

As the Ranger held the documents to the light, young Prestridge bounded off the bed and, with all of his might, slammed one fist into the side of Hughes' jaw. Hughes paid absolutely no attention to the blow, but merely glanced at the angry young man and went back to looking at the collection of very revealing photographs that had been hidden among the papers. He was so engrossed in the pictures that when young Prestridge hit him in the jaw again, the Ranger merely backhanded the teenager without even looking at him. The force of the blow sent the young man flying across the room where he bounced off of the partially open closet door crashed into the wall.

What had so captivated Hughes attention was the fact that he was looking at several very fetching nude photographs of Eva Prestridge, her wrists tied behind her back and a gag in her mouth, hidden among the papers that Prestridge had been trying to sneak out of the foreman's cottage. At first glance it appeared to confirm that she had been kidnapped. However, a closer study revealed from the way that the bound and gagged young lady was looking at the camera and arching her back to show her breasts in the best light, it was apparent that young Eva was no stranger to bondage or being in front of a camera. It was also very apparent that young Eva was on much better terms with the foreman than even her parents knew.

Suddenly, with a berserk howl, young Prestridge, who had been helped back to his feet by the solicitous Sheriff, twisted free, grabbed for Mosley's sidearm, pushing the Sheriff across the room, and swung around to point the stolen pistol at Hughes' head.

"Give me those pictures right now or I will kill you, you bastard!" yelled the young man, his voice quivering. "You have no right to see those!"

Hughes merely glanced at the angry young man and looked back down at the pornographic photos, completely ignoring the pistol pointed at his head. Mosley had frozen across the room as if afraid to say or do anything. He was positive that young Prestridge was going to shoot the Ranger in the head and then there would be hell to pay. In spite of his threat, Prestridge, paying no attention to Mosley, took two steps closer to the Ranger, and prodded him roughly in the ribs with the barrel of the stolen pistol.

"I said give me those pictures right now or I will blow your God damn head off!" yelled Prestridge, grabbing for the pictures still clutched in the Ranger's hands with his free hand. For just a moment, his eyes left Hughes and focused on the pictures he wanted so desperately to get from the Ranger.

Suddenly Hughes whirled and threw the pictures in Prestridge's face. Surprised, the young man stepped back, grabbing for the naked pictures of his sister, the gun in his hand seemingly forgotten. Taking advantage of his opening, Hughes again backhanded the young man with his left hand. Prestridge was rocked to his heels by the force of the blow, the gun falling to the floor. Drawing back, this time Hughes hit Prestridge square on the chin with one big fist, watching his legs collapse and his opponent fall face forward to lie unconscious among the nude photographs of his sister scattered once again about the floor.

"My God, you've killed him!" breathed Mosley, his face white as a sheet. "What are we going to do now?"

"Mosley, you are a jackass!" snapped Hughes, not even bothering to look at the Sheriff. He hooked the toe of his boot beneath the pistol lying on the floor beside Prestridge's limp hand and sent it sliding across the floor toward the trembling, white faced Sheriff. "Pick up your gun and shut up!"

Reaching down and once again gathering up the photos and papers on the floor, Hughes calmly stepped over the prostrate young man and returned to the bed. Slowly he reached down and lifted the set of keys to study them carefully. He was suddenly aware that he was looking at a set of keys to a Rolls Royce, a model of vehicle that he had not seen on the ranch. Next he shifted through the small pile of Indian jewelry, an idea forming in the recesses of his mind. He seemed to remember that the Daniels women had stopped to buy some Indian jewelry in mesquite.

Turning, ignoring both the young man lying on the floor and the confused looking Sheriff still standing just inside the bedroom door, the Ranger strode over to the closet and jerked open the door that had been slammed shut by Prestridge's flying body earlier. Slowly and carefully, he shifted through the contents, pausing when he found a bundle hidden far back in the closet. Pulling the bundle from its hiding place, he took it over to the bed and opened it. There, he found some bloodstained clothing.

Grunting to himself, Hughes, quickly and efficiently continued his search of the bedroom. When he finished, in addition to the jewelry, the keys, and the bloodstained clothes, the Ranger had laid a set of bloodstained driving gloves and a .45 automatic on the bed. It had taken only one whiff of the barrel to tell Hughes that the gun had been fired recently. The eight shot magazine had only three rounds remaining, plus one in the chamber. Someone had recently fired five shots with that gun. The last thing he had dropped on the bed were two cheaply printed brochures for the Cloudcroft Inn in Cloudcroft, NM, one of them had a folded piece of paper used as a bookmark. The page marked was for the bridal suite.

As he had been searching the room, Hughes had been mulling everything over in his mind. It was pretty brazen for Kennedy, a mere foreman working for someone as powerful as Judge Prestridge to take off with the Judge's daughter. He was almost positive that the Rolls Royce keys would fit the car that the Daniels women had been driving. Based on the keys alone, there was no doubt in his mind that Kennedy was involved in the disappearance of the Daniels women. He just couldn't figure out the connection between Kennedy and young Eva Prestridge, other than the obvious one based on the sexy pictures. Then one possible explanation dawned on him, he suddenly knew what had motivated Kennedy.

At that moment, the Prestridge boy lying on the floor moaned and tried to sit up. Hughes glanced down at the young man and held out one hand toward Mosley.

"Give me your handcuffs," he snapped, stepping over to grab the young man's collar and pull him closer to the bed.

"Uh, what are you going to do?" asked Mosley in some confusion, making no move to respond to the Ranger's demand.

"Just shut up and give me your cuffs!" ordered Hughes, holding out one big hand.

Fumbling nervously with the handcuff case on his belt, the Sheriff finally handed his handcuffs to the big Ranger. Hughes leaned down and, taking the young man's left wrist, handcuffed it to the wrought ironed headboard of the Foreman's bed. Assured that the young man was not going anywhere anytime soon, Hughes gathered up all of the items on the bedspread and started for the door.

"Let's go!" he ordered the Sheriff, not even bothering to look at the corpulent Sheriff or at the young man handcuffed to the bed.

With one last glance at the groggy youth half lying on the floor, one wrist handcuffed to the bed frame, Mosley meekly followed the Ranger out of the cottage. He had the feeling that there would be hell to pay when Judge Prestridge found out about this.

"Where are we going?" Mosley finally demanded from the Ranger when he caught up with him. They were rounding the house, heading for the Sheriff's car in which they had arrived. "We need to talk to Judge Prestridge and tell him about his son. You might have hurt him when you hit him."

Hughes glanced at the puffing Sheriff with some amusement.

"You would have preferred that young Prestridge shot me, instead?" he asked mildly, his face passive as he glanced at the Sheriff. "I knew that you were an ass kisser, but Jesus Christ, man. Show at least some backbone!"

Mosley turned even redder than his normal complexion and he stammered in some confusion.

"Uh, no, of course not; I certainly did not want the boy to shoot you," he finally gasped, almost running to keep up with the long stride of Hughes. On the other hand it would have certainly solved the problem of splitting that reward money with the Ranger.

"But the judge is going to awfully mad at you for punching out his boy. Besides, where are we going in such an all fired hurry?"

"To interrupt a honeymoon and catch a killer before he kills again!" snapped Hughes as he arrived at the car and tossed the items he carried into the back seat. "You can drive or I will, but we are going after that man before he hurts that girl."

"But where are they?" demanded Mosley, leaning against the car as he panted for breath. "Unless you have some type of special power that none of the rest of us do, ain't nobody got any idea where they done got off to."

"Get in and I'll tell you where they went, while we drive," ordered Hughes, sliding into the passenger seat.

Still mystified, Mosley went around to the driver's side and side behind the wheel. He started up the car as he heard a high-pitched male voice screaming profanity behind him. Glancing in the rear view mirror, he saw young Prestridge, the source of the never ending stream of profanity that filled the air, struggling to get through the door of the cottage, the wrought iron headboard to which he was still handcuffed clutched in both hands.

At about the same time, the front door of the main house flew open and Mosley saw the Judge charging down the front steps, a shotgun clutched tightly in one hand as he ran toward the car. Trailing behind him was the rest of his family. His other son was waving a handgun over his head.

"Drive on, if you want to save that girl!" snapped Hughes, looking out the rear window of the squad car, watching the antics of the Prestridge family unfold behind them. "Otherwise, I will have to hurt somebody."

"But-----," breathed Mosley, clearly undecided about what to do.

"Your funeral," observed Hughes, leaning back in the seat as if he had not a concern in the world. "But I thought that you wanted that reward for finding the Daniels women."

"Jesus Christ," swore Mosley as he made a decision and stomped on the gas pedal. The powerful patrol car fishtailed as it went tearing down the gravel drive, leaving the Judge waving a shotgun and his younger son trying to chase them down the drive, dragging a wrought iron head board behind him.

CHAPTER SIX

At that moment, the young lady that was the cause of all of this confusion was sitting casually in the passenger seat of one of her father's cars, her long, deeply tanned, dancer's legs crossed at the ankles, her head back against the headrest, her eyes closed as Bertram Kennedy hummed happily beside her. Kennedy was feeling on top of the world, he knew that his days of just scrapping by were over. Once the two of them were married, the Judge would have no choice but to promote Kennedy to a much better job so that he could support his new wife.

Eva Prestridge was a beautiful young lady, just reaching her 16th year. Her hair was long and blonde, her eyes a deep blue and her long tanned legs and full hourglass shaped figure could stop traffic. She was also daddy's little girl and as spoiled as they came. Normally, she was someone who planned everything out, but this particular action was really a spur of the moment act. She hoped that she had judged everyone's reactions correctly.

At that moment she was distracted from her thoughts by Bertram Kennedy running one hand up and down her bare leg to finally rest it on her left knee. Not opening her eyes, but instead allowing a smile to play around her full lips, she allowed her legs to part slightly, encouraging him to explore higher, beneath her casual knee length dress. From the slight tremor she felt in his roving hand, there was no doubt that Kennedy was going to jump on her as soon as they were alone. She didn't mind his attention since she loved sex, which she used to control the men around her.

The two of them had been secretly "keeping company" as the older folks called it, since she had turned fourteen. Even at that relatively young age she had been a beautiful girl, with a detailed knowledge of, and a liking for, sex that rivaled someone twice her age. Since that first time in the loft of the barn, the foreman had made love to her in every position she had ever heard of, and a few that she was sure he had made up; the randy foreman never seemed to get enough of her. Everything was progressing according to her plan.

At that moment, her naturally randy disposition exerted itself as she felt Kennedy's hand slide slowly between her legs and the car begin to slow. Her eyes flew open and her lips parted softly as she slid her own soft dainty hands along his powerful forearm, stopping his further explorations of her nubile body. She was well aware that if her daddy caught them before they arrived at the hotel he would kill Kennedy and that would ruin her entire plan.

"Soon, Bert, soon," she panted, as she grabbed his roving hand with both of her. Her low-pitched sensual voice shook as she spoke, her own lovely features showing her sexual arousal. "As soon as we get there you can do anything you want to me, my dear. But, remember, until we get where we are going my father can still stop our plans. You know that he would never agree to this!"

"I guess you're right," grunted Kennedy, as he removed his hand from the moist warmth between her full thighs and mashed down once again on the powerful auto's gas pedal. She felt the powerful car pick up steam and watched the speedometer crawl toward sixty miles and hour. "The sooner we are there the better. Once we are married, he will have to accept me."

Neither of them noticed the mounted cowboy sitting his mount among a small copse of trees near the road watching them intently. Once the car was out of sight, the silent rider kicked his mount into motion, heading toward a nearby country store at a fast trot. Once there he swung from his horse and ran toward the pay phone mounted on the side of the building. Dropping in the correct change, the rider quickly dialed a number from memory.

"Judge Prestridge, please," he blurted quickly before the person that had answered the phone could say a word, almost dancing with nervousness as the phone was answered. After a moment, he heard the well-remembered voice of one of the most powerful men in the country come on the line.

"This is Judge Prestridge," came the low powerful voice of the man that had sent him to prison for five years. "Who is this?"

"Judge, this is Laney Larson," began the rider, nervously. "I've heard from one of your men earlier that you are looking for that Bertram Kennedy."

"That's true," responded Prestridge cautiously. "Have you seen him?

"I have," he responded, gathering his courage at the suppressed eagerness he detected in the Judge's voice. "I saw him and a woman in a car that passed here not more than five minutes ago."

"Where are you?" asked the Judge quickly.

"Kennedy is one of those that lied about me to you, Judge," barked Larson, ignoring Prestridge's question. "He got away with lying and you sent me to prison for five years. I want my name cleared and your man also said that there would be a reward for the person that found that bastard."

"That's right, there is a reward and if you help me find Kennedy, I'll personally clear your name," responded the Judge impatiently. "Where are you and where did you see them?"

"Oh, I'm sorry Judge, I'm at Claridge's store on the back road to Cloudcroft," Laney responded, elated that Kennedy was finally going to get his and this time it would be Laney Larson that would profit. "Like I said, that Kennedy bastard went tearing by here in a big fancy black car with some female."

"Did you recognize the woman?" suddenly demanded Prestridge.

"Fraid not, Judge, she had her head back against the headrest like she was sleeping. But I saw him, there is no doubt that it was Kennedy driving the car," responded Larson, turning to look down the road.

"You wait there and I will have someone come give you the reward," said Prestridge. "I won't forget this, Larson. You can be sure that I will not forget your help."

Without waiting for a response, Prestridge broke the connection. Larson held the dead receiver for another moment before he dropped it back into its rack and immediately slid his finger into the coin return to see if his money had by some miracle been refunded. He was a bit disappointed to find the coin return to be empty. But he suddenly brightened as he considered the reward that he had coming from Judge Prestridge. He bet it would be at least a hundred dollars. Why, with a hundred dollars, he would be rich, maybe he would even be offered a full time job at Prestridge's New Mexico ranch. Why he could even become foreman of the home ranch in place of Kennedy.

He was still dreaming about his possible rewards thirty minutes later when a big saloon car pulled into the parking lot of Claridge's store. Larson recognized Judge Prestridge sitting in the passenger seat. Hitching up his pants, the bantam sized cowboy walked across the graveled lot to claim his reward. He never expected what he received; he never saw the barrels of the sawed off shotgun poking out of the back window. The shotgun fired as Larson leaned forward to talk to the Judge, the double load of double ought buckshot hit the cowboy in the center of his face, almost tearing his head off. The blast was still echoing across the parking lot as the big car roared out of the parking lot down the road toward Cloudcroft, NM.

Joe Claridge was on the phone to the Sheriff's office before the big car was out of sight. His description was complete, right down to the license number of the car. Eva's little escapade had sat many things in motion that would continue to be issues in this area for decades to come.

IN THE SHERIFF'S PATROL UNIT

"OK, Ranger," began Mosley in some frustration. "Now that we have really pissed off Judge Prestridge, slugged and handcuffed his son, would you mind telling me where we are going?"

In answer, Hughes tossed one of the hotel brochures he had taken from Kennedy's cottage into Mosley's lap.

"We're going to Cloudcroft, Sheriff," responded Hughes, never taking his eyes off of the road. "From the papers and the pictures that we found in Kennedy's bedroom, it is clear that Miss Eva is not the innocent that her family tried to make her out. I think she has run off with this Kennedy to get married and they are going to Cloudcroft for a Honeymoon. But if her father gets there first, the girl may be a widow."

"Oh, now, Ranger," protested Mosley, taking his eyes off the road to look at Hughes. "I've known that girl since she was born. She might not be as pure as the driven snow, but she is not the type to run off and marry some saddle tramp like Bertram Kennedy."

Hughes shrugged; his own eyes were still locked on the road ahead of them. His mind was racing, planning for the upcoming confrontation.

"Maybe yes and maybe no," he responded indifferently. "Maybe she ran off with him and maybe she didn't. However, what I do know is that we have two missing women in this area and there is no way to mistake those Rolls Royce keys that I found on Kennedy's bed. I don't know of any other Rolls in this part of the country, but those Daniels women were sure as hell driving one. I will also be willing to bet my pension that those keys will fit the Daniel's car. If Kennedy killed those women, then Eva Prestridge's life may be in jeopardy. Bertram Kennedy may be both a kidnapper as well as a cold blooded killer."

"Jesus," gulped Mosley as he considered all of the implications of the Ranger's statements. The first thing that flashed through his mind was that saving Eva Prestridge would make the Judge indebted to him for life. He suddenly flipped a switch on the dash and pushed the gas pedal all of the way to the floor. The quiet of the countryside was suddenly disturbed by the high-pitched wail of the siren as the big car suddenly surged forward. If Kennedy was a killer, there was no way he was going to let the Foreman kill that pretty little girl.

He leaned forward and pulled the radio microphone from its clip and keyed the transmit switch.

"Headquarters, this is Sheriff Mosley!" barked the Sheriff.

"This is headquarters," came the immediate response. "Sheriff, I've got Mrs. Prestridge on the phone –."

"Stow it, Parkman! No, you listen to me and you listen good," snapped Mosley as the headquarters radio operator paused for a moment and released his transmit switch. "I want you to call Johnny Quinton, the Sheriff in Cloudcroft and tell him that Bertram Kennedy, a suspected killer, is going to be checking into the Lodge with a hostage. Tell him not to try and arrest Kennedy, as we do not want the hostage hurt.

"Ask him to make sure that Kennedy is assigned one of those cottages on the backside of the property. Ranger Hughes and I should be there in about forty minutes and we will take care of the situation."

"Uh, sure thing, Sheriff!" responded Headquarters. "But Sheriff, I need to let you know that Mrs. Prestridge said that her husband just took off with some of his men to get their daughter. She said she was afraid someone would get hurt since they took guns."

With a grunt, Mosley returned his microphone to its clip on the dash, not even bothering to respond to the statement.

"Told you that old man would be out for blood," remarked Hughes mildly.

"Now you will see how we do things in El Paso, Ranger!" Mosley boasted, as he laughed loudly, picturing what he would demand from Judge Prestridge as a reward for saving his daughter. Around here, a man steps on his own snakes. The judge is doing what any father would do. But we will get there first and resolve it before anyone gets hurt."

Hughes' response was only a grunt as he settled more comfortably in the corner of the seat. He could picture what he was sure that he would see about the way things were done in El Paso, but even he could not have anticipated what would happen before this day was done.

THE AUTOMOBILE CONTAINING JUDGE PRESTRIDGE

Judge Prestridge sat forward in his seat, as if his leaning forward would make the car go faster. He was intent on reaching Cloudcroft before any of the authorities could find out about his daughter's newest stunt. He was determined to protect the dignity of the family name, a name that would be a laughing stock if it was known that his daughter had run off with a mere Ranch foreman. If a few of the local riffraff had to die to protect the Prestridge name, then so be it.

Turning slightly, he glanced at his two men in the back seat of the car. Rafe McEntire, the man who favored the sawed off shotgun sat placidly, chewing on a piece of straw. Beside him was a hulking figure, over eight feet tall in his stocking feet, called only Tiny. Prestridge was the only person that Tiny had ever looked up to and obeyed. These two would insure that no one lived to spread any negative tales about his daughter.

"Can't you go faster?" he demanded of Ron Artnot, his driver. "We have to get to Cloudcroft before that fool Sheriff can get there!"

CHAPTER SEVEN

THE LODGE, CLOUDCROFT, NEW MEXICO

The hotel, now known as the Lodge, was originally constructed in 1899, by the Alamogordo & Sacramento Railroad as a resort for its workers who supported the Railroad's never ending search for suitable timber. When opened to the public, the hotel was immediately successful as it's breathtaking location in the lushly wooded Sacramento Mountains offered a welcome cool retreat to literally thousands of visitors from Texas, New Mexico, Oklahoma, and Arizona.

An article published in the Albuquerque Journal-Democrat near the completion of the Lodge in 1899 stated, "*This beautiful building will be known as Cloudcroft Lodge and it's interior will be furnished with a lavish hand, yet in keeping with the character of the place. Fireplaces, with wide, hungry mouths, will sparkle, crackle and dart forth welcome tongues of flame to hundreds of merry guests, who will find new pleasure in life during the long, sultry summer." In 1908 the El Paso & Southwestern Railroad System- the Lodge's new owner- advertised that the hotel, restaurant, dancing pavilion, tennis court, golf links, bowling alley, billiard parlor, burro trips and children's playground were accessible for "weekend rates of $3.00 round trip," and that Lodge rates were "$12.50 and up" per week.* Unfortunately, on June 13th 1909, a raging fire blazed through the Lodge, utterly destroying it.

By 1911, the Lodge was completely rebuilt and reopened on it's current site, and it's appearance has remained virtually the same since then- a historic, timeless gem suspended in time. Over the long, distinguished history of the Lodge, it has played host to numerous famous folk- including Pancho Villa, Gilbert Roland, Judy Garland, and Clark Gable (in fact the last two carved their names into the wall of the Lodge's

Tower, where they can still be seen to this day). But by far the most infamous guest of all at the Lodge is the specter of Rebecca. Rebecca was said to be a gorgeous red-haired chambermaid who worked and lived at the Lodge in the 1920's/30's.

Similar to her fellow Lodge employees, she lived in the employee's rooms, which were located in the basement at the time. She was by all means a very friendly and flirtatious young lady, and unforgettably lovely. There was some rumor that Rebecca moonlighted as a prostitute, although no proof of this claim existed.

Whatever the case, according to the story, Rebecca's jealous lumberjack boyfriend caught her in the arms of another man at the Lodge (possibly in Room 101, also called the Governor's Suite) and became enraged. Shortly after this unfortunate event, Rebecca disappeared from the Lodge, never to be seen again. However, soon after her disappearance people began to report having some very strange, even ghostly, experiences in certain areas of the hotel.

Over the years, there have been many sightings of an auburn haired apparition floating through the halls, a vision seen by both employees and guests alike. One guest heard scraping sounds in the hallway late one night and opened the door to see a red-haired woman in a 30's style nightdress rearranging flowers in a vase on top of an antique chest. Another guest was shocked when he went to take a shower, only to find a "vaporous female" reclining in his bathtub.

There have also been reports of objects such as watches, ashtrays, and silverware sliding across surfaces untouched... doors opening and closing on their own... lights and other appliances turning on and off by themselves... furniture moved inexplicably... and even faucets turning on and toilets flushing for no apparent reason. But perhaps one of the strangest events happened one Halloween night, when a man dressed in a tuxedo came into the Lodge's dining room and sat alone at an intimate, two-chaired table. He ordered two dinners and two glasses of wine. Everyone in the room watched closely as the man ate his meal and carried on a conversation with someone who wasn't there. No one ever saw anyone sit with the man or even go near him, yet at the end of his meal, both wineglasses and both plates were empty.

Rebecca's manifestations are many. One of her favorite areas is called the Red Dog Saloon- an old-west style saloon with rough-hewn walls and Southwest decorum- which is located in the basement, where the employee's showers used to be. This is a very active spot- lights go off and on untouched... 1930's-era poker chips have been mysteriously found in the middle of a floor which had been clear only minutes before... Lodge patrons have called the front desk to complain about the loud music coming from the saloon at times when the saloon was empty and wasn't even open... an apparition of a twirling woman has been reportedly seen on the dance floor... and a bartender claimed to have seen the reflection of a beautiful red-haired woman wearing a long dress in the mirror behind the bar- yet the woman wasn't there when the bartender turned around to look at her.

Another paranormal hotspot seems to be found in the "Tower"... a three-story structure that stands tall above the Lodge itself. The Tower is kept locked, with two levels of small sitting rooms with windows that yield a panoramic view of the lush mountains. Some people have reported feeling cold spots and a "presence" in the Tower, and on the third floor, where there is a locked door leading to the Tower, there are reports of paranormal activity as well. Additionally, there is also said to be a lot of activity surrounding Room 101, the Governor's Suite. Some have theorized that Rebecca carried on her "trysts" in this room and was perhaps even caught in the act there by her lumberjack boyfriend one fateful day. Whatever the connection, the Lodge staff has gotten calls from Room 101 where no one is on the other end, even when no one is in the room at the time. Despite having a modern, computerized phone system, the phone calls from Room 101 persist. The light in the ceiling fan just outside of Room 101 is also said to turn off and on at will. A former housekeeper claimed that after making up a bed, she would come back only to find an indentation as if someone had just laid or sat there. She also said that guest's shoes would mysteriously move a few rooms down from where they were supposed to be. It would seem that even in spectral form, Rebecca is a very fun-loving and mischievous spirit. To this day, employee and guests alike are still reporting strange and mysterious encounters at the Lodge such as toilets in the ladies rooms flushing by themselves.

Into such a historic scene, Bertram Kennedy strode in through the ornate front doors and went up to the registration desk. He waited patiently until Jimmy Montrose, the Registration clerk finished with the elderly lady to whom he was explaining some of the history of the historic old hotel and moved down the counter to wait on him.

"Yes sir, what can I do for you?" asked Montrose cheerfully. His eyes locked on Kennedy's, but he was still watching for a young lady matching the description he had been given by the local Sheriff.

"Need a room for two," responded Kennedy, with his own bright smile. "One that is sort of off to itself. We just got married and we might be a, uh, little noisy, so to speak."

Montrose smiled knowingly, as a lot of honeymooners came to the Lodge and quite often the ladies, especially some of the younger ones, were what were politely known as screamers. His daddy had always told him that there were two kinds of women in the bed, screamers, or biters. He'd take a screamer any day.

He laid a registration card on the counter in front of Kennedy and moved over to get a room key. Kennedy was still slowly filling out the card when Montrose returned with the room key so, like most clerks being able to read upside down, he scanned the information Kennedy had already written. Everything appeared to be in order, so he decided not to ask for a large deposit in advance.

At that moment, the phone rang. Montrose laid the room key down on the counter and moved over to answer the phone.

"The Lodge, Jimmy Montrose speaking."

"Jimmy, this is Sheriff Quinton,"

"Yes sir, how are you?" responded Montrose cheerfully.

"Just fine. Listen, have you had someone named Kennedy check in there with a pretty young filly named Eva?"

Montrose paused, not wanting to let Kennedy, standing only a few feet away, know that the Sheriff was asking about him in case he was a wanted man or something similar. It just would not do for the Lodge to have a shootout in the lobby. It would be bad for business.

"Uh, yeah, I think so, is there a problem?" responded Montrose cautiously.

"Is he there now?" asked Quinton intuitively.

"Exactly!" responded Montrose, relief evident in his voice.

"I want you to assign them the old caretaker's cabin at the rear of the property, away from the main hotel," instructed the Sheriff carefully, his voice revealing nothing. "Don't do anything else."

"Uh, sure, no problem," responded Montrose, turning to glance at Kennedy who was looking at him curiously, clearly impatient to get a room key. "Listen, I've got a customer, so I have to go."

"OK, call me when they have gone to the cabin," ordered Quinton, breaking the connection.

Montrose hung up and returned to the counter.

"Some kind of problem?" asked Kennedy, concern on his face.

"Oh, no," Montrose hastened to answer. "There are never any problems at the Lodge, just a few matters that the staff has to deal with."

Montrose paused a moment and turned back to the key cabinet.

"You said that you wanted privacy, so I have just the place for you. It used to be the cabin for the caretaker years ago. Now it is sometimes used as a honeymoon suite. I assure you that no one will hear you from there; you and the little lady can make all of the noise that you want. Just follow the drive around the hotel and you will find the little cottage at the rear of the property."

"Just the thing!" exclaimed Kennedy, holding out his hand for the key.

"Here you go, sir!" boomed Montrose as he handed Kennedy an antique key unlike any of the other room keys. "The cabin is actually older than this hotel since it was built at the same time as the original hotel in 1899. The original hotel burned and was rebuilt in 1911. So that old place is historic if you know what I mean. Have a good time and look out for Rebecca."

"Rebecca?" asked Kennedy in some confusion. "Who's Rebecca?"

"Oh," began Montrose. "I see you haven't heard about the ghost that haunts the hotel. Her name is Rebecca."

Kennedy laughed in derision. "Well I don't believe in ghosts and besides, I will be otherwise involved. I won't have any time for ghost hunting."

Montrose smiled and waved as he turned to wait on another guest.

"Well, enjoy."

He paused as he watched Kennedy exit the hotel and run down the steps to enter a dark car. He could tell that there was someone else waiting in the car. Asking the new guest to wait, he turned to the phone and dialed the Sheriff's office.

"Sheriff's office," answered a female voice.

"Sheriff Quinton, please," said Montrose.

"Who is calling?" queried the voice.

"Tell him it is Jimmy Montrose," responded Montrose, his voice low as he turned, glancing around the lobby to make sure that Kennedy hadn't slipped back inside to eavesdrop.

"Sheriff Quinton," came a deep voice almost immediately.

"I did like you said, Sheriff, I put them in the old caretaker's cottage. There was someone waiting in the car for him, but I couldn't get a good look at that person. They just went back there now," blurted

Montrose quickly, his voice almost quivering with excitement. "Is he some kind of big time criminal?"

Quinton snorted in derision.

"Now Jimmy, don't go letting your imagination get the best of you," began Quinton. "Never you mind why we want him, just keep people away from the cottage until we get there, and don't you go snooping around there!"

"Uh, sure thing, Sheriff," responded Montrose, disappointment evident in his voice. He had read so many stories about bank robbers and their molls that his imagination had populated the surrounding forests with every criminal from Baby Face Nelson to Ma Barker. Now that it appeared that there might be an honest to god criminal registered at the Lodge, the Sheriff was refusing to let him in on the secret. One day, when he was a member of the FBI and working for J. Edgar Hoover he would know where the criminals were, but until then, he was just a desk clerk.

IN THE OLD CARETAKER'S CABIN

As Bertram Kennedy brought in the luggage that filled the back of his borrowed car, Eva Prestridge made the rounds of the little cottage, investigating each nook and cranny. She noticed that it was somewhat isolated and not in the hotel proper, smiling to herself, dismissing this as Bert Kennedy planning on some very noisy activities. She was finally admitting to herself that she might finally be able to get free of her parents. Her granddaddy's will had left her a fortune but she had to be either 21 or married to get it free of her daddy's control. She didn't want to wait another four years for that money and she figured her daddy would kill Kennedy for messing with her, leaving her free to enjoy her wealth, so, in her mind, marrying the poor schnook was the best course of action. Besides, he was hung like a horse and certainly knew how to use his equipment. She paused to glance out the window, her eyes drinking in the beauty of the pristine wilderness.

As she stood at the window, Kennedy came up behind her, sliding his arms around her, his big hands cupped her full breasts. He rubbed against her, only his pants and her summer dress between them. Turning, she put her arms around his neck and raised her full lips for the kiss that she knew was coming. One thing that she liked about Kennedy was that he could never get enough of her.

She moaned softly, as she felt Kennedy's fingers begin to lower the zipper on the back of her dress. Obligingly she lowered her arms so that Kennedy could slide her dress off of her shoulders and drop it to the floor. Quickly, this time his hands visibly shaking, he unfastened her bra and let it drop to the floor on top of the dress pooled at her feet. Slowly he ran his hands down her back and hooked his fingers in the waistband of her wispy panties. In seconds the lacy panties joined the rest of her clothes on the floor. Now she stood before him in just high heels, a garter belt, and hose.

Growling softly, Kennedy scooped her up in his powerful arms and carried her to the bed. He lowered her gently to lie sprawled on top of the bedspread as he began to remove his own clothes. Eva Prestridge watched each movement with smoldering eyes. Her turgid nipples and flaring nostrils showed her own rising sexual excitement. Finally, naked, he lowered himself into her waiting arms. Soon they were lost in the world all their own.

CHAPTER EIGHT

Mosley kept the gas pedal floored until the entrance to The Lodge was in sight. There had been very little conversation between the two lawmen, each concentrated on their own thoughts. Hughes was gratified to see that the local Sheriff was waiting in the entrance to the hotel drive, leaning against his car. Very little bothered Hughes, but when he acted outside his jurisdiction, he always made sure to obtain the cooperation of the local authorities. It certainly made for less problems in the long run. Now that he was in New Mexico and not Texas, he was really a civilian, not a lawman. He was a little surprised to see that Mosley also worked with other Sheriff's when he left his jurisdiction. This was actually more intelligence than he had credited Mosley for having.

Mosley braked the big cruiser sharply to a stop mere inches from Quinton's own unmarked cruiser. Before Mosley could exit the car, Sheriff Quinton came up to the open window.

"OK, Mosley, Kennedy and the young woman with him are in the old caretaker's cottage on the back of the property. Now what is all of this about?" began Quinton, using his sleeve to mop the sweat from his forehead.

"I'm Texas Ranger Captain, Hughes," interrupted the big Ranger before Mosley could speak. "The suspect is believed to have abducted an underage woman and brought her across state lines for immoral purposes. He is also suspected of being involved in the kidnapping and possible murder of two other women."

"Well," whistled Quinton, "this could really be something interesting. I had no idea what this was all about, but I have sent men to block all of the exits from the hotel grounds. We can rush the place it you want."

He paused for a moment and grinned.

"One of my men slipped up and listened at the window. I doubt that they would even hear us coming if we rushed the place. That girl is a real screamer, if you get my meaning. The two of them wouldn't know if a bomb went off outside that cabin."

"Might I suggest that Sheriff Mosley and I try to talk him into surrendering so that we do not endanger the girl by trying to rush the place?" suggested Hughes tactfully, tucking what Sheriff Quinton had said away for future use. He wanted to be very sure that he did not step on any sensitive toes in this jurisdiction. "Who knows what could happen if a gun battle breaks out."

Quinton thought about it for a moment and then shrugged. If the two visiting lawmen wanted to make themselves targets for a possible kidnapper then it was no skin off of his nose. He stepped away from the car and swept one around toward the hotel.

"Just follow the drive around the hotel. The cottage is on the right at the rear of the property."

"Much obliged, Sheriff!" called Hughes as Mosley, a sour look on his face, drove slowly along the driveway. Quinton's cruiser fell in behind their car.

"Ranger, I want to make it clear that I am in charge of this here operation," began Mosley, his voice quivering with anger. "Prestridge will have my ass if something happens to that girl of his!"

Hughes favored the Sheriff with a steady stare, personally he felt that Mosley in charge guaranteed that someone would die, but legally, as a Texas Ranger, he was only in the area to adviser local law enforcement. Mosley was the El Paso County Sheriff and they were in New Mexico, but his badge was the one the locals would cooperate with.

"Oh, by all means, you are in charge," quipped the Ranger. "If something happens to the girl, you can explain it to her father."

Braking to a stop behind a small stand of trees, Mosley and the big Ranger exited the car, softly closing the doors so as to not alert their quarry. Hughes started to move softly toward the cottage, when to his total shock, Mosley walked out into the open drive, facing the cabin. He glanced back and saw that Sheriff Quinton was also regarding Mosley with total disbelief.

"Bertram Kennedy," shouted the pompous El Paso County Sheriff, his fists on his hips in what Hughes was sure that Mosley thought was a commanding stance. "This is Sheriff Mosley from El Paso, I am here to arrest you for kidnapping and taking a minor across state lines for immoral purposes. Now you come out of that cabin right now and surrender before I have to come inside and get you!"

For a long moment, there was total quiet; no movement could be detected from the cabin. Mosley ignored attempts by the local Sheriff and the Ranger to get him to take cover. This was his moment of glory, where he showed that he was a take-charge type of lawman who could be depended upon to get his man. Rescuing that girl would certainly get him a big reward and probably a fancy state job. Finally, growing impatient, Mosley drew his pearl handled sidearm and started for the door to the cottage.

As his right foot came down on the first step that led to the small porch of the cottage, the window closest to the door was broken from the inside and two bullets came whistling through the air. Both of the bullets hit Sheriff Mosley in the chest. The Sheriff was knocked backward a few steps, but he stayed on his feet. Slowly he turned to face Hughes, who had prudently stepped behind a tree when the shots had been fired. At first Hughes was uncertain if Mosley had actually been hit as he had his pistol still clutched in his hand, but pointed at the ground. Then like a mighty oak tree that had finally been struck down, Mosley finally dropped to his knees and fell face forward into the dirt of the driveway.

Suddenly the cabin door burst open and a partially naked man literally sprang through the door and paused then started running toward the nearby car, a revolver clutched in one hand. Hughes heard a car screech to a halt behind him as he stepped out into the open, but paid it no mind. As far as he was concerned traffic control was the responsibility of local law enforcement.

"Kennedy," he bellowed. "Texas Rangers! Drop your weapon or I will shoot you down where you are."

Bertram Kennedy, wearing only his pants, but no shoes or shirt, stopped and turned toward Hughes, the pistol still clutched tightly in his hand.

"Wait," Kennedy yelled, raising the pistol. "You don't understand!"

Determined to take no chances, Hughes drew his own pistol and fired at Kennedy. His bullet struck Kennedy in the upper right side of his chest; the pistol that he clutched in one hand fell to the ground and Kennedy fell to his knees, his left hand clutching his bleeding right shoulder. Hughes, weapon ready, took two steps toward the kneeling man when he heard a shotgun roar from behind him. The Ranger ducked as something whistled close by his left ear and from the corner of his eye, he saw Kennedy rise up from his knees and flip over backward.

Dropping to one knee, Hughes spun and fired instinctively. The skinny man who had fired the sawed off shotgun at the fleeing man had a look of total shock on his thin face as the shotgun fell from his nerveless fingers. Slowly he looked down at the hole in his chest that was spurting blood and then he fell over backward.

There was a maniacal scream from the right and Hughes looked over to see the biggest man he had ever seen in his life running at him, a club raised over his bald head. Not wanting to stop and ask questions, Hughes fired twice, knocking the big man's right leg, which was the size of a tree trunk, out from under him.

Hughes rose to his feet, relieved to see that Sheriff Quinton now held a gun on the driver of the car that the two killers had come from. What puzzled him was Judge Prestridge standing beside the car; his hands also raised in the air, a Cloudcroft Deputy Sheriff holding him at gunpoint.

"You all right, Ranger?" yelled Quinton, his eyes never leaving his prisoner.

"Doing fine," responded Hughes holstering his weapon as he walked over to kneel beside Mosley's rapidly cooling body. Mosley had wanted to play the big shot and he had gotten more than he had bargained for. With a sigh, Hughes rose to his feet and walked over to kneel beside Kennedy. Hughes' bullet, intended to disable the suspect, had hit him squarely in the shoulder. Unfortunately, the sawed off shotgun had been loaded with double 00 buckshot and the blast had hit Kennedy squarely in the face. There was no question that the man was very dead.

Rising slowly, Hughes drew his weapon once more and stepped cautiously toward the partially open cabin door. Reaching out, he slowly pushed the door open with the barrel of his pistol. He neither saw nor heard anything inside the cabin. Cautiously, weapon at the ready, he stepped inside the cabin, that at first, appeared empty.

He was on the verge of holstering his weapon when he heard a sound from beneath the bed. Dropping to one knee, he peered beneath the bed to see that there was someone crouched down on the other side of the bed.

"Come out of there or I will fire!" Hughes snapped, his pistol held at the ready, the hammer back.

Over the years, Hughes had seen a lot of things and been in a lot of high-pressure, life or death situations. However, none of this prepared him for what happened next. For from the dubious protection of that rumpled bed rose the most beautiful woman Hughes had ever seen.

From the top of her head to the tips of her dainty painted toes, Eva Prestridge was absolutely gorgeous. Her long red hair was mussed and there were some bruises on her face, her eyeliner was smeared and her wrists were handcuffed behind her back. She was wearing only her hose, which were torn, making it look like she had been worked over thoroughly. She stood with one foot slightly in front of the other, the pink tip of her tongue just visible between her moist, ruby red lips.

For a long moment, Hughes just stood and stared at the young lady, who continued to stand as if posing, meeting him stare for stare. Finally, Hughes holstered his weapon and stepped over to the window.

"Sheriff Quinton!" he yelled.

"Yes, Ranger!" responded the Sheriff looking up from trying to fit standard handcuffs on the huge wrists of Tiny.

"Send Judge Prestridge in here," Hughes responded.

There were a few minutes of discussion in the group of Deputies gathered around the three prisoners before Hughes heard slow footsteps on the small stoop leading to the cabin. In a moment, Judge Prestridge walked calmly into the cabin. His suit was rumpled and his hair was in mussed and his expression was resigned. Like Hughes, he froze when he caught his first glimpse of Eva. It was at that moment that Judge Prestridge realized that Daddy's little girl was now all grown up.

Hughes regarded the Judge with a calm, stony stare until the Judge began to flush slightly. Eva Prestridge still stood silently, almost nude, posed as if on display for the two men, her wrists cuffed behind her. Neither made any move to help her cover her nakedness.

"Judge Prestridge, you and I need to talk!" began Hughes, his muscular arms crossed over his broad chest.

PART II

THE SALE

CHAPTER NINE

It has long been said that military service changes people. Normally this remark refers to the broadening of experiences and the priceless opportunities that can come with military service. However, some individuals are changed in very unexpected ways. Some of these unexpected ways are very much outside the understanding of man. Such a person was Anna Ortiz, a lovely, 25-year old, Hispanic woman who had seen service in Operation Desert Storm as a Helicopter pilot. A member of the reserve only recently promoted to Captain and allowed to achieve her dream of flying military helicopters, Anna was one that had no fear, to her no mission was impossible, only a greater challenge.

The mission had been touted as routine, picking up a squad that had been marooned by mechanical breakdown of their Bradley Fighting Vehicle. As she circled the area, Anna could see no signs of any of the enemy, but as she approached the LZ (Landing Zone), a Stinger missile had come from a nearby building to slam into her tail rotor causing her to lose control of the aircraft. The Huey helicopter had spun and smashed into the side of a two-story building at the edge of the marked LZ. Luckily there had been no fire and, as the soldiers they had come to pickup raced to deal with the insurgents hidden in the deserted buildings, her co-pilot had pulled her unconscious body from the wreckage. Four of her passengers had died in the crash, while Anna had suffered several broken bones and a severe head injury.

Her injuries were much more severe that they had appeared at first, and in spite of everything the doctors were able to do, Anna slid into a coma the second night in the field hospital. She had been medivaced to a hospital in Germany and then airlifted to Beaumont Army Medical Center at Fort Bliss, Texas, the military post located at El Paso, Texas. It was also her home; the Army had sent her home to die.

For several weeks, Anna lay in a coma in a small hospital room, life support machines hooked to her body. No one expected her to ever regain consciousness, but her grandmother, her closest relative, refused to give up hope. Each day, 73-year old Elena Granado Espinosa made the trip from her home in Ciudad Juarez to her granddaughter's hospital room at Beaumont Hospital with high hopes. Each night she went home saddened and in mourning. In spite of the doctors' firm belief that Anna was already dead but her body didn't know it, her grandmother refused to give up hope and Anna managed to take one breath after another. As long as she still lived, her grandmother would not authorize the removal of life support. Where there is life, there is hope.

It was on October 31st, Halloween, the day when traditionally the barrier separating the living from the dead is at its weakest when Anna's condition changed for the better. On that day, as if she was answering a call, Anna opened her eyes to see an older man with a very kind face, leaning over her. He studied her intently for a long while and then slowly reached down to check her pulse. His hand was so cold that it startled her, causing her to try and pull her hand away from him. To her surprise, she was so weak that he had no trouble retaining his grip. Apparently realizing what had caused her reaction, he smiled and released her wrist.

"No cause for alarm, Ms. Ortiz. My patients always complained that my hands felt like I kept them in the freezer," he said with a kind smile.

"Where am I?" she asked him weakly. She remembered nothing after catching sight of the Stinger missile coming at her aircraft from the edge of her vision. "Why am I so cold?"

The doctor, she saw his nametag read Johnson, pulled the sheet up to her neck and wrapped it around her snuggly.

"There is no need to worry, my dear, you are going to be fine," he paused as if searching for the words. "Your injuries were very severe and the Army returned you to Fort Bliss. You were not expected to live, but from this point forward, you will get stronger each day. You will also find that you will experience some, shall we say, differences once you leave the hospital. But these differences are nothing to be concerned about. In time you will become accustomed to these changes."

He rose and walked over to glance out of the window. Over his shoulder she could see that the sky was beginning to brighten in the distance, meaning that it was the early hours of a new day. She glanced toward the little travel alarm sitting on the bedside table and saw that her guess had been correct; it was a few minutes after 5:00 in the morning.

The sight of the little alarm gave her a warm feeling. It had been a gift from her to her grandmother last Christmas. She guessed her grandmother had left it in the room for her.

"As for the reason that you are so cold, my dear, man was not meant to cross the barrier. You have been allowed to cross the barrier twice and in the process you have been given a wondrous gift, but it is not without price. Do not fear the changes for you will come to embrace them."

She was still very weak and groggy from the medication for she was having trouble following the conversation.

"Barrier?" she tried to ask, but her voice sounded a million miles away as she drifted off the sleep. The last sight she saw was the kind face of Dr. Johnson leaning over her, studying her with his deep set eyes.

When he spoke, Anna heard him as if from a long way off.

"Tell Mason that Maurice is sorry that Beatrice died, but he should know that she did not suffer."

Then everything went black.

When next Anna opened her eyes it was morning and a nurse in a starched white uniform with a pert little cap on her crown of blond hair, was bustling about the room, making things tidy. The squeaking of her white shoes on the tiles floor was actually soothing to Anna as they reminded her of similar sounds that her grandmother made when she walked around their kitchen. Without moving her head, Anna's eyes followed the Nurse as she bustled around the room. The curtain around the bed was partially drawn to keep the bright light from hitting Anna's face. Satisfied with her cleaning job, the woman, she was really little more than a girl, with blonde hair and bright blue eyes finally turned her attention to the bed.

"Well it's about time you woke up, young lady," the nurse said firmly. "You've slept long enough. A lot of people are waiting on you to assume your duties. According to Dr. Johnson, you will be going home shortly to begin your new work."

"Duties?" asked Anna in some confusion. "What duties?"

The nurse started to answer and then paused, a frown on her lovely face. Finally, she glanced at the doorway leading into the hallway and then stepped back behind the curtain so that she was out of Anna's line of vision. At that moment, the door opened and a young man bustled into the room, a stethoscope draped around his neck. He was studying a chart that carried in his hands, not looking up until he reached the bed. With a sigh and a shake of his head, he closed the chart and laid it on the table beside the bed. He placed the earpieces of the stethoscope in his ears and leaned toward Anna. It was only then that he realized that she was watching him.

"Uh-------," he said, a look of total shock on his face as he froze, stethoscope extended out toward Anna. "You, uh ----------."

He looked so comical that had she the energy to do so she would have laughed in his face. As it was she favored him with a tired grin and a raised eyebrow.

"Is there something wrong?" she asked curiously. "You seem surprised to see me."

"Uh, yes, I mean, uh," he paused clearly at a loss for what to say and then he finally stepped away from the bed as if she was contagious. "Uh, wait here, I'll be right back."

With those last words, he almost bolted through the door back into the hallway. Anna was puzzled by his reaction, but felt too tired to do anything about it. She assumed that someone would soon explain everything to her. She turned to a more comfortable position and realized that the nurse was still in the room. The young woman stood beside the bed looking down at Anna, a green plastic water pitcher in her hand.

"Nurse, what got into him?" asked Anna, reaching for the glass of water she suddenly noticed sitting on the edge of the nightstand. She realized that she was very thirsty.

The nurse glanced toward the door and sniffed in disdain as she carefully placed the green plastic pitcher on the bedside table.

"The younger doctors have no real understanding of how thin the line is that separates life from death. That young man is right now trying to understand the miracle that he just saw."

"Miracle?" asked Anna in bewilderment, the plastic cup poised near her mouth. "What miracle?"

The Nurse smiled, revealing for the first time that her upper front tooth was chipped, but when she smiled, that flaw did not mar her beauty only emphasize it.

"Oh, it was the first time he has ever had a dead woman talk to him."

Before Anna could respond the room door literally burst open to admit a mob of people. The young doctor that had run from the room was accompanied by a half a dozen nurses, dressed in scrubs and three other older doctors. All of them skidded to a halt and simply stared at Anna in utter amazement. Anna frowned in return and turned back to ask the Nurse to do something, but there was no one beside her bed. The pretty nurse in the white uniform had vanished.

Puzzled she turned back to look at the group that were standing at the foot of the bed.

"Is there a problem?" she finally asked, a little testily. She had never liked being stared at.

Rather than answer, the doctors looked at each other and then back at the nurses behind them. No one seemed to want to say anything. How much longer this standoff would have gone on is a question that would never be answered for at that moment her grandmother came through the door, being led by the family's Priest, Father Ramon. Her grandmother was crying into a handkerchief and looking down toward the floor. It was some little time before the grieving woman finally looked up and found her granddaughter staring back at her. The scream of joy could be heard all over the hospital.

"Madre de Dios, it's a miracle!" breathed the priest as he crossed himself before stepping back to allow the older woman to rush to Anna's bedside.

Soon Anna was being smothered by her grandmother as tears streamed down both of their faces. The gathering of medical personnel finally began to break up as the first doctor flipped open the chart, looked at the death certificate for Anna Ortiz that had even been witnessed by two other specialist who were present when the woman had died the night before and shook his head.

"It's impossible," he mumbled to himself. "There is no doubt that she quit breathing over five hours ago. That girl was dead!"

THE HOSPITAL ROOM OF ANNA ORTIZ

The Director of Nursing and the Charge Nurse for the floor descended on the crowd gathered at the door of Captain Anna Ortiz, trying to peer inside at the woman that had come back from the dead and quickly restored order in Anna's room. The Charge Nurse very firmly ushered everyone out except for Anna's Grandmother, the Priest, and her treating physician, Dr. Edmund Ramey. Dr. Ramey was giving Anna a thorough physical exam and hooking her to every machine that he could think of. He really didn't want to take any blood for lab work until she was stronger but short of that, he put her through every test in the book. Finally, he removed his stethoscope, draped it around his neck, and dropped into a nearby chair with a deep sigh.

"Well, Doctor?" asked Anna, "How am I?"

Dr. Ramey made no secret of the fact that he was baffled at her remarkable recovery.

"Young lady, I am absolutely baffled," he began, crossing his arms and studying the slightly built young woman in the hospital bed. "Yesterday your vital signs were barely visible and to be perfectly frank, at about 3:00 AM this morning, you stopped breathing. According to every medical standard that I know, at that point in time you were dead!"

"What?" she demanded, sitting up to stare at the people sitting beside her bed, "Are you serious? I died?"

It was her grandmother that answered that question.

"My dear," she began in her accented English, "I was here when it happened. You had been sinking all afternoon, so Father Ramon and I stayed here last night until you stopped breathing. It happened about 3:00 this morning. Nothing the doctor did could get you breathing again. Father Ramon gave you the last rites and you were pronounced dead. I asked the doctor to allow you to stay in this room until I could get the arrangements made to transport your –uh, well, your body to the funeral home."

Anna rubbed her eyes for a moment trying to make some sense out of the story.

"But grandmother, it can't be true," she began in protest, "ask Dr. Johnson, he was here examining me at 5:00 this morning and I didn't see any of you here."

She stopped when Dr. Ramey suddenly sat bolt upright in his chair and stared at her with a strange look on his face.

"Who did you say examined you at 5:00 this morning?" he asked slowly. The normally dark complexioned physician was suddenly very pale appearing.

Anna took a deep breath, fighting the rising fear that lurked at the edge of her mind. There was something very strange about this entire situation, but she had no idea how to deal with it. She had no idea why she should feel fear, but something about Dr. Ramey's tone of voice raised the hair on the back of her neck.

"There was a doctor here early this morning, he gave me an examination and seemed to feel that I was fine. His nametag said that his name was Johnson. While he was here examining me I glanced at the travel clock on the bedside table and saw that it was a few minutes after five. I saw none of you here at that time and since I was talking to him and he was responding, I certainly wasn't dead. So you need to ask Dr. Johnson about my condition at that time."

She paused and thought a moment, then it hit her; the nurse, she had mentioned that Dr. Johnson had said that Anna would be going home soon, so she could confirm that Dr. Johnson had been here.

"Don't take my word for it, ask that blonde nurse that was in here earlier," she offered. "I don't know her name, but she apparently talked to Dr. Johnson because she told me a little while ago that he had said that I would be going home soon."

"What blonde nurse?" asked Dr. Ramey skeptically, "I don't know of any blonde nurses who were on duty here either last night or this morning. Could you describe her?"

Anna shrugged her fear and puzzlement getting even bigger as they talked.

"Well, she was of medium height, wearing a starched white uniform with one of those little caps on her head. She was very pretty, her eyes were blue, and her hair was blonde."

Anna paused for a moment, trying to picture the lovely young woman in her mind. Then she remembered the chipped tooth.

"Oh, yes, one of her front teeth was chipped," she finished, "you couldn't see it until she smiled, but her tooth was definitely chipped. Or yes, her shoes squeaked when she walked on this tile!"

The three visitors silently studied the young woman lying in the bed for a long moment before Anna broke the silence. It was clear that something was going on that she did not understand. She had never liked being kept in the dark.

"Surely someone saw her!" she suddenly protested, pausing to take a sip of water from the glass at her elbow. "She has been here ever since I woke up. Ask that young doctor that came in and then ran out earlier; she was here when he came in."

Then she noticed that the doctor was staring intently at the water pitcher that the nurse had left. He started to say something and then paused. Finally, nodding to himself Dr. Ramey slowly got his feet and took a deep breath.

"Anna, I'll be right back," he said as he walked out of the room.

As the doctor left the room, Anna turned toward her grandmother.

"I'm not crazy, you know," she said earnestly, needing at least one person to believe her. "I don't know what is going on here, but I really was being examined at 5:00 this morning. I know that you wouldn't lie to me, but if I had died, Dr. Johnson would surely have noticed."

Suddenly Father Ramon stood and came to the side of her bed.

"My child, you must not get upset," he soothed, patting her hands where they lay on top of the sheet, "I am sure that after everything that you have been through, it is perfectly understandable that you would be confused."

Her anger starting to show on her otherwise beautiful face, Anna jerked her hands away from the Priest and pushed herself up in the bed. It was even more frustrating at how week she was; she could barely push herself up in the bed. Her grandmother rushed to grab the bed remote and raise the head of the bed so that Anna could lean back.

"Father Ramon," she began in an icy tone, her voice very strained, "I can assure you that I am not dead now nor did I die this morning. You can ask Dr. Johnson or track down that nurse that was here earlier. I do not know what is going on, but clearly you are all are either mistaken or you are trying to play some kind of sick joke on me."

They were interrupted by the return of Dr. Ramey, who was accompanied by the Director of Nursing and an older man that Anna had not seen before. The older man wore the uniform of an Army Colonel, over which he worse the usual white lab coat. The three came to stand at the foot of her bed, intently studying her without speaking.

"Anna," began Dr. Ramey, taking the chart from where it had been left at the foot of her bed and handing it to the older man. "This is Ginger O'Connor, the Director of Nursing."

"We've met," responded Anna shortly.

"And this," continued Dr. Ramey, "is Colonel Mason Delbert, the Director of Medicine for this hospital. In view of your, uh, shall we say, miraculous recovery, he wanted to talk to you."

Anna looked at Dr. Delbert inquiringly.

"Yes, Colonel?" she replied, shortly. In spite of her growing unease and smoldering anger, Anna was reassured to see that he had the kindest eyes of anyone she had ever met. Something about the man put her at ease.

"Captain Ortiz, or if I may, Anna," he began, as if searching for words. "I understand that you do not believe that you died here this morning. But based on the medical evidence that I have reviewed, and all of the reports made by the physicians on duty this morning, there is no question that at 3:00 AM you were medically dead. You were pronounced as such as a death certificate of signed."

Anna started to protest once again, but he raised one hand to signal that he had more to say.

"It has been my experience," he continued, "that many times, people who have experienced near death experiences are unable to psychologically deal with the thought that they actually died, and denial sets in. It is much better for you emotionally to admit to your mortality and work through these issues."

Anna took a deep breath and let it out with the sound of a sigh. She leaned back against her pillow and closed her eyes against the light.

"How many times do I have to tell you all that at 5:00 this morning I was having an examination by Dr. Johnson and I could not have died at that hour or any other time?" she responded between gritted teeth. "I think that even a mediocre physician would be able to tell if the patient he was examining was dead, don't you."

When Colonel Delbert did not immediately respond, Anna opened her eyes at looked at him. He was looking at her with an expression of total bafflement, tempered with what she judged to be real concern.

"Anna," he began kindly, "Dr. Ramey took the liberty of telling me your story and I am sorry to say that it cannot be true. You see we have no Dr. Johnson on staff and have not had anyone of that name in a very long time."

He motioned toward Nurse O'Connor. "We have also checked the nurses on duty last night and this morning and none of them match the description of the blonde that you describe. Additionally, nurses at this hospital have not worn starched white uniforms and those little caps since the late 1970s."

"But I am not making this up!" protested Anna in growing anger. "I was actually examined by a doctor whose nametag said Johnson."

Dr. Delbert was quick to reassure her.

"No one is saying that you made anything up, my dear," he responded quickly, coming around the bed to take one of her too thin hands between his. "The mind can play tricks on you during periods of great stress. No one is really able to explain what happens at or during the death experience. Perhaps you saw an alternative ending of your life, perhaps your mind refused to accept that you were dying and conjured up Dr. Johnson in order to reassure itself. Anything is possible.

"But one thing that is not possible," he continued raising one finger for emphasis, "was for you to have met a Doctor Johnson here last night or early this morning. The only Doctor Johnson that I am aware of that has ever been affiliated with this hospital was Maurice Johnson and he died in 1952."

"But Colonel, that was his name, I remember now!" she struggled to sit up straighter as her grandmother rushed to adjust the pillows behind her. "As I was going to sleep, he said tell Mason that Maurice is sorry that Beatrice died, but that she did not suffer."

Colonel Delbert's mouth dropped open and he looked at her in complete and total shock. "What did you say?" he finally demanded in a hoarse voice.

"The last thing I remember was that Dr. Johnson said was that I was to tell Mason that Maurice was sorry that Beatrice died but that she didn't suffer," she repeated softly, aware that the message, if that was what it actually was, had a tremendous impact on the Colonel. In fact, the man trembled as he backed away and then suddenly sat on the foot of her bed, clutching tightly to the railing that ran along the foot of the bed.

"Colonel, what's wrong?" demanded Dr. Ramey, stepping over to take Colonel Delbert's pulse. The Colonel's face had gone white as a sheet. Nurse O'Connor grabbed the water pitcher from the bedside table and then dropped it as if it were hot, her eyes bulging out of her head as she stared at the pitcher in disbelief.

Finally, the Colonel's color returned and he pulled his wrist away from Dr. Ramey. Nurse O'Connor slowly backed away from the bedside table and the pitcher that had clearly spooked her. Anna's grandmother and Father Ramon simply sat and stared in bemusement at the totally unexplainable actions taking place in the hospital room.

Colonel Delbert took several deep breaths and then stood, looking at Anna with a totally different attitude.

"My dear," he began slowly. "I am at a loss to understand how you could make something like this up, but Dr. Maurice Johnson was not only one of the most brilliant physicians that I have ever come in contact with but he was also my mentor when I was a young physician stationed here in the 1950s. My bride of only a few months was named Beatrice. One night I worked the late shift. When I arrived at home that night, she had been murdered. I almost lost my mind in my grief and I have always tortured myself with the belief that she had to have suffered horribly. Only the support of Dr. Johnson kept me from killing myself in my grief.

"Unfortunately, a few months later, Dr. Johnson called to tell me that he had found out something about the person that killed Beatrice. He wanted me to meet him at the hospital as soon as I could. When I arrived here, I found him in his office, dead of an apparent suicide. I have always believed that he was murdered."

Colonel Delbert paused, looking at Anna's stunned face carefully.

"There is no way you could have known any of this or that I would become involved in your case. I am baffled as to the why or the how, but it appears that you actually did have a conversation with the dead!"

CHAPTER TEN

THE HUGHES MANSION

Chelsea Mallard was only in her late thirties, but she had everything going for her; she was beautiful, rich, and today, she very pleased with herself and she had every reason to be. Her real estate business had been moving slowly, when six months ago she had inherited the estate of her distant cousin, former Texas Ranger Ezra Hughes. She had been his only living relative and she had thought that the rich old bastard would never die, but finally at age 97, he had been found dead, lying at the foot of the stairs in that big old mausoleum he had lived in on Montana Avenue. The house was big, full of valuable stuff and it was now all hers.

Not one to let grass grow under her feet Chelsea had immediately arranged for an invitation only estate sale and placed the house on the market for sale. Her office had handled the sale of the real property and she and her staff had also handled the estate sale. The return had been staggering. She had discovered that some of the paintings were extremely valuable and those had been immediately shipped off to her contacts at various New York Auction houses. The Texas Ranger memorabilia that Hughes had collected had brought in ten times her estimate during a silent auction held during an invitation only luncheon. Finally, those items that had not sold had been donated to Goodwill for the tax deduction. Now, as she made one last tour of the mansion before tomorrow's closing, she was walking on cloud nine.

The truth be told, Chelsea Mallard really cared for no one except herself. She had married her high school sweetheart, Art Mallard, who went on to local fame as a high school and college football star. He had joined his father's business as an insurance executive and, after his father's unexpected death he managed a portfolio of several million dollars worth of commercial property that his father had amassed. During a domestic dispute, four months ago, Art Mallard had been shot through the head by Chelsea, in what was ruled a case of self-defense. Her later engagement to Judge Prestridge, the presiding judge at her trial was looked at as just one of those things in El Paso. Now she was a grieving widow, who still looked good in mini-skirts, and worth over five million dollars in insurance money plus the twelve millions dollars she had received for the Hughes estate.

Sentiment had nothing to do with this last tour of the old house that she was taking. She had hated the house and she had hated old man Hughes, but she wanted to make certain that she was not overlooking anything that she could take out of the house to sell for a few extra dollars. However, it looked like she had already found everything of any value, so she was empty handed as she headed for the front door, briefcase in hand. She would certainly be glad to get this white elephant closed and her money in the bank.

She walked past the open door of the library and noticed a lamp burning on the desk. She didn't remember leaving it on, but she probably had. There were a few pieces of unique furniture that had been purchased with the house and the furniture in the library was part of that sale. Humming a popular tune to herself, she entered the library and was approaching the desk when she heard movement behind her. Before she could turn, something hit her in the back of the head and the lights went out as Chelsea Mallard collapsed in front of the desk.

The figure that had struck her was dressed all in black, wearing a rubber Halloween mask with a likeness of Richard Nixon over its head so it was impossible to tell if the figure was male or female. For a long time, the masked figure stood quietly over the fallen form, just contemplating the unconscious woman. Finally, the black clad figure made a decision and moved quickly.

First the high backed desk chair was pulled around in front of the massive oak desk. It was a high back, brown leather chair similar to those used by judges in the courtroom. Once the chair was in place, the figure knelt down beside the unconscious woman and unbuttoned her blouse to reveal her white lace bra. Grabbing a handful of Chelsea's long auburn hair, the figure pulled her into a sitting position so that the blouse could be pulled down her arms and removed. The bra quickly followed, leaving the unconscious woman naked from the waist up.

Next the figure wrapped her arms around the torso of the limp woman and wrestled her into the chair. Leaving the captive unattended for a moment, the dark clad figure walked over to the desk and pulled out the bottom drawer to reveal a black bag. The figure set the bag on the desk, unzipped, and opened it, revealing several pairs of handcuffs, several lengths of strong cord and several rolls of duct tape on top.

Taking a pair of handcuffs, the figure handcuffed the unconscious woman's wrists together in front of her. Leaning down, the figure removed Chelsea's high heeled shoes, leaving her wearing only her stylishly short skirt. Grunting with the effort, the figure pulled the unconscious Real Estate Agent forward so the zipper in the back of the skirt could be lowered. Then by draping Chelsea over her shoulder and slightly raising her form the chair, the skirt and thong bikini panties were worked down to her knees. With a sigh of relief from the masked figure, the unconscious woman was allowed to drop back into the chair. The clothing bunched at her knees was removed from her legs and dropped on the floor. Chelsea Mallard was now naked as the day she was born, handcuffed and unconscious in her late cousin's desk chair.

THE LIBRARY IN THE HUGHES MANSION

The first thought that came to Chelsea as she regained consciousness was that she had a hell of a hangover. She didn't remember even going out, but lately her drinking had gotten somewhat out of hand and she experienced periods of not being able to remember things. Her head was pounding and her scalp was tender on the right side of her head. Then she remembered hearing someone behind her and feeling pain on the side of her head. Finally, she forced her eyes opened and, though still groggy, found that she was still in the library, sitting in her cousin's fancy desk chair. She certainly did not remember sitting down. She started to move and realized that she was actually tied in the chair. She was also gagged with something shoved in her mouth and what appeared to be duct tape, wrapped around her head, covering her mouth, several times. Glancing down, her eyes widened when she saw that she was also naked.

Terrified, she fought to get out of the massive chair. Finally, after coming to the realization that she could not get loose she studied her bonds. Her arms were stretched above her head and secured at the top of the chair. She had played enough bondage games with Art to remember what handcuffs felt like, so she knew that, at least, her wrists were handcuffed together. Her legs were bent at the knee so that her feet were off of the floor. There was a handcuff on each of her slim ankles and then each ankle was then secured, somehow, to one of the arms of the chair. She could also see that each of her legs was secured to the arm of the chair by a length of cord that circled each leg and then was secured to the arm. She was not only firmly secured, but she was also exposed. She had always been proud of her sensual body, but now she was not happy with the way her position made her already prominent breasts stand out.

At that moment, the library door opened and a masked figure came into the room. Chelsea tried to yell, but the gag was secure enough to make any sound she made come out so muffled that she was sure it could not be heard outside the room. Finally, exhausted, she fell silent, her full breasts rising and falling rapidly as she struggled to pull enough air into her lungs to sustain life.

The masked figure walked over to stand in front of the captive woman and studied her through the eye slits of the mask for several moments.

"Nice to see you," rasped the figure in a hoarse voice, "I have enjoyed you from a distance many nights."

Chelsea was a very intelligent woman; she quickly caught onto the fact that this was someone that she knew. This was someone that had every reason to hide behind a mask for fear of exposure. She tried to respond, to offer anything to be let loose, but it only came out as a muffled grunt.

The figure reached forward and gently took one of Chelsea's exposed breasts in a gloved hand. With the thumb, the figure began to tease the already turgid nipple. Chelsea, whimpered and tried to pull away from that teasing hand, but was held in position by the tightness of her bonds.

"Now, my dear," continued the figure, all the while teasing the sensitive nipples of the captive, "you and I are going to have a talk. If you give me the correct answers then things will go well. If you give me the wrong answers, then I will punish you. There is no one here but you and I so do not expect anyone to come save you. The cavalry only arrives to save the day in the movies."

The speaker paused for a moment, concentrating on bringing Chelsea's nipples to their full erectness. The captive struggled against the bonds holding her, but finally gave up and allowed the liberties. There was no doubt to her captor that in spite of her helpless position, Chelsea was beginning to become aroused. Maybe she liked being helpless, thought the masked figure.

Chelsea was angry at being stripped and tied up. She did not like being restrained. She had gone in for a little S&M with some of her past lovers, but she was the one that was always the dominate partner in a relationship, and she was not used to being restrained. However, she had to admit, that the mask figure was certainly a knowledgeable lover and in spite of herself, she was feeling the first rush of arousal. She finally nodded her understanding. The gag prohibited any other communication.

The figure reached into a pocket and pulled out a spring loaded clothespin such as was used to hold washing on the line. Slowly the figure held the simple wooden clothespin in front of Chelsea's disbelieving eyes, and slowly opened and closed the spring loaded pinchers.

"Now I am sure that if I placed this on your nipples it would hurt, don't you agree?"

Realizing what was in store, Chelsea nodded rapidly. She had always had very sensitive nipples; to her, having one of those things placed on her nipples would be torture. She decided that if this lunatic would let her talk, she would tell this nutcase whatever she was asked.

Her captor nodded, for no particular reason and lowered the clothespin until it just touched Chelsea's right nipple.

"So now that we understand each other, my dear, let's have our little talk."

The masked figure paused to run the tip clothes pin once more around the left nipple of the captive.

"Now at this invitation only estate sale that you had; do you remember seeing a set of several leather bound notebooks? There would have been six or seven, maybe more."

Franticly, Chelsea thought back to all of the things that had been found throughout the house and marked for sale. Try and she might, she would not remember seeing a set of leather bound notebooks. Not wanting to lie to her captor and not knowing if this was a test question or not, Chelsea finally shrugged and shook her head no. She had not been the only one to price items, but she could not tell her captor that due to the gag.

Rather than answer, her captor simply opened the clothespin and firmly attached it to Chelsea's erect left nipple. The pain was so bad that Chelsea thought that she would pass out. For a long moment, she struggled and moaned her torment. A stinging slap to the face made her focus her eyes back on the figure in front of her.

"That was the wrong answer, my dear," rasped the black clad figure, eyes glittering through the slits in the mask at the sight of the woman writhing in pain. "I know they were here, and I want to know who bought them. So once again where are those notebooks? Remember, I have several more clothespins."

Chelsea tried to make herself understood through the gag, but to no avail. She had a list of who bought what items and how much they paid in her briefcase, but that list ran to over 100 pages. There was no way she could remember every single thing that had been in this huge house. She had also had a dozen of her employees working for her during the sale and each of them priced certain rooms. The notebooks could have been in any room in the house or not in the house at all.

With a sigh, the figure removed another clothespin from a pocket and attached it to Chelsea's other nipple. This time the pain was so intense that even the gag could not stop her agonized scream from being heard, in spite of the gag. The pain in her breasts was worse than anything she had ever felt. At that point she would have gladly told her captor anything and then kissed his feet. Her body was covered with sweat and her face was streaked with her tears and her mascara that had run down her face in dark streaks.

Another stinging slap gained her attention once again. This time the masked figure was holding a silver egg shaped device in one hand. A long cord ran to an oblong box. This item Chelsea immediately recognized as there was one in her bedside table that she used many nights when she woke up horny and was not able to go back to sleep.

"You sluts seem to be guided by your sex, so perhaps this will help me get your undivided attention," said the figure with a sneer. "Make no mistake bitch; I will have the answers to my questions before I leave here!"

Ignoring Chelsea's attempts to stop the questing hand, the figure took the silver egg and reached between her wide spread legs. Slowly, roughly due to Chelsea not really being fully aroused, the gloved hand slid the silver egg deep into her vagina. No matter how Chelsea squeezed her internal muscles to try and expel the intruder, the egg was placed where it would have the most effect on her. Then with a sound approaching a chuckle, the figure turned the knob on top of the oblong box to the halfway mark. The little silver egg began to vibrate at a fairly high rate of speed. Chelsea reacted as if she had received a severe electrical shock. Her eyes bulged in her head, as every muscle in her body went taut.

With her legs tied off of the floor, the captive was unable to even brace her feet so instead she strained against the chair itself. Chelsea worked out at the gym regularly to keep herself in shape, so there was not an ounce of fat on her well developed body. The heavy wooden frame of the chair creaked like a tree in a gale as her lean muscles contracted in a powerful orgasm. Finally, overcome with the intensity of the orgasm she had undergone at the hands of this masked figure, Chelsea passed out and hung limply in her bonds. Her head sagged and her long hair hid most of her sweat covered face. The masked figure grabbed Chelsea by her long hair and pulled her head up. This time a stinging slap failed to rouse her. With a grunt of annoyance, the figure contemplated her captive for a few minutes before coming up with another idea.

This time when Chelsea regained consciousness, she found that she was now lying face down across her cousin's desk. The heavy judge's chair had been returned to its customary place, though it was now tiled back on its legs so that all that kept the back of chair from lying flat on the floor were her bound wrists, one of which was handcuffed to each arm. She was not physically strong enough to pull the heavy old chair upright, so the sheer weight of the chair kept her face down on the desk. She could also tell that her ankles were tied to the legs of the desk so that her legs were spread wide apart. She also realized that her ass now felt sore as if she had been whipped, though her body was such a mass of pain that it was hard for her to tell for sure.

The little vibrator was still going to down, and now it felt like something had been stuffed inside her to keep the vibrator in place. She was just glad that now the intensity of the vibration had been reduced, so that while she was now certainly aroused, she was in no immediate danger of another orgasm. She had to get away, but found that after so many orgasms, her muscles were a little slow to obey.

Suddenly, she detected an aroma in the room that that teased at her memory for a moment and then she realized that the smell was of a cigar. Someone in the room was smoking a cigar and the same brand as her soon to be husband, Judge Prestridge, if she had to guess at the brand. With a grunt, she tensed her stomach muscles and tried one more time to straighten, but the weight of the heavy old chair kept her pinned to her stomach.

"Now, my dear, let's talk again," rasped the hoarse voice, as a gloved hand began to squeeze her sore ass cheeks. "Shall we?"

Chelsea felt something large push against her exposed anus and screamed her shock and pain into the gag filling her mouth. The only response was hysterical laughter from her captor.

ANNA ORTIZ'S HOSPITAL ROOM

Anna was very tired after the barrage of questions that Dr. Delbert and Dr. Ramey had thrown at her. She had been asked to tell and retell everything she remembered about her examination by Dr, Johnson, and the nurse that no one knew. Nurse O'Connor had finally calmed down enough to say that the water pitcher in Anna's room was identical to those that had been used in the old hospital wards in the 1970s and that so far as she knew that there were none like it currently in use or even left in the hospital. She was also adamant that since Anna had been in a coma that there had been no water placed in her room. All in all, the entire scenario had been incredibly spooky. Father Ramon had said very little, but he had excused himself as quickly as possible to "go consult with the higher authorities of the Church."

For her part, Anna was certain that she was losing her mind. She was having trouble understanding what had happened to her; perhaps the head injury had left her deranged in some fashion. Had she really talked to a dead man? She wasn't sure that she believed that and frankly the pounding in her head was making it hard for her to even think. There was no doubt that she needed time alone to sort all of this out in her own mind.

Late that afternoon, seeing how tired Anna was looking, her grandmother had left saying she needed to go home for a time, but that she would be back later than night to sit with her granddaughter. Left to herself, though to be sure someone checked on her every few minutes as if they were afraid she would fly out the window, Anna finally began to doze. When she awoke, it was night outside and the lights in her room were dim. On the far wall, she could see shadows that looked for all of the world like those of a large number of people, grouped as if they had all gathered to watch her speak. To her surprise, she was not frightened, though she was certainly puzzled. What was happening to her?

Movement to her left caused her to turn her eyes in that direction. Though she had not heard anyone enter, an old man stood there wearing a brown floor length robe. Most of his face was covered with a long white beard; only his bright gray eyes and his wide, firm mouth were free from any facial hair. He carried a long wooden staff in his right hand. He was leaning on the staff; his serene gaze directed at her.

"Who are you?" Anna asked softly. For some reason, it seemed only proper to whisper.

"I am your teacher," he responded in a very faint tone of voice, as if speaking from a great distance. "I am here to help you."

"Teacher?" she responded in puzzlement. None of this was making any sense to her. There was no longer any doubt in her mind that she had suffered some severe brain damage.

In answer the old man smiled and raised his staff toward her.

"You need to sleep, my daughter," he said softly. "There is time to talk later."

As if the raising of the staff was a signal, in spite of her best efforts, Anna was not able to stop her eyes from closing. In moments, she was sleeping deeply, her drawn features now relaxed as her tense muscles relaxed. The old man stood for a long time looking at her and then glanced toward the wall covered with shadows.

"She must rest, my friends," he said addressing the shadowy figures. "Soon she will begin her work, until then she needs time to fully recover. I ask you to go."

Slowly, as if in protest, the shadowy figures that had been so visible on the wall of the hospital room seemed to blur and then blend into the wall. Soon the room was empty of figures, filled only with the soft glow of moonlight through the window. Finally, the old man's outline began to blur and he, too, faded away. Anna slept peacefully; blissfully unaware of just how much her life had changed.

CHAPTER ELEVEN

THE HUGHES MANSION ON MONTANA

Rosa Madrid walked slowly up to the cracked driveway to the side door of the silent old three-story house. Even though the day was just starting, the heat and humidity promised that this would be a scorcher of a day. She had left her home in Cuidad Juarez feeling fresh and chipper, but the long bus ride and the two-block walk from the bus stop had just tired her out. She could feel her blouse sticking to her back as she began to sweat.

Now that the old man was dead, she thought to herself sadly, her job would soon end. She was sorry that the old man had died, but she was more sorry that that bitch that had inherited the place wanted her out. Jobs were so hard to find in El Paso and this had been a good one.

Opening the screen door, she struggled to balance her purse, her sack lunch, and the ring of keys clutched tightly in her left hand. With a tired sigh, she eventually found the correct key and slid it into the lock. As usual, the antique lock did not want to open and she had to struggle to force the key to turn the tumblers. Rosa finally got the stiff old lock to turn and pushed the heavy door open, stepping into a house that felt twenty degrees cooler than the outside. That bitch that had inherited the property refused to allow her to run the coolers, but the construction of the house was such that it normally stayed cool in the summer. That was one of the things that old Mr. Hughes had liked, she remembered fondly.

It is hard to believe that the old man was dead, she thought to herself sadly as she put her purse and lunch bag into the butler's pantry, off of the kitchen, and picked up the plastic bucket of cleaning supplies.

She was not really looking forward to working in this historic old house today, though she was well aware that the work before her was not difficult, she thought to herself. Old Mr. Hughes, Ranger Hughes everyone had called him, even long after his retirement, had liked everything to run on a schedule and this was the day that she was supposed to mop the floors and wax the gleaming woodwork on the first floor. Every Monday for the last ten years, it had been her job to clean the study, the library, living room, kitchen, and the three additional empty rooms that made up the lower floor and then mop all of the floors. On Tuesdays, she was supposed to clean the rooms on the second floor and then on Wednesdays, she would clean the third floor rooms.

Rosa had been very fond of the old man and it had broken her heart to discover his wasted body lying at the foot of the stairs, his neck broken. Though dead, it strong personality still pervaded the old house, since the old man had lived here for over forty years. She remembered him from when she had been a little girl, going shopping with her mother. Ezra Hughes had been a famous Texas Ranger and then after the murder of the Sheriff, he had become the Sheriff of El Paso County. From that time forward, Ranger Hughes had been a part of the county, just as solid as the Franklin Mountains that towered over the City. She still expected to hear his shuffling walk as he descended the stairs each morning precisely at 9:00 AM to go into his study to work on his book. In fact, she still thought that she could smell those cigars he always smoked.

Suddenly, she paused, her hand on the door to the library, and sniffed the air. It wasn't a memory, she realized, she really did smell one of the old man's cigars, but no one had ever smoked in this house except Ranger Hughes. Since his death, no one had smoked in this house at all.

Suddenly, the thought hit her that someone could have broken into the house. After all, that bitch that had inherited the estate had discharged all of the people that had worked for Ranger Hughes, so there was now no one in the house at night. She was also very much aware that there was no one in the house now except her. She sniffed the air again and there was no doubt in her mind that someone had smoked one of the old man's cigars very recently. Moving a few steps away from the library door, she sniffed again, confirming her suspicion that the smell was the strongest at the door. Someone had been smoking in the library, she told herself.

Taking a deep breath, she reached out slowly and turned the ornate old doorknob until the door moved slightly inward. She sniffed softly at the slight opening she had formed and the somewhat stale aroma of cigar smoke that floated through the small opening, left no doubt in her mind that someone had been smoking in that room very recently.

Turning her head so tht her right ear was by the slight opening, she listened intently, trying to even stifle the sound of her breathing that might mask the sound of movement in the room. She heard nothing. Finally, gathering her courage, she slid her hand through the slight opening and simultaneously flipped on the lights and pushed the door open.

As she stepped into the room, the slightly stale odor of the cigar was strong, but nothing seemed out of place though she was puzzled by what she saw at the desk. In fact, it took her a second to realize what she was actually seeing on the old man's desk. Though she was aware that Ranger Hughes had been something of a ladies man in his youth, she could think of no reason why a naked woman would be draped over his desk, especially now that he was dead and gone. Cautiously she approached the naked figure, noting that the woman was actually tied to the desk in some fashion. Then she reached the desk and reached out a hand to touch the woman. It finally dawned on her what she was seeing and her horrified screams filled the silent, empty room of the old house.

The shapely, naked body of Chelsea Mallard was still bent over the desk, her wrists were still attached to the heavy old chair, and the gag was still filling her mouth. Though now her sightless eyes were fixed on the wall behind the desk. The floor beneath the desk was bright red with the slowly drying pool of blood that had run from the sliced throat of the once lovely young woman.

THE LIBRARY OF THE HUGHES MANSION

Police Lieutenant Caleb Morgan rose from his crouched position behind the big library desk, stifling an oath as his left knee popped. For about the hundredth time, he thought to himself that he was getting too old for this shit. He glanced over at his partner, Sergeant Juan Estrada, who had just entered the library. Two evidence technicians were carefully examining the floor around desk, being very careful to avoid the congealing pool of blood beneath the desk.

"What'd you find out?" asked Morgan, rounding the desk with a slight limp. Much as it pained him to admit it, he was getting old, he thought.

Estrada flipped open his pocket notebook, pausing to watch the M.E. and his assistant enter the room and approach the desk with its silent victim. Dr. Archie Raney had been the county medical examiner since before Estrada had been born and was a well liked figure in town. He knew and could remember the names of most of the police department.

"Juan, Caleb," greeted the old man, carefully sitting his bag on the corner of the desk. Without touching anything, while he pulled a pair of latex gloves from his pocket, Raney began to carefully examine the bloody body that was all that was left of what had been an unusually beautiful woman. Now, bled out as she was, she looked like a side of beef.

Interlacing his fingers to ensure that his gloves were securely in place, Dr. Raney carefully separated the smoothly rounded globes of the victim's ass checks and stared for a long moment. Finally, nodding to himself, he rounded the desk to examine, first a dark spot on the side of the victim's normally bright blonde head and then her bound wrists and the way that they were secured to the arms of the old chair. Finally, with an audible creak, the old man straightened and stepped away from the desk.

"Well, boys, do you have an identity for the victim?" asked Raney, glancing toward the door to see the police photographer pausing at the doorway. Horace Lathrup was young, but a good photographer. He just tended to get sick a lot at murder scenes.

"Horace, I want pictures of the room, the desk and the body from every angle," directed Morgan. "I especially want pictures of the way the legs and arms are secured."

.   Morgan turned his attention back to Dr. Raney.

"Sorry, doc," apologized the Lieutenant, his eyes still following the photographer who was cautiously approached the desk as if he was afraid the corpse would bite him. "What were you saying?"

Raney nodded toward the victim.

"I asked if you had an identity for this young lady, yet," he repeated. "I had rather examine her thoroughly as she is before I turn her over to get a good look that her face. But, I know how quickly you boys like to be able to identify the victim."

Morgan shook his head slowly.

"No reason to rush, doc," he responded. "The identity is not a mystery this time. That's Chelsea Mallard, Judge Prestridge's main squeeze. She was also the listing agent the sale of this old house."

Raney looked back at the horribly exposed victim with a new appreciation. A slow whistle escaped him.

"So that's the delectable Ms. Mallard, is it?" he mused, a certain appreciation on his florid face. "I never had the pleasure of meeting her prior to this, but I guess I now understand all the stories about her. She is, or was, a stunning woman."

"Was," agreed Morgan, distaste visible on his craggy face. He glanced back at his partner.

"Get anything from her office?" he asked.

Estrada suddenly remembered his notebook that he had been holding, forgotten at his side.

"Oh, yes," he said slowly, as he flipped to the appropriate page. He reviewed the information and then glanced back at his partner.

"She left her office at about 3:00 yesterday afternoon for a meeting and mentioned that she was planning to come back by here after the meeting for one last check. The sale of this place was to close today and apparently the new owners plan on taking possession of this property next week and she wanted to make sure that nothing important had been overlooked. When she did not show up this morning, they assumed that she was sleeping in or she had found a guy and had a long night."

Morgan crossed his arms over his broad chest and lowered his head in thought. Finally, he looked back at Estrada.

"Did her office tell you what she was driving," he asked; a frown on his face. "I mean there are no cars here, so either someone dropped her off here or she took a cab here from some other location. Either way, we need to find the person that drove her here."

Estrada nodded and returned his notebook to his coat pocket.

"Or the killer stole the car," offered the Sergeant. "According to her secretary, she was driving her fire engine red Mercedes 460 when she left the office. She had one of those personalized plates on her car that said

Mall01. No one at her office has seen either her or that car since she left yesterday."

Raney sighed deeply and turned back toward the victim.

"I guess I had better get back to work," he said over his shoulder.

He paused for a moment and then turned back to the two officers.

"Boys, you need to find whoever did this and quickly. The killer was not only deadly, but had a very sick mind. I'm no shrink, but I would have to guess that someone this brutal will kill again."

"How so, doc?" asked Morgan, his interest clear from his expression..

Raney rubbed the back of his right glove against his chin as he considered his answer.

"Well, first, my initial belief is that the victim was alive when her throat was cut, otherwise, there would have been more blood pooled on the desk top and not on the floor. You can also see blood splatter on the wall behind the desk which indicates that the blood was actually gushing out of the wound. This would indicate that she was very much alive at the time her throat was cut.

"Secondly, I can't tell you if she was raped until we can do a proper exam in the lab, but there is no question that she has been violated every way possible. If you look closely, you can see that the killer shoved something very large up her anus. That accounts for the reddish stains on her ass cheeks. The pain from being violated like that would be excruciating.

"Frankly, if I had to guess, I would say this woman has been beaten and tortured and it went on for some lengthy period of time."

AT THE DOME RESTAURANT, CAMINO REAL HOTEL

The list opened on the table had thirty names on it; thirty names belonging to some of the most prominent people in El Paso. The killer, impeccably dressed as befitted the killer's social standing, slowly sipped coffee from a china cup, nodding politely as the mayor called out a greeting, calling the killer by name. Isn't it ironic, thought the killer, if not for a car wreck, there would have been thirty-one names on the list and all of this death would be unnecessary. Of course, it would not be nearly as much fun for the killer.

Those damn books, swore the killer quietly, and that bastard Hughes. If anyone got those books and read what that old fart had written, then the killer, and a number of the killer's close friends would be facing serious charges. If the killer had only been able to get to that estate sale, then the books could have been purchased from the estate and quietly destroyed. But being rear ended by a drunk trucker had put the killer into the hospital for a week; the same week in which the estate sale had taken place. So others had purchased what by rights should never have existed in the first place.

Damn Hughes, anyway, thought the killer for the hundredth time that day alone. Why did he have to go and dig up that old disappearance anyway? Who would have guessed that the old man had realized what had really happened to those Daniels women or would try to use that knowledge as a lever? Those two bitches got what they deserved and no one had even realized the killer's involvement. The death of the Prestridge foreman should have ended the matter, and it had for law enforcement.

The murders of the two Daniel's women had been the first of a long list of murders that the killer had indulged in over the years, but certainly, they had been the most memorable. Just thinking about how the lovely Dorothy Daniels, naked, bound, and gagged, her eyes covered with a blindfold, had humped that vibrator was enough to get anyone excited.

The blood lust flooded the killer's system, though to anyone looking, the killer would appear to just be enjoying a good cup of coffee. The thought of finally killing that bastard Hughes after over forty years of giving in to his demands had been the most satisfying feeling in the world. It had taken very little effort to push that old bastard down the steps in his own home. Now there was no one that had any idea that beneath the genteel appearance that the killer presented to the world lurked the soul of a cold-blooded killer. Except for what the old man had written in those damn journals.

With an effort of will, the killer returned to the list of names lying on the table. Well, there's no time like the present, thought the killer. The first name on the list was that of Celia Rosenberg, someone well known to the killer. Trust her, with that money she picked up when her husband had that heart attack on the golf course, to be attracted to that old junk that Hughes had collected. Putting the list carefully into the leather briefcase lying on a nearby empty chair, the killer picked up the briefcase, dropped some money on the table to cover the tab and walked slowly from the fashionable restaurant.

BEAUMONT HOSPITAL

Across town at Beaumont Hospital, Anna Ortiz stirred restlessly in her hospital bed and muttered softly "Daniels, dead."

Her grandmother sitting across the room looked up sharply at the sound of Anna's voice and crossed herself. She hoped to God that it was not starting with her granddaughter. She knew from experience that no good would come from it.

CHAPTER TWELVE

REAL ESTATE OFFICE OF CHELSEA MALLARD
Lieutenant Morgan glanced at the woman across the desk with true appreciation. Lisa Nettleton, the executive assistant for the late Chelsea Mallard, was a stunning woman, even more eye catching that her late boss. Though Nettleton was only twenty-two, she conducted herself with the mannerisms of someone much older and more sophisticated. Frankly, to Caleb Morgan, a widower for the last ten years, her appearance was so distracting he was having a hard time keeping his mind on business.

"Lieutenant?" asked Ms. Nettleton, with an amused smile on her lovely face, prompted him for the next question. Morgan had an idea that she was well aware of what he was thinking. It jerked him back to the present from a delightful fantasy involving the well-endowed Lisa Nettleton.

"Was there something else?"

"Was Ms. Mallard a hard person to work for?" he finally asked having run out of his list of standard murder investigation questions.

The very self-possessed young woman across from him favored the Lieutenant with a rueful smile.

"I'll say that she was," she responded emphatically. "While she was not well educated in the formal sense, she was one of the most intelligent people that I have ever known. She lived to amass power so that she could use it to make people feel small. A lot of people in this town hated her."

"Enough to kill her?" he asked quickly.

Nettleton was slow to respond to that question, but finally shrugged and leaned forward to rest her elbows on the top of her desk. The view down the front of her low cut blouse was certainly distracting.

"Actually, yes," she finally responded. "Chelsea was not above taking advantage of her looks, her position or her relationship with Judge Prestridge to get what she wanted. She hurt a lot of people in this town in her climb to the top. There were also a lot of rumors that she had the dirt on a lot of the movers and shakers in this town. That alone would be enough to get her killed, I would think."

"Any prime candidates come to mind?" he asked with a raised eyebrow. He was again favored with that half smile as the lovely young lady shook her head.

"There were certainly a lot of people who will not regret that she is dead, but I can't say that I can think of anyone special at the moment; but let me sleep on it."

A thought hit Morgan and he shifted his line of questioning.

"Ms. Nettleton was there some place where Ms. Mallard kept private papers, or did she have a diary or some other type of record system that would not be part of the company files? I mean, if she had this "dirt" on the movers and shakers she couldn't very well keep it at her house or in her office files. That would be too obvious and the first place that someone would look."

Lisa Nettleton started to shake her head, but then a sudden thought hit her. She remembered something that she had seen one day by accident. She rose from her desk and beckoned to the Lieutenant.

"Come with me," she said turning to lead the way into Mallard's private office. "I may know where she keeps her private papers."

Lieutenant Morgan was glad to follow the young woman because the view she presented as she moved away from him was stupendous. He would happily follow her all day if she wanted him to. She led him into the inner office and then softly shut the door.

The office was very much in keeping with Mallard's ostentatious lifestyle. The desk was ornately carved from a single piece of mahogany; the carpet was off white with a thick pile. To his left was a large, built in wet bar, well stocked based on the well known labels he could read from his position across the room. Morgan watched, somewhat puzzled, as she went over to the bar and slowly ran her hand along the ornate tile inlay that formed the right end of the bar. Whatever she seemed to be looking for eluded her because she had to do it several times before there was an audible click and the entire bar section actually slid to her left, revealing a door sized opening. With a triumphant grin, Lisa Nettleton stepped back and looked over her shoulder.

"I knew it was here, I just had to find it," she said. "I passed her doorway one day and the door was not closed all the way. I could see a small section of the office and she just seemed to appear from the area of the bar. I knew that there had to be a hidden room of some sort, I was just never able to find it until now."

Morgan tipped an imaginary hat to the grinning executive assistant and stepped up to the opening. The interior of the hidden room was dark, so he ran his hand along the inside of the opening until he found a light switch. When he flipped the switch, the room was bathed in soft light that revealed a row of filing cabinets along the far wall. However, it was the items sitting inside the hidden room that literally took his breath away. Morgan was certainly no expert, but he believed that he was looking at a fortune in works of art and collectibles. He had hit the mother lode.

SECRET ROOM IN CHELSEA MORGAN'S OFFICE

Eight hours later, Caleb Morgan, Juan Estrada, and another dozen or so officers finished conducting a thorough inventory of the items hidden in the secret room behind Chelsea Morgan's office. There was so much hidden in that room that the completed list covered fifteen pages. As each page contained space to list all of the vital statistics for 45 individual items, that meant that the officers found 675 items stored in that hidden room.

As each page of items was completed, it was handed to two evidence technicians who compared the information on that page to a thick book of items that had been reported as stolen and never recovered. After completing the comparison, the senior technician walked over to the Lieutenant.

"Lieutenant, out of the 675 items listed on the inventory, we matched the descriptions of over four hundred of them to items reported stolen either here or in Cuidad Juarez. So I guess there is little doubt that Ms. Mallard was running a first class fencing operation here."

Morgan glanced at the technician, a slight smile on his otherwise tired face. Oh, to be that young and enthusiastic again.

"Officer -," he looked at the technician's nametag a moment. "Benson, one should not jump to conclusions in police work. In spite of appearances, we don't know that she was an actual fence, but we do know that she was certainly a receiver of stolen property. There is a major difference."

Benson blushed slightly at being corrected by a senior officer, but covered it up very well.

"Yes, sir, sorry for jumping to conclusions," he paused a moment as if gathering his thoughts. "Is there anything else you need us to do before we pack this stuff into the vans and transport it to headquarters? I would also point out that we still have not thoroughly gone through those filing cabinets. Who knows what we will find there?"

The enthusiasm of the young technician made Morgan feel even older and more tired than he normally felt. He glanced at his watch.

"Officer Benson, it is now 11:15 on a hot West Texas evening and I am sure that you and the others are tired. It's been a long day. Whatever is in those cabinets has certainly been there for a long time. Getting a good night's sleep and a fresh start in the morning is not going to delay things," Morgan paused at the crestfallen face of Officer Benson.

"Besides," he finished, "we need this art and all of these other things out of here before we start digging into those cabinets. I wouldn't want anything to get damaged with people moving back and forth carrying out files."

Taking the hint, and glad to escape from the intimidating presence of Lieutenant Morgan, Officer Arnold Benson turned to the technicians gathered around the temporary worktable that had been set up in the outer office.

"OK, let's get these things loaded so we can go home!" he called to the other officers.

As if glad to be doing something, the team of technicians descended on the hidden room and in very short order removed every last item that had been found. In less than an hour, the room was empty except for the mysteries that might be hidden in the locked filing cabinets.

Sergeant Juan Estrada watched the last of the vans pull away from the real estate office parking lot before turning back to his friend and partner.

"Well what time do you want meet here tomorrow?" he asked, reaching for his jacket, carelessly thrown over the back of a nearby chair.

Morgan smiled slight, as he turned toward the entrance to the hidden room.

"Now, Juan, you've known me for years," he replied, walking over to examine the lock on the closest filing cabinet. "You didn't believe that bullshit about getting a fresh start tomorrow did you?"

Estrada moaned softly and tossed his jacket in the general direction of the chair where it had earlier rested. Just his luck to have a partner that never seemed to need to sleep, he thought sourly as he watched Morgan pull a small green velvet bundle from on pocket. Deliberately the Lieutenant pulled what he thought was the proper lock pick from the set and delicately inserted it into the lock. A few deft movements of his hand and there was a click that signaled that the lock was now open.

It was going to be a long night, Estrada thought to himself as he watched Morgan pull a thick manila folder from the top drawer of the cabinet and open it up. Without waiting for an invitation, Estrada stepped over grabbed a visible file and carried it over to Mallard's desk. At least he would sit down to read.

CHAPTER THIRTEEN

THE BEDROOM OF CELIA ROSENBERG

Everyone in town thought that Anson and Celia Rosenberg had the perfect marriage. Both were in their late forties, both were very good looking and most of the men in town in their social circle envied Anson's marriage to Celia, a well endowed, long legged beauty. Her cleavage alone got them invited to almost every party in town and her own special sexual talents had endeared her to most of the area's politicians. Few knew that the appearances were very deceiving. Anson and Celia had not slept in the same bedroom in over ten years and in fact, that they actually barely tolerated each other.

They had returned from the party at the Mayor's house rather late on this hot evening, the picture of a loving couple until they had entered their own home and the door was shut behind them. As if a switch had been flipped, their visible, smiling affection for each other had vanished. Without a word, Anson had immediately headed for his study to crawl into his nightly bottle of Scotch and Celia had marched up the stairs, undressing as she climbed. She could be followed by the trail of clothing she left strewn behind her. She was so looking forward to relaxing in her hot tub and then crawling into her king size bed for a long night's sleep.

Entering her room, she kicked her stiletto heels off and finished undressing, dropped her very expensive, sweat stained clothes into a pile at the foot of her bed. Curling her toes into the thick pile of the carpet, she stretched and ran her hands slowly from her narrow waist up to cup her full breasts. Finally, completely nude, she padded over to stand in front of her full-length mirror. Though she was not one of those who obsessed over getting older, each night she made a point to stand in front of this mirror and study her body with a critical eye.

She wasn't a girl any longer, but she had to admit that she was still in good shape for a woman of her age. Her long, tanned dancer's legs were still shapely and firm. Hell, she thought, there were enough people that wanted to get between them, both men as well as women to make her feel justifiably proud. Her shapely ass didn't sag much, and her waist was not as slim as it had been in her twenties, but it was still smaller than that of most of her friends. Then she turned her attention to her what she knew was clearly her best asset, her eye-catching chest.

Though most of her friends were starting to sag by the time they reached their late forties, her own breasts were still as firm and as soft to the touch as they had been when she had first developed at age eight. From the time she was twelve years old, living in that cracker box tract house on the outskirts of Dallas, others had enjoyed getting their hands inside her old fashioned blouses and a lot of them had even been willing to pay her to strip to the waist so that they could enjoy her breasts without any barriers.

The sight of so much money being paid to her for the opportunity of feeling her breasts had quickly destroyed any inhibitions that she had about nudity. In fact, very few people knew that she had worked her way through college and even started her first business using those tremendous assets. More than one of her professors had been willing to trade grades for time alone with her.

As her feeling of her own full breasts turned to a more sensual touching, she decided that perhaps she needed to have the edge taken off of her passion before turning in. After all, after his Honor had gotten through groping her in the safety of his kitchen and the Mayor's wife had trapped her in the powder room for a little girl on girl slap and tickle, Celia had found herself unusually distracted. It was too bad that her husband was too much of a drunk to get it up any longer. She had entertained such hopes for him when they had married, but over time, his fondness for Scotch had rivaled his father's. Unfortunately, Anson was not able to handle his liquor as well as the old man had, or his wife either for that matter.

She decided that she would have Maria join her for some late groping after the bath. Gliding over to the house phone, Celia punched in the extension for her personal maid. After two buzzes, the receiver was lifted.

"Si?" came a sleepy sounding voice.

"Maria, I want you to come up here in about an hour," ordered Celia, who dropped the receiver back into the cradle without waiting for an answer. She and Maria had an understanding. "I need some relaxing."

THE BEDROOM OF MARIA TORNILLO

According to what Celia told everyone, twenty-nine year old Maria Tornillo was a Mexican Exchange student who took classes at the local college. In return for room and board in the mother in law's quarters of the big house, she cleaned, cooked and took care of Ms. Rosenberg's more unusual "urges". She also gave massages that could take care of almost any ache or pain, or at least take the recipient's mind off of the pains.

Anson Rosenberg also liked having the tawny haired, well-built young woman serve at parties, suitably dressed in a very skimpy maid's outfit designed to display her truly superb legs and excite the imaginations of his wealthy friends and business associates. More than one of them had later been caught, and photographed, with Maria, in very compromising positions, resulting in Anson having preferential treatment almost all over town.

Maria, unknown even to Anson Rosenberg, had only recently become a college student and was certainly not an exchange student from Mexico or anywhere else. She was a first class call girl that had been seen by Ms. Rosenberg plying her real trade outside a fashionable restaurant in Cuidad Juarez. Feeling in the mood for a little roll in the hay of the type that she dared not indulge in while in El Paso Celia had rented the girl for the afternoon. She had been expensive, but well worth the price. In fact, Celia had been so impressed with the girl's hidden talents and the way that she used them, that they had been together ever since. A week or two later, Celia had moved Maria into her home.

Unknown to Celia, it had not been Maria that had answered the phone when she had called. In fact Maria was not able to do much of anything, for at that very moment, Maria was very naked and tied spread eagled to her bed, a thick wad of her own silk panties shoved into her mouth as a very effective gag. A black clad, masked figure sat casually on the edge of the queen-sized bed, one gloved hand clamped tightly around Maria's very exposed, left breast. An ornate engraved, silver cigarette lights burned merrily in the other gloved hand.

"Well," rasped a whispery voice, "it would seem that your employer has need of your, shall we say, special talents. I am afraid that she will be somewhat disappointed, since you are otherwise involved, as it were."

Maria struggled to free herself, her wide opened eyes riveted on the burning lighter, but it was clear that she had been tied too tightly. It had happened so fast that she had not really realized what was going on until it was too late. She had been cleaning up from having her own small dinner for a few lose friends in the kitchen when she heard a gentle tap on the door. She thought it was perhaps one of her "friends" coming back for a late night visit and opened the door without bothering to check the security cameras. Instead of a familiar face, she found herself falling, a cloth pressed tightly over her face. Then that was the last thing she knew until she woke up, naked and tied to her own bed.

"However, let me see if I can find a way for us to pass the time," finished the rasping whisper that so grated on Maria's nerves.

Slowly, the black clad figure brought the flame of the lighter closer to one of Maria's wide nipples. The girl struggled to pull away, but was helpless to avoid the hot lighter coming in contact with her sensitive nipple. Her scream of agony was loud in spite of the gag stuffed deeply into her wide mouth.

Laughing softly, her captor stood up and began to undress, until the figure was naked except for the mask. Then with a flourish, the mask that covered her captor's face was removed and Maria was shocked to see that she knew her captor. The identity of the masked person left her speechless, as this was the last person she would ever expect to have done such a thing to her. Wait until she was free and able to tell people, no one would believe it she thought to herself.

Forcing Maria's wide spread knees even further apart, her captor crawled between them and began to administer to Maria's most private regions. This was a liberty that Maria rarely allowed to even her best customers and even then the charge was very high. Most thought it was because she was, in spite of her past history, still somewhat inhibited, but it was really because a tongue sliding into her most private recesses sent her into fits of orgasms that left her weak and almost comatose. In spite of the agonizing pain in her breasts, in only a few seconds, she felt the first wave approaching and then she ceased to care what was going on around her.

It was some time later, before the naked figure rose from ministering to the now unresisting woman tied to the bed. Maria's head was thrown back, her eyes had rolled back in her head, and she had actually passed out from the succession of orgasms that had coursed through her system. Pausing a moment, until the world stopped spinning, and the hands stopped shaking, that the intruder slowly resumed the black garb and the mask.

It was not until the masked figure was completely dressed that Maria made a sound that showed she was not actually dead. The young woman, still drugged by the powerful orgasms slowly raised her head and looked groggily at the masked figure towering over her, her eyes wide. For a moment, she was puzzled by what her ravisher was doing, but then she realized that the item held in the gloved hands was a syringe.

"It is too bad, my dear, we could have had a lot of fun together," murmured the intruder. "But you saw my face and I can't have you telling people. The sad thing is that I just can't trust you."

It was at that moment that Maria panicked and began to frantically pull at her bonds. She tried to make the intruder understand that she promised not to tell; she would do anything not to die. But it was all to no avail. The syringe held lightly between two fingers, the intruder sat back down on the edge of the bed. Leaning over to examine Maria closely, her masked captor captured her injured breasts tightly in one hand and captured the throbbing nipple between strong white teeth. With no warning, those teeth sank deeply into the soft skin of Maria's breasts, grinding as the captive woman screamed her intense agony. Finally, pulling away from the now bleeding breasts, the masked figure jabbed the needle deeply into the underside of the left breast, pushing the plunger home.

The captive young woman froze a moment, her screams of agony died in her constricted throat as her eyes bugged out of her head in fear and then she went completely limp. One last time, those beautiful hazel eyes looked at her killer and then slowly closed. In a few moments, her breathing increased dramatically and then she took one final deep breath and lay still. Maria was not dead, but she would be soon enough.

Rising from the edge of bed, the masked figure reached down beside the bed and picked up a small bag that was carefully placed in the spot only vacated by the killer. The used syringe was dropped into it and a 9-millimeter automatic was removed from a separate compartment of the unusual bag of tools. Rummaging into the bag for a second time, the killer then removed a long cylinder that was expertly fitted to the end of the barrel and screwed tightly into place. The pistol held very competently in one gloved hand was now silenced, an assassin's weapon.

A glance at the clock on the bedside table showed that it was still twenty minutes until the mistress of the house expected Maria to come minister to her. That would be plenty of time to take care of a few other chores. Silently, the killer crossed the room and cracked open the door enough to see that the hallways to the kitchen was empty. Not even the killer's keen senses could detect any sound or any movement.

Slowly, alert for anything out of the ordinary, the killer's form almost flowed through the partially opened door. A few steps brought the masked figure to the kitchen where the small bag was placed by the back door. The dimly lit kitchen was silent, everything in its proper place.

There were two other maids that lived in a large suite immediately off of the kitchen; the closed door to their suite of rooms was beside the door to the pantry. Crossing to the door, the killer slowly turned the knob and eased the door opened. There was a shot flight five carpet covered steps leading down to what appeared to be a small sitting room. Off of this sitting room were two doors, the killer knew from tidbits of information painstakingly gathered that the far door led to the room of the older woman and the nearer door led to the room occupied by the younger maid. The door to the older maid's room was closed, but the door of the younger was partly opened.

Cat footing across the room, the killer pushed the partially opened door further opened and peered inside. From the moonlight filtering into the room, the killer saw that the bed was empty. With a sound of annoyance, the killer moved to the closed door. Slowly the knob was turned and the door slowly pushed open. This time, the moonlight showed that the older woman was sound asleep, the cover thrown back. Her nightgown was pulled up around her waist, revealing a surprisingly nice set of legs, a thick bush where they joined. The woman's thick even breathing showed that she was deeply asleep.

Slowly reaching down, the killer removed a small plastic bag from a cargo pocket and from the bag removed a damp cloth. The sharp pungent odor of chloroform filled the room, though the sleeping woman did not notice. Slowly the killer approached the bed, stopping only when towering directly over the sleeping woman. Carefully, the silenced pistol was slid into the belt of the masked figure. Then slowly, almost not breathing, the killer leaned forward to suddenly grab the head of the woman, clamping the damp pad over the sleeping woman's mouth and nose. Startled into wakefulness, and completely disoriented, the woman on the bed struggled only for a moment, before the fumes overcame her senses and she lay limply, at the intruder's mercy. Her stocky legs had opened even further during her struggle; her most intimate recesses were even more on display for her attacker to see.

Letting her unconscious victim fall back onto the bed, the killer crossed room, and silently closed the door so that no one could see what went on the in the room. Returning to the bed, the masked figure quickly stripped the nightgown from the unconscious woman and rolled her over on her stomach. Tearing a strip from the discarded nightgown, the killer reached around the woman's head and shoved the wad of cloth deeply into her mouth, securing the thick wad of cloth by tying another strip tightly around her head, covering her mouth.

Reaching into a pocket, the masked intruder removed a plastic tie such as the police sometimes use in lieu of handcuffs and bound the woman's thick wrists behind her back. Reaching into another pocket, another plastic tie was removed to secure her surprisingly slim ankles, but at that moment, the killer glanced up and saw, lying partially concealed by the pillow, an egg shaped vibrator. So, the killer thought, that's why she was sleeping so soundly, she had been amusing herself.

Taking the vibrator from beneath the pillow, the killer carefully reached between the woman's plump thighs and slid the egg shaped vibrator part of the device deeply into the woman's most private moist recess. Before turning on the sex toy, the killer finished binding the ankles and then raised the woman's bound feet, using another plastic tie to secure them to the bound wrists, effectively hog tying the captive. Another strip of the discarded nightgown was used to tie the plump thighs tightly together to ensure that the little vibrator could not be pushed out by any contractions.

Next the killer thumbed the control knob of the vibrator to high and turned it on. Though unconscious, the movement of the little silver egg had to be driving the woman crazy. Removing a glove to run one hand over the surprisingly smooth skin of the plump thighs of the bound maid, the killer made a small sound of regret, murmuring, "Next time."

Assured that no matter what noise was made, this woman would not be either coming to investigate or calling the police, the killer replaced the chloroformed soaked cloth in the plastic baggie and the baggie back into one of the many cargo pockets on the dark pants. As the killer left the room, closing the door softly, the only sounds were the muffled grunts of the bound maid as the little vibrator left on its highest setting, quickly brought the woman to the edge of her senses. Even as the killer watched the bound maid began to pound her hips against the bed like a jackhammer. She was certainly out of action for the night.

Smiling beneath the mask, the intruder slowly moved through the hallway, moving toward the staircase at the front of the house. Suddenly, the killer froze at a sudden noise from behind the closed door to Anson Rosenberg's study. Pistol held ready, the intruder gently eased the door to the study open far enough to peer into the room. Seated behind his desk, chair turned to the side was the great Anson Rosenberg.

What was that bastard doing up at this hour, cursed the killer? His appearance was unusual, and his head was thrown back and his back arched as if he was having a seizure. Both of the puzzles were quickly solved as a head covered with long dark hair suddenly appeared over the edge of the desk.

"You like?" asked the young girl coyly.

"Damn you bitch!" growled the normally unruffled Anson, grabbing the girl's head with both hands and forcing it down. "You know I do, now bring me off."

The intruder recognized the girl as the younger maid whose bed had been found empty. There was no doubt that the young woman couldn't be over 17 or so. She was a tiny thing, no taller than 4'11", and even though it was clear that she had a knockout body, she actually appeared much younger than her actual age. The outfit that she wore as a maid hid the treasures of this young woman's body, but clearly not from Rosenberg.

So Anson Rosenberg liked them young, did he, mused the masked figure quietly. That was certainly interesting information. He was married to a woman that could give a marble statue a hard on and yet he had to diddle the help. There is no doubt that you just can't know what goes on behind closed doors in this town.

Fairly certain that in his present condition, Anson would not know if a marching band came into the room, the intruder quietly approached the desk. The killer paused when close enough to see the bobbing head of the girl, who was on her knees between the man's outstretched naked legs. Taking careful aim, the intruder shot Anson directly between the eyes, the silenced pistol making less noise than the girl's licking and sucking. He never knew what hit him. It took the girl a few seconds to realize that something was wrong. Finally, holding his limp member in one dainty hand, she looked up at him with a puzzled looked on her pretty face.

"Is something wrong, Senor?" she asked coyly, looking up and actually batting her eyes at her employer. The intruder had not seen someone bat their eyes in a long time. "You are going soft. Do I not pleasure you?"

"I am afraid that something is definitely wrong, my dear," interrupted the masked killer in a gentle voice. "He seems to have lost interest in your little activities."

The startled girl started to rise; her tiny hands trying futilely to cover her very large, bare breasts. She was wearing a very skimpy nightgown, but the narrow straps had been pushed off of her slim shoulders, and the top was now bunched around her narrow waist, held up only by the wide flaring of her hips. The girl was only flustered at being discovered until she glanced at Anson Rosenberg and saw the blood streaming down his face from the hole between his staring eyes. At that point the panic was visible on her face.

Knowing full well that the girl was going to go into hysterics any minute and with a great deal of regret, the intruder fired once and a third eye appeared just above the girl's own large brown eyes. The pretty Mestizo stood for a moment, her tiny hands cupping her own full breasts as if offering them to the intruder, before her legs finally gave out and the dead woman, really nothing more than a girl, fell. Ironically, her head come to rest in Anson's crotch.

Now that was a very appropriate position, thought the killer, backing from the room and turning out the light. Having accounted for the husband and all of the hired help, the killer walked boldly across the entry hall and ascended the stairs, stopping outside the door to Celia's room. Pressing one ear against the wooden panel, the intruder could faintly hear water running down the drain. Talk about perfect timing, thought the killer as the door was opened and the masked figure slipped inside.

Just as the intruder approached the bathroom door, it opened and a robe covered Celia Rosenberg swept into the room. Spinning counter clockwise, the intruder stuck out one dark clad leg and swept both of Celia's out from under her. The startled woman hit the floor on her back, her breath knocked from her lungs, leaving her fighting for air.

Before Celia could react, the intruder rolled her over onto her well-developed torso, grabbed the collar of her terry cloth robe, and stripped it from her warm, damp body leaving her completely nude. Both wrists of the stun woman were roughly jerked behind her and secured with another plastic tie. As a final act, the killer dropping onto Celia's broad back with full weight, which again forced her breath from her lungs and also caused her to open her mouth to gasp for air; taking advantage of the opportunity, the killer shoved a small red ball into her open mouth and secured it with the two attached straps. In record time, Celia Rosenberg had been stripped, bound, and gagged.

Rising to a kneeling position astride Celia Rosenberg, the intruder used another plastic tie to secure her captive's shapely ankles. Finally, satisfied with the way the woman was bound, the killer rolled the terrified woman over onto her back once more, sat back on booted heels and gently put the muzzle of the silenced pistol under the chin of the terrified woman and pushed her head back.

"Now, Celia, we need to talk," came the wheezy, rasping voice of the killer. "I think you have something I want."

CHAPTER FOURTEEN

LUCY'S COFFEE SHOP

The next day dawned hot and overcast, a thick haze filling the air as the pollution from the many factories south of Ciudad Juarez came north with the early morning breeze. Lieutenant Caleb Morgan had always been an early riser and so, in spite of having not gotten home until two in the morning, he arrived at Lucy's Diner on Mesa at a little after five in the morning. He started every day with at least one cup of Lucy's special blend of coffee.

As was always the case, after his first cup of Lucy's steaming coffee, he felt more human and pulled some papers from his jacket pocket. He had read them twice the night before, and now he read them once again. Once again he read the spidery scrawl that marched across the papers, the writing every bit as direct as the man he was sure had written those lines.

The cover page stated that this was the Last Will and Testament of Ezra Hughes, former Captain of the Texas Rangers and long time sheriff of El Paso. Caleb had known the old man very well and had come to look up to him as a second father. He had known that the old man had a rather checkered past and the part of this document he had written had reinforced that belief.

"I have only one living relative that I know and frankly she is a first class bitch who has little love for me. She only comes by to check on me to see if I am dead so that she can sell off what I have spent a lifetime acquiring. So for this reason, I leave Chelsea Mallard the grand sum of one dollar and that it too damn much.

I have done a lot of things in my life that I have since regretted, but one thing that I do not regret was my affair with Elena Granado Espinosa. When I met her she was working for the Alcalde in Juarez; her father was the Chief of Police across the border and a very proud man of the old school. When I first saw her, I knew that I had to have her and at the first opportunity, I took her. I am not sure that her family ever knew about our relationship, but if not for my own entanglements, I would have certainly married her, propriety be damned. Even though I was more than forty years her senior, I loved her and I know that she loved me. Elena told me that she was going to tell her father and insist that he bless out marriage, however, I never found out if she did.

"The Viper found out about our relationship and I knew that there would be trouble, perhaps very serious trouble. I knew that at this age, I am not much use to anyone and certainly not able to protect Elena from the Viper. Much as it pained me, I gave Elena a large sum of money and pleaded with her to get out of town until I could take care of matters. I never saw her again. I tried to find her, however, her father refused to even talk with me after Elena disappeared. I have heard a rumor that when she left, neither of us knew that she was pregnant. If I am not able to make amends before my death, then by way of showing my feelings for her, I leave her, or if she is dead, her heirs, my entire estate.

"In honoring a promise, and accepting what I knew was a bribe, I never used what I discovered as I should have to bring a criminal to justice. I reckon not being able to live out my last years with Elena is my punishment for turning my back on my duty. However, I was weak, the amount of money offered to me was a fortune even today and in those days things were done a lot different than they are now. I thought that I could watch things and make sure that the Viper killer no more. I was wrong.

I leave it to Elena to do what is right with the information contained in my diaries. Signed Ezra Hughes."

Morgan slowly folded the documents and returned them to his coat. He had grown up when the name of Ezra Hughes could send the bravest criminal running for the woods. This Viper must have been some kind of enemy for Hughes to feel that he was too old to handle him. Even in his declining years, Hughes had still be a man to ride the river with. No wonder the old man had never married, he was afraid that this Viper would kill his wife.

It was disheartening to think that the great Ezra Hughes would cover up a crime, but even Hughes was human Morgan thought to himself. What crime could have been so heinous that it would still be causing repercussions after all these years? To Morgan's knowledge, Hughes had solved hundreds of serious crimes over the years, and there were probably thousands more in the old man's long career that Morgan had never heard about.

He had heard that Chelsea Mallard had inherited the old man's estate, which had been something of a surprise to a lot of people. It was common knowledge that Hughes had despised the woman, not even wanting her to even so much as set foot in his house. Then after his death, the surprise Last Will and Testament had surfaced leaving everything to Mallard. So Morgan was somewhat surprised to find this second, and earlier, Will in one of the hidden filing cabinets inside Mallard's secret room. Perhaps he needed to pay a visit to the Lawyer that had represented Mallard in her claim for the estate.

At that moment, Lucy Calderon, the owner of Lucy's walked in the front door and headed for the back of the diner. She and her daughter, Esmeralda, had run Lucy's since before Morgan had been born. His earliest memories were of his father, Jeff Morgan, bringing him here on Saturday mornings for an early breakfast. A sudden thought hit him.

"Lucy, can I see you a moment?" he asked taking a sip of his coffee.

"Si, Senor," the old lady responded, crossing the spotless linoleum floor with that distinctive squeak of her rubber soled orthopedic shoes. She reached out, snagged the coffee pot on the way, and immediately refilled his partially empty cup. "What can I do for you?"

"Lucy, how long have you lived in El Paso?" he asked, as he poured sugar into his freshly filled cup.

"Oh, all my life and I will be sixty years old next week," she said proudly. "My ancestors were some of the first to settle in what is now Ciudad Juarez."

"Congratulations, Lucy," responded Morgan with a smile. "And here I thought you were no more than thirty."

This brought a peal of laughter from the old woman as it always did. Morgan planning to marry Lucy because of her great tasting coffee had been a running joke between them for over twenty-five years.

"Caleb Morgan you are as big a flirt as your daddy ever was," the old woman giggled as she started to return to the counter. Caleb had long heard stories that she and his father had been "very" good friends before his father married his mother.

"Lucy, have you ever heard the name Elena Espinosa?" he asked, his attention focused on carefully pouring fresh cream into his cup. He didn't notice the old lady stiffen and hesitate at the question. Finally, she carefully replaced the coffee pot on the warmer and then stood motionless behind the counter.

When she did not answer, he finally glanced up. To his surprise, Lucy was staring off into space, her face covered with a wistful smile.

"Lucy?" he prompted, to regain her attention. "Did you know someone named Elena Espinosa?"

"Oh yes, Lieutenant, I once knew someone by that name, she was once my good friend, many years ago, before you were just a gleam in your daddy's eye," she responded in a very soft voice. "Our families lived near each other in Ciudad Juarez, so we became very close."

"Where is she?" he asked, curiously. He was fairly sure that it could not be the one that Ranger Hughes had written about in his Last Will and Testament, but then in El Paso anything was possible.

Lucy passed as if to answer and then uncharacteristically she shrugged and began bustling about, cleaning the already spotless counter top.

"That was many years ago and I have not seen her in over twenty years," she returned, making every effort to not meet his bemused gaze. "The past is dead, it is best to leave it so. Now, I have no more time to talk. I need to get ready for my customers. They like a clean place to enjoy their morning coffee."

Morgan's gaze sharpened, as it became clear to him that Lucy wanted to avoid talking to him. He was currently the only customer in the diner, just as he was always the first customer of the day; her busy time did not start until after 7:00 am when the regulars would begin to arrive for their breakfast. With the instinct of ten years as a police officer, he was positive that Lucy knew a lot more than she was telling.

"Lucy, it is important. I need to know," he said quietly, "this involves a police matter."

With a clear reluctance, Lucy slowly returned to his table and sank into the chair across from him with a deep sigh.

"Oh, let it rest, Caleb" she pleaded. "It was a long time ago. Enough lives have been ruined."

He did not respond, just gazed at her steadily. Finally, she dropped her eyes and began to toy with the fork lying in the center of the little Formica table.

"Oh, very well," she finally gave in quietly. "Like I said, Elena was my friend. We went to school together and, when we were older, we went out on dates together. In those days a proper young lady of our social class did not go on a date without a chaperone. Elena was a beautiful girl, her parents were very well off, and she had many wealthy suitors.

"When she was 19, she was offered a job as an assistant to the Mayor of Juarez. Her English was very good, so when he had meetings with those from this side of the border, she always went along as his translator. So it was that, one day, the Mayor of Juarez and the then Sheriff of El Paso, Ranger Hughes, had a meeting. Elena was with the Mayor as usual. For Hughes and Elena, it was love at first sight."

"Wasn't there a large difference in their ages?" asked Morgan curiously.

Lucy smiled at him with the same impishness that she must have shown in her twenties. "Oh, yes, my friend, she was barely 20 and he was probably in his mid sixties at the time. But you have to remember that in Mexico the age differences between a man and a woman is not as big an issue as it is among you gringos. For a long time the fathers would arrange marriages for their daughters to older, wiser men."

"So it caused no problems?" he pressed.

Again Lucy gave him that impish smile, a reminder that in her day she had probably been a hell of a looker herself.

"Elena kept me informed of their relationship, Caleb," she continued, her eyes showed him that she was lost in memories. "Even though he was about forty years older that she, according to Elena, Ranger Hughes, even at that age, was muy toro. She called him her bull because she said he was such a great lover. She very much wanted to marry him."

"Did her parents accept the arrangement?" questioned Morgan, his interest certainly raised by the possibilities that ran through his mind.

"Oh, no," responded Lucy emphatically, leaning back in her chair to shake her head. "Her papa, he was a descendant of a long line of Spanish nobles and was livid that his daughter had taken up with what he called that "bastard Texas Ranger." According to local rumor, the two of them had once been very close friends, but had a falling out over something long before Elena was born. However, Elena persisted and finally won her parents over. When I last saw her, she was so excited that they were finally going to let her marry the man."

She paused for a moment, wrinkling her brow.

"So did they marry?" prompted Morgan curiously.

"No, I don't think they ever did marry. I know that she was determined to marry him, but then something happened, I never knew what it was. Elena disappeared the day after she told me that she and Ranger Hughes were going to be married, and I never saw her again. There were rumors that she was pregnant and her parents sent her off to have the baby somewhere else, but I was never able to find out the truth."

She looked at Morgan with an earnest expression on her broad face.

"That's all I know, Caleb, I swear. None of this was ever secret. Elena and her family were once very well known in society on both sides of the River. It is just something that has never been talked about, especially with a gringo. If she became pregnant without getting married, that was something that would have never been admitted by the family and if she eloped and married without the blessing of the Church it would have been a sin and her family would certainly not let anyone know. So in either case, it would have been a deep secret."

Morgan rubbed his chin for a moment, considering Lucy's story. It seemed to fit all of the facts that Ranger Hughes had written in his Last Will and Testament. Of course, he needed to talk to Mallard's attorney, but it would appear that the Last Will and Testament of Ranger Hughes that had gone to probate had been a forgery. He had always heard that Chelsea Mallard was one of the old man's last living relatives, but he also had heard it said that he hated her. It looked like she had found the actual will, hidden it, and then decided to steal the estate for herself, and had a phony Will drawn by some shyster attorney making her the sole heir. He gulped the rest of his coffee and stood.

"Are Elena's parents still alive?" he asked as he dropped some bills on the table to cover his breakfast and the tip. This type of fraud was really not something he was supposed to get involved in, but he had really liked that old man and felt a need to make sure that his wishes were carried out as he had intended.

"I do not know, Caleb. However, I did notice in that news story about that female pilot that was returned to Beaumont, that her grandmother was named Elena Espinosa, perhaps she is a relative and would know if my Elena's parents still live."

LAW OFFICE OF DUNCAN RENALDO, ESQUIRE

When the Courthouse opened that morning, Lieutenant Caleb Morgan was the first one into the probate records. It took him only thirty minutes to confirm the identity of Chelsea Mallard's attorney. In fact, he had already been fairly certain of his identity, but he just wanted to be thorough and make absolutely sure that his theory was solid. Based upon what he had found in the hidden files, he now knew that the purported Last Will & Testament of Ezra Hughes submitted for probate was a forgery. The question was who had been involved in the forgery.

It is said that every town has at least one lawyer that is well connected with the underworld and, for a price, can arrange anything. In El Paso, that lawyer was Duncan Renaldo. He had been City Attorney six or seven times and represented every major criminal that had appeared in the El Paso's courts. His record of winning cases had very few in the loss column, and in fact, several of his better known wins had appeared to the uninitiated to be nothing short of miracles. Like many others before him, everyone knew that he was crooked, but no one had ever been able to get anything on him.

The probate records confirmed that not only had Duncan Renaldo had represented Chelsea through the probate process, but he had also helped her sell off much of the valuable art that had belonged to Ranger Hughes at the time of his death. Now that it appeared that the validity of the Will that was submitted for probate was in doubt, this placed a new light on things. Perhaps Attorney Renaldo had finally made a mistake.

As Morgan made ready to leave, he was struck by a sudden idea. He wondered how many other large probate cases had been handled by Renaldo. Perhaps they also needed looking into to see if the Last Will and Testament was valid. He spent another hour looking up cases and having copies of records made that he could take back to his office.

From the Courthouse, Morgan had driven straight to Renaldo's Office. Though it was common knowledge that Renaldo was a millionaire many times over, the building where Renaldo had his offices was a rather non-descript building on a side street. In fact the building had certainly seen better days, now it looked rather rundown. Even the hallway from the front door to the wing of the building occupied by Renaldo was in need of repair and smelled faintly of stale urine.

However, when Morgan entered Renaldo's office there was no doubt that this was the office of a very wealthy man. The rich walnut paneling provided the perfect backdrop for some of the very expensive paintings that decorated the outer office. Even the furniture in the small waiting room spoke of wealth. Feeling somewhat out of place, Morgan crossed the carpeted area between the door and the receptionist's desk as quickly as possible.

"May I help you, sir?" inquired the young lady sitting primly behind the large receptionist desk before Morgan could say anything. She was Hispanic and had a 1000 watt smile which she immediately flashed at him. His practiced eye also noticed the diamond studded wristwatch on her left wrist as she rested her forearms on her desk. That was a pretty expensive bauble for a receptionist's salary, he mused to himself. Her see through blouse was also rather risqué for a lawyer's office, but perhaps it helped explain the expensive watch. Of course, he certainly approved of the view of her assets allowed by the thin material of the blouse.

In answer he laid his credentials on her desk.

"Lieutenant Morgan, El Paso Police Department to see Mr. Renaldo," he responded formally.

Being confronted by a police Lieutenant did not fluster the young lady a bit, showing Morgan that she was probably as smart as she was attractive.

"And what is the nature of your call?" she asked officiously. He realized that she was not going to give an inch until her made her do so.

"Official business," responded Morgan returning his credentials case to his pocket.

With just a hint of a frown on her pretty face, the receptionist regarded him for sometime before she picked up the phone and pushed the intercom button. She turned partly away from Moran as she spoke.

"There is a police Lieutenant by the name of Morgan here to see you," she said, partially cupping her hand over the mouthpiece. "No, he only said official business."

She listened for a time and then lowered the phone.

"I am sorry sir, but if you will make an appointment for a more convenient time, Mr. Renaldo will give you a few minutes. He is getting ready for a trial and really cannot be disturbed at this time," her pretty face made it clear that he was being given the brush off, though her tone was apologetic.

In response, he smiled and turned back toward the door.

"No thank you," he responded over his shoulder, his hand on the doorknob. "I thought I would give him the courtesy of explaining a few things to me before it all hits the papers. At least he can't say that we did not try to give him a break."

His last backward glance showed that she was just sitting there, her mouth hanging open. She clearly had no idea what to say at this point.

He had started his engine and was letting the air conditioner run for a while so that it would start blowing cool air instead of warm, when there was a rapid tap on his driver side window. He turned to see the receptionist bending down looking through his car window. His response was not immediate because the view down the neckline of the blouse was even more spectacular than through the sheer material. Finally, after lettering her sweat a bit in the 100 degree heat, he rolled down the window.

"Lieutenant, Mr. Renaldo found that he did have some time to see you after all," she said rapidly; she must have run after him because she was breathing rapidly and sweat already beginning to soak through her fancy blouse. This was clearly one of those girls built for the indoors. She didn't appear to fare well in the heat.

"Would you follow me please?"

Morgan exited his car to see that the young woman was also wearing stiletto heels, which, coupled with her short skirt, made her long legs look spectacular, but also made it hard for her to move rapidly. She must have really been frantic to catch him to have moved so quickly.

They re-entered the plush office, the cool temperature a welcome relief after being out doors. She led him across the carpet, more sure of herself now that they were back on familiar ground, to a paneled door off to one side. She tapped on the door gently and pushed it open.

If Morgan had thought the outer office was plush, Renaldo's private office looked like a museum. Morgan was not an art collector, but he knew a good bit about it and there was no doubt that the picture hanging on the wall above the leather couch was probably worth more than Morgan made in ten years. This was a man who liked to show his wealth, but only behind closed doors.

Morgan had of course seen Renaldo in court many times, but he had never before met him. Renaldo was of middle years, probably in his late forties, tall, with thinning blonde hair that he combed back to cover his bald spot. His charcoal pinstripe suit was very expensive and his shoes carried the distinctive Gucci logo.

Renaldo came around his desk to offer his hand to Morgan and then led him to some plush chairs arranged in a sitting area in one corner of the large office.

"Bring us some coffee, Janey," Renaldo ordered in a soft voice as he sat down in one of the chairs, gesturing for Morgan to also sit. Morgan noticed that he was so certain of obedience that he did not so much as favor the girl with a glance. For her part, the receptionist literally scurried to obey.

Renaldo just observed his guest in silence until the coffee was brought and both men had been served. Morgan studied the cup for a moment, noticing the gold rim and the family crest on one side. Renaldo glanced at the young lady who was now standing uncertainly in the center of the floor, her hands clasped behind her back, her assets on full display for both men as she waited for more orders.

"You may return to your desk, Janey," he said, his voice flat, showing no emotion. "Hold my calls."

Janey exited the office as fast as she could move on the stiletto heels. Morgan wondered what else Renaldo usually ordered her to do. That girl was clearly completely under the lawyers thumb.

"Now Lieutenant, how may I serve you?" began Renaldo, taking a small sip of the steaming coffee from his own matching cup.

"Mr. Renaldo, I am with the Homicide Department. I am afraid that this visit is about one of your clients," began Morgan, ignoring his own cup of coffee.

Renaldo raised one eyebrow, "Indeed. Well, Lieutenant Morgan, I am sure that you are well aware that because of attorney-client privilege, I cannot release information to you, or anyone else for that matter, about my clients' affairs." His voice had taken on something of a condescending note. "So I am afraid that you are wasting your time."

"Oh, I am well aware of attorney-client privilege, counselor, but I also know that this does not apply when the client is dead," Morgan observed, casually taking a sip of his own coffee. "I want to know about one of your deceased clients."

Renaldo's startled expression showed that Morgan had finally cracked his shell of studied indifference.

"I am not aware of the recent death of one of my clients," Renaldo finally responded, the barest hint of perspiration now showing on his wide forehead. "And even if one has died, I am not sure how I would figure into your investigation. As for older former clients, I am afraid that I have sent those files to storage. It would take some time to retrieve those files, of course."

It was Morgan's turn to feign indifference. He had to draw this man out and get him to talk.

"Well, the deceased is Chelsea Mallard, who I understand you represented in the probate of Ezra Hughes' estate, not too long ago. I think that I also heard that you arranged for the sale of a lot of the assets of the estate on her behalf."

He glanced at Renaldo and was amused to see that the man had almost stopped breathing. The attorney was just sitting and staring at Morgan, his condescending expression frozen on his face. Knowing that the first one that speaks in such a situation loses, Morgan continued to enjoy his coffee, though it was not as good as that served at Lucy's.

"Uh, well, yes, I did represent Ms. Mallard in the probate of her relative's estate and in the sale of a good portion of the physical assets of the estate," the attorney finally admitted cautiously. "Do you think that this had something to do with her death?"

"I am surprised that you are not more curious about how she died, Mr. Renaldo," observed Morgan, leaning back in his chair and crossing his legs. "I would imagine that it is not everyday that one of your clients dies."

"Oh quiet right, quiet right, Lieutenant," Renaldo was suddenly turning on the charm. Morgan could see that the thought of Chelsea Mallard dying really upset this normally very self-assured man. "How did she die?"

"She was murdered," responded Morgan bluntly, "very brutally murdered. In fact, according to the M.E. she was tortured to death in the library of Ezra Hughes' mansion."

Renaldo paled, and leaned so far forward that for a moment Morgan thought he would topple from his chair. Then, like the consummate professional that he was, Renaldo pulled himself together and turned the discussion to a safer topic.

"So how do you think that I might help you solve this heinous crime?" asked the attorney, his voice still just a bit shaky. "It is so sad to hear about the death of Ms. Mallard. Of course, as her attorney, I will naturally take charge of her estate for her next of kin. I am not sure whether or not she had any heirs."

"First off," began Morgan, leaning forward to spear Renaldo with a direct stare, "you can tell me what you know about the forged Last Will and Testament that you submitted to probate on Ms. Mallard's behalf in regard to Ezra Hughes' estate."

"Forged?" demanded Renaldo, his voice almost cracking in his shock. "I know nothing about a forged Will."

"Well, whether you knew it or not, the Will that you submitted to probate was forged. There is little doubt that it was a forgery. We found the real one in a hidden room in Ms. Mallard's Office, along with a fortune in stolen works of art and several cabinets of personal information on various people in the area."

At the mention of the hidden room, Renaldo had turned white as a sheet and swayed in his chair for a moment.

"Hidden room?" repeated Renaldo weakly. "Uh, were there ---?"

He never finished the question because Morgan had anticipated what the attorney would ask and nodded in agreement.

"Oh, yes, Mr. Renaldo," agreed Morgan. "Your very able assistance in helping to fence valuable stolen artifacts was mentioned in many of those files. It made for very interesting reading and I am sure that both the District Attorney and the State Bar Association will find the information in them as interesting as I did."

Now Renaldo did moan and topple from his chair. Morgan sat quietly drinking his now cool coffee waiting for the attorney to get up from the floor. It was a new Renaldo that revived from the dead faint. He could not wait to provide information on the forgery and a list of all of those collectors that had paid high prices for what were actually stolen works of art, since neither Mallard nor Renaldo had the right to sell them.

As he left the office with a treasure trove of information, Morgan could only think that he hoped that Janey had some other talents that she could fall back on, as he did not think she would be employed by Mr. Renaldo very much longer. There was little need for receptionists or private secretaries where the attorney would soon be going.

CHAPTER FIFTEEN

The little detour by Renaldo's office meant that Morgan arrived at Chelsea Mallard's real estate office well after the rest of the personnel assigned to the investigation. That was about the only benefit running an investigation allowed; he could come and go as he pleased. He entered the private office to see Juan Estrada deeply immersed in a thick file. Lisa Nettleton, the late Chelsea Mallard's executive assistant was across the room filing several coffee cups from a large silver coffee urn that had been installed on a temporary worktable. She flashed him a bright smile as he entered.

"Anything new?" he asked as he tossed his own jacket over the back of the nearest chair. He smiled his thanks as Miss Nettleton came over to hand him a cup of steaming coffee.

Juan leaned back in his chair and stretched his back muscles. He found this reading of old files boring; he had always preferred action to being behind a desk.

"Well what I have found is not really new; but these records leave no doubt that she had her finger in almost every major crime that has occurred between here and Dallas in the last year. She also kept very detailed records of who stole what and how much she paid for the items she received. These records are so detailed that it looks almost like she expected an IRS audit at any time."

"Any names we should know here in El Paso?" he asked idly, his eyes following the young assistant as she carried a try of coffee cup into the secret room.

"A few," Estrada responded. "No major players, but she does list a lot of mid level fences, dealers and receivers of stolen property. A couple of them had kept such low profiles that we were not aware that they existed. She also outlined one of the primary routes for moving heroin from here to Atlanta. The feds should be very interested in all of this information."

Estrada paused a moment and shifted through some of the stacks of papers and files that littered the top of the large desk. Finally, he pulled a leather bound book from beneath a file and tossed it across the desk to Morgan.

"Thought you might like to see this," he remarked, rubbing his eyes and picking up the file he had been reading once again. "It's certainly seems to be more interesting that these files."

Grinning, Morgan glanced down to see that what Juan had thrown him was a leather bound journal. The journal was clearly very old; in fact, the leather was darkened with age and cracked in several places. However, neither age nor the darkening of the leather could conceal that embossed on the front was a large Texas Ranger's Badge and below the badge was the name Ezra Hughes, Captain, Texas Rangers. They had found one of the old man's personal journals, a rare glimpse into the mind of one of the most legendary law enforcement officers to ever wear a badge. Almost reverently, Morgan opened the cover to the first page. Unfortunately, at that moment, his cell phone rang. It would be a while before he would be able to read even so much as the first line.

"Morgan," he answered, flipping up the cover of his cell.

"Caleb, this is Captain Jackson," the gruff voice of the Chief of Homicide could be heard several feet away from the little phone. He wasn't necessarily angry, that was just his normal tone of voice.

"Yes sir, Captain," responded Morgan, letting the journal fall into his lap. "What can I do for you?"

"Did you have a talk with Duncan Renaldo this morning?" the Captain demanded gruffly.

"I did, sir," responded Morgan, very shortly. "His name came up in regard to the Mallard murder case."

"Well I have always let you run your investigations as you saw fit, but this time, whatever you said to that shyster was enough to upset him to the point that he called in the big guns. Caleb, I have told you time and again that there are certain people in this town that you can't roust and Renaldo is probably at the top of the list," rumbled Jackson. "Like it or not, this is a Hispanic town and there are a lot of interfamily connections that carry a lot of weight."

The Chief of Homicide paused for a moment.

"You and your sidekick are to meet with Congresswoman Prestridge for lunch at the Lancers Club," directed the Chief of Homicide.

"She is expecting you at noon precisely. For once, listen to some good advice and try and be on time.

"I am sure that she is going to try and change the direction of your investigation. I also want you to know that you are on your own; I can't help you with that female barracuda. She has the clout to make the Governor turn back flips and you know what kind of sorry excuse for a backbone the Mayor has. So you watch yourself, boy! That woman eats police lieutenants for breakfast!"

Having said his peace, Captain Jackson broke the connection, leaving Lieutenant Morgan wondering just what kind of trouble his spur of the moment visit to attorney Renaldo was going to bring. Of all of the people he would have thought that sleazy bastard would call for help, he had never figured it would be Congresswoman Eva Prestridge. More than one promising career had ended in getting crosswise with that power broker. Suddenly, the day did not look too promising.

THE LANCERS CLUB, CORONADO TOWER

The west side of El Paso was relatively flat the further out Mesa Street one drove. The highest building on the west side of town was twelve stories tall and on the top floor was the well known Lancers Club. This was the gathering spot for the town's movers and shakers and it was the almost exclusive domain of the local Congresswoman, Eva Prestridge, who also happened to be the younger sister of the most senior superior court judge, Neil Prestridge.

Morgan and Juan paused in the entryway of the Lancers Club, unsure of which way to turn. When one exited the elevator, there were two ways to turn, one way led to the buffet line and the seating area, while the other way led into the small bar. As Morgan tried to decide which way to turn, a very slick looking young man with a small pencil thin moustache approached.

"Lieutenant Morgan?" he asked politely, studiously ignoring Detective Estrada, standing just beside Morgan. It did not take a genius for Morgan to know that the arrogant upstart in front of him did not like Hispanics.

"Yes," responded Morgan, shortly. This guy looked like he had just walked off of the cover of GQ. His suit, alone, probably cost him as much as Morgan made in a month.

"Right this way, if you please," directed the young man, turning to walk away as if he never doubted that Morgan and Juan would follow as ordered. Morgan made it a point to walk slowly in the general direction that the slick young man had gone. He hated being ordered around by someone a fraction of his age. He also noticed that Juan had not said a word, a clear sign he was not happy with the borderline insolence either. Last time that had happened, Estrada had put the guy that had insulted him through a window.

Finally, seeing the oily greeter standing impatiently across the room, they approached a table sitting in the corner, framed by two large windows that contained a spectacular view of the lower valley. Of course, the view out the windows had trouble competing with the view inside. Eva Prestridge was sitting with her back to the windows, facing into the room, the sun behind her, bringing out the coppery reddish tints in her long hair and throwing her face into shadow.

Though she had to be in her late fifties or early sixties, Eva Prestridge was still a beautiful woman. Her dark hair was full and worn long; her skin was clear and only a few wrinkles showed, primarily around her large eyes. However, it was her manners and her body that elicited the most comment. With her long dancer's legs, her shapely body and her full, firm chest, Congresswoman Prestridge still turned men's heads when she entered a room. There were a lot of rumors connecting her with various national personalities, but none of them had ever been substantiated and surprisingly, she had never married, though the local rumor mill reported that she had received a number of invitations.

Even Morgan, fully prepared to be barely civil to what he felt was a blatant attempt to influence him in his duties, felt the power of her gaze when she turned her sparkling green eyes on him. For a moment, time seemed to stand still and everyone else in the room vanished, as the two of them locked gazes. Morgan did not realize that he was just staring at the Congresswoman, until Juan had to poke him in the ribs.

Though she was fully aware of the effect she had on the detective, as if nothing had happened, Eva Prestridge rose and held out her hand toward him.

"I am Eva Prestridge," she said in a warm husky voice. "You must be the police Lieutenant that I have heard so much about. Your ability has been much remarked on by some of my acquaintances. I thought it was time that I meet this remarkable young man."

He took her pre-offered hand and brought it to his lips in an old world way of greeting a beautiful lady. Some sane portion of his mind watched from a distance, as the rest of his senses were overwhelmed by her beauty. The little voice in his mind said that he should go slow, but the rest of him was moving ahead at full speed. There was no question that she had loads of sex appeal and certainly knew how to use it.

"I am Caleb Morgan, Congresswoman and this is my partner, Juan Estrada," he introduced his partner, in a way that he knew annoyed the slick used car salesman assistant standing nearby, but never released her hand. There was something about this woman that drew him like a magnet.

With one last noticeable squeeze of her long fingers, Eva slowly pulled her hand away and motioned them both to sit across from her.

"I was not aware that you were such a gentleman, Lieutenant and Detective Estrada, I am glad to meet you, as well," she responded graciously, turning to look at her assistant hovering nearby. "Have them serve, Larry."

Like a well-trained puppy, her assistant trotted off toward the Manager who was waiting patiently near the door to the kitchen. A nearby waiter stepped forward to take the drink order of Morgan and Estrada. Within seconds the drinks appeared by their plates as if by magic.

"I do appreciate you both taking time from your busy schedules to join me for lunch," began Eva Prestridge, her eyes coolly surveying Morgan. "I know that you both have many more important things to do than go to luncheons. But, I am a servant of the people just as you are and one of my biggest supporters has asked me to look into a matter for him."

She paused, a slight smile playing at the edges of her full red lips, "I also want to stress that this is not an attempt to influence your judgment or direct your investigation in any way. When I was asked to look into the matter, my initial response was that I had no control over local law enforcement, but that I would look into the matter as a courtesy."

"And your supporter would be?" asked Morgan quietly as if he was not already aware that she had to have been called by Duncan Renaldo.

The Congresswoman fluttered her eyelashes for a moment as she took a small sip of her iced tea.

"Actually, I was called by my brother, Judge Prestridge. He said that he had been contacted by a very prominent local attorney, Duncan Renaldo. It seems that Mr. Renaldo had somehow gotten mixed up with something about a forged will and wanted to make sure that everyone knew that he had not been involved with the forgery, that he had just been representing a client."

Morgan nodded, his face giving away nothing. From time to time, he could catch a faint whiff of her perfume and it was certainly distracting. In spite of their wide difference in age, he found himself strongly attracted to this woman, even though she was old enough to be his mother.

"Well, Madam Congresswoman," he began in his most professional voice.

"Oh, call me Eva, please," she interrupted, to ask with a dimpled smile on her face, "and I believe that your first name is Caleb, if I may be permitted to call you Caleb."

Morgan was thrown off his planned statement by her gesture. He hesitated a moment and then continued.

"Oh, yes, uh, Eva, and my friends call me Cal, Caleb sounds so old fashioned," he almost stammered he was so flustered at her familiarity. He was feeling a little foolish at his lack of poise and the grin that he saw Juan direct his way certainly didn't help matters.

"Oh, thank you, Cal," she responded with a girlishness giggle that literally took his own breath away. "I am sorry for interrupting, please continue."

Morgan looked blank for a moment and then picked up his prepared speech where he had left off, "Yes, well, as you say, my questioning of Renaldo is part of an ongoing criminal investigation and I really can't go into the details with a non-police officer until I have permission from my superiors, but, suffice it to say that there does to be some indication that Mr. Renaldo may know more about the matter of a forged Last Will and Testament than he intimates," finished Morgan, for some reason feeling reluctant to disappoint this captivating woman.

"Well, will you at least keep me informed of what you find?" she asked, being very careful not to make any demands that might cause Morgan to dig in his heels. She was well aware that a few words in the right ear and a story of her attempt to interfere with a local criminal investigation would be front-page news.

"If it turns out that he is definitely guilty of some impropriety, both my brother and certainly myself need to distance ourselves from any appearance of impropriety on our parts. I am sure that you understand, Lieutenant."

Morgan glanced up as a waiter appeared at his elbow to carefully place a bowl of soup before him. He glanced up at Eva Prestridge who dimpled with a small smile.

"I hope you both do not mind, but I took the liberty of ordering the buffet for all of us."

CHAPTER SIXTEEN

POLICE HEADQUARTERS, PIEDRAS AND MONTANA

Lieutenant Morgan was in something of a pleasant daze when he and Juan Estrada arrived back at Police Headquarters. Their boss had wanted them to come by and brief him on the outcome of the luncheon before he heard any repercussions from his own superiors. Morgan was a little smug in feeling that he had acquitted himself very well with Congresswoman Prestridge.

Though Eva, as she insisted that he call her, was old enough to be his mother, she had shamelessly flirted with him for the entire two hours that they had spent over the luncheon. Even Juan had to admit that the old girl could turn the sex appeal like no one he had ever seen before. She had been gracious to Juan, unlike her staff members, but she had positively doted on Morgan. She had gone out of her way to touch his arm as they had talked, and laughed her sensual laugh form time to time. Morgan had been a little overwhelmed, not being used to having attention from such a beautiful woman literally showered on him. He was normally someone who stood lightly back and watched others, but she had not given him the opportunity to achieve the space he needed.

Juan, on the other hand, certainly had the time to step back and watch the rest of the party. As the only Hispanic at the little gathering, he was rarely engaged in conversation. He divided his attention between the outstanding buffet and watching the interplay of the others at the table. In addition to the Congresswoman, there was her chief of staff, Marvin Winkler and her press secretary, Sandra Winston. Both of them had tried to sound out the Lieutenant in what he thought about the involvement of Mr. Renaldo in the smuggling of stolen property, however, neither gave Juan more than a passing glance. Even the Congresswoman, who went out of her way to be gracious to both of them, spared him only a little of her attention. It is quite a remarkable performance.

He glanced at his partner, who now had a spring in his step that Juan had not seen since before Morgan's wife had died in a car wreck two years before. Perhaps, he mused to himself, something good will come out of this dalliance. There was no question in his mind that Prestridge was setting Morgan up to use him for information, but on the other hand, her show had certainly raised Morgan's spirits.

As the two left the ninety degree heat of the west Texas afternoon for the air conditioned comfort of the Homicide Division squad room, they were met halfway across the squad room by Captain Nathaniel (Nate) Jackson, Chief of the Homicide Division. Jackson was a massive man, standing over 6'4"" tall and weighing over 250 pounds. More than one person had thought his weight was flab, but had been shown the error of their ways. The power in his massive frame resulted in him rarely having to pull his weapon.

He was normally a very graceful man, who moved with an economy of motion, but at the moment, he seemed flustered. When the two detectives spotted him, he was in the somewhat difficult process of trying to talk on his cell phone at the same time he tried to pull his jacket on over the over sized Desert Eagle semiautomatic that he carried in his shoulder holster. He was having some trouble accomplishing both at the same time.

He stopped both trying to get his jacket on and walking when he met his two subordinates in the center of the room. They could only hear his side of the conversation which consisted primarily of yes sirs and no sirs. There was no question in the mind of the two detectives their there superior was not a happy camper at this particular moment. Finally he snapped the flip top of his cell phone closed and dropped it into his pant's pocket.

"Damn I hate politics," he growled at no one in particular as he completely removed the offending jacket and carefully slipped it back on over the bulging shoulder holster.

"Just coming to see you Captain," began Morgan, before Jackson cut him off with a shake of his shaggy head.

"Well, it is just going to have to wait," the Captain snapped. "I have been called to a meeting with the Mayor and the Chief received a call from the Head of the Chamber of Commerce asking for a favor and of course the Chief thinks that his Homicide Division had nothing better to do than favors for political bigwigs."

The Captain paused for a moment, chewing on the ends of his Fu Manchu moustache as he considered the matter for a moment. Finally she shook his head and sighed.

"I was going to send you two to meet with the Mayor, but he'd never go for it," said Jackson sadly. "So you two will just have to take care of the favor that I was planning to do for Pete Rosenberg on the way down town."

Juan allowed a small grin to play at the end of his wide mouth. He knew that Caleb Morgan hated do favors for politicians even more than Jackson. So he was not surprised when Morgan tried to get them out of the request.

"Uh, well, you see Captain," began Morgan, starting to back toward the door through which they had entered. "I was just going to say that we came by to tell you that we had some hot leads on the mallard murder and that we would be out of the office for a couple of days running them down."

"Oh, you did, did you?" snapped Jackson, smiling in a fashion very similar to the smile that a shark would give if a shark could smile. "Well, Mallard is dead and not going anywhere and these hot leads can wait for an hour or two while you two take care of the little favor that I am ordering you to take care of for Mr. Pete Rosenberg."

Morgan looked as if he was going to continue the argument, but Juan knew that Morgan knew that there was no way he was going to change Jackson's mind. At the same time, Jackson expected Morgan to argue, it showed that he was a man that knew his own mind. Or at least that's what Jackson always said when Morgan would argue with him, right before he would always throw Morgan out of his office. To the surprise of both Jackson and Estrada, Morgan threw in the towel without too much more arguing, something he rarely did.

"O.K., Captain," he said, with a tired sigh. "What's the favor that Pete Rosenberg wants from the Police Department?"

"What's the matter, boy?" asked Jackson with some concern. "You off your feed again? Where's your fire? You don't seem enthusiastic to help El Paso's elite."

Morgan made a face and shook his head.

"Oh, I guess I'm just tired, Captain," he finally responded. "It seems that the requests for favors by the Mayor's circle of friends will never end so why fight it. It'll save me a lot of time if I just go along with the program."

Jackson speared the Lieutenant with a hard suspicious stare.

"If I didn't know better I would think that you are up to something."

Morgan didn't answer, but merely gazed at the Captain quietly, he expression unreadable. This approach always resulted in Morgan being thrown out of the office and this was no exception. Rather than continue to pry, Jackson sent the pair to see why Celia Rosenberg was not answering her phone or her door bell. As the self proclaimed hostess with the mostest in El Paso, as well as a woman with a stupendous chest, killer legs and convenient morals, Celia was always in demand. So when Pete Rosenberg had asked for the Police Chief to check on his brother and sister-in-law since Anson had missed a very important meeting at noon, the Chief had been happy to oblige. As Rosenberg said, whatever people said about his brother, Anson Rosenberg never missed a meeting.

Finally, Jackson snorted and shoved a slip of paper at Morgan.

"OK, we'll deal with this later. I was given this information by the Chief's office. In addition to the Rosenbergs, there is an exchange student and three maids living in the Rosenberg home. Go find one of them and see what's happened to El Paso's first family, as the Chief called them. Call me as soon as you know anything, I'll be at the Mayor's office."

So the result of the conversation between the two Detectives and their Captain was the Homicide Captain heading for the Mayor's Office while Morgan and Estrada headed for the Rosenberg Mansion on Montana. The elder Rosenberg's mansion was one of the massive houses in the block that also held the unique home of Ezra Hughes, the late Captain of the Texas Rangers. It was certainly an ironic turn of events that reasons continued to surface to return to that historic old neighborhood, thought Morgan but everything seemed to lead back to the area around Hughes' old house.

It was not far from Police Headquarters to the Rosenberg home on Montana to it was not quite four o'clock when Morgan pulled up to the curb at the foot of the Rosenberg driveway. The house appeared deserted.

THE HOME OF VIRGINIA TURNER

In the house located directly across the street from the Rosenberg house, a gloved hand pulled the front curtains open just enough so that a pair of probing eyes could watch Lieutenant Morgan and his partner exit their car in front of the Rosenberg house. With a low pitched oath, the watching figure turned away from the window to study the slim, naked, blonde woman tied tightly to the very expensive, very old chair in the center of the tastefully decorated living room. Strands of her expensively styled blonde hair now hung down over her bruised face. If the police found the bodies in that house, then their investigation would intensify. It would become more dangerous for the killer to search for those incriminating dairies. Maybe the killer would get lucky and find the diary here.

Virginia Turner was a very wealthy, very well known society matron in El Paso. She was the widow of one of the largest builders in the area and had trebled his fortune since her husband's death. She was also a person with a true nose for bargains at estate sales. She was one of those on the list that the killer had gotten form Chelsea Mallard.

The killer had long ago learned that for most women, it broke their spirit to be forced to undress for a captor. Once their spirit was broken, they became somewhat easier to handle. So it was that when Virginia Turner had returned from her luncheon date with "the girls" she had walked into the air conditioned comfort of her very expensive home to find herself looking down the barrel of a rather large handgun.

The intruder had said only one word, "Strip!"

Virginia Turner had at first refused, but after being slapped upside the head by the barrel of the deadly looking pistol, she had shakily complied. It was a very warm day, so she was not wearing much and thus was very quickly reduced to bare skin. In fact, the killer though that she looked very fetching standing nude in the middle of her living room, her arms stretched high above her head.

Rumor had it that Virginia Turner, who had just turned fifty-eight, had a string of young studs from the University of Texas at El Paso football team come to late night parties at her house. There were usually five or six football players and just Virginia. Rumors held that the boys all left exhausted. Her figure was certainly good enough to keep their attention.

After forcing the distraught matron to pose in various suggestive positions, the intruder forced her into the chair to which she was now tied. Once the woman's wrists were tied tightly together and further secured to the chair, the intruder had softened her up with a few hard slaps across her face. Finally, satisfied that the captive understood that she was at the intruder's mercy, another chair was pulled up in front of the bound woman and the intruder sat down for some conversation.

"Now, Virginia," began the killer in a wheezy voice, "I believe that you have something that I want."

CHAPTER SEVENTEEN

THE ROSENBERG HOME

The two police officers standing on the front porch of the grand old mansion looked at each other in puzzlement. Since their arrival there had been absolutely no sound from the home, nor any sign that anyone was inside the home. In the middle of the day, it was highly unlikely that, not only the owners, but the entire staff would be gone at the same time. Most of the owners of these large historic homes normally ensured that at least one member of the staff was at home at all times to discourage break-ins.

"Doesn't look like anyone is home," observed Juan Estrada as Morgan rang the doorbell for the third time.

The only sound to be heard from within the large house was the echo of the doorbell. Finally, Morgan began to pound loudly on the ornately carved front door of the historic old home. Of the possible five people who lived in that house, surely one of them would be home. He stepped to the side of the wide porch and tried to peer through one of the windows flanking the ornate front door. He could detect no sign of movement of any type nor hear any sound from the interior of the home.

As he straightened from trying to peer through the small window, he used the back of his right hand to wipe the sweat dripping down his forehead. He guessed the temperature had to be pushing a hundred and it was only early May. It was going to be one hell of a summer, he thought to himself. At that moment, it suddenly dawned on him that he was not hearing a sound that he should. Stepping off the porch, he crossed the yard, halfway to the street and then turned back to try and look on top of the two story historic home. He could see four air coolers spotted about the pitched, tile roof, but he could see little, if any, detail. Finally, he gave up and walked back to the relative cool of he shaded front porch.

"What was that all about?" asked Juan curiously, having stayed in the deepest shadowed part of the porch.

"Listen carefully and tell me what you don't hear?" asked Morgan, as he returned to the window flanking the front door.

His partner stepped off the porch onto the hot sidewalk and listened intently. He could make out traffic sounds, the sounds of children laughing in the distance and a couple of dogs barking down the street. However, he had no idea what sound he should heard but wasn't. Maybe the heat was getting to his partner. Finally, he rejoined Morgan by the front door.

"I have no idea what you are talking about," he finally responded to the broad back of Morgan as the Lieutenant cupped his hands around his eyes and tried once again to get a good look inside the unlit entry hall.

"Would you agree it is somewhere close to 100 degrees at the moment?" asked Morgan without taking his eyes from the window.

Estrada shrugged.

"Sure, but I don't see -----," he responded.

"And would you agree that anyone in his right mind wants to come home to a cool house when the temperatures are close to being triple digits?" Morgan continued as it Estrada had not interrupted him.

"Uh, yeah," responded his partner, resigned to wait until Morgan finished his verbalized thought process. He was used to Morgan using him as a sounding board in situations that did not make much sense.

"Then why would the Rosenbergs, one of the wealthiest families in town, not have at least one of their coolers running?" Morgan finished, straightening up from trying to peer through the window. "With the temperatures at this level, by tonight this house will be like an oven. I don't know about you, but I hate to sleep in a hot house and I am sure that someone like Celia Rosenberg does too."

Estrada peeled his ears and realized that Morgan was right; the swamp coolers at the Rosenberg home were not making their distinctive humming sounds. That meant that the air conditioning system for the mansion was not activated. So the inside of the house had to be like an oven.

Moving past Estrada, Morgan stepped off of the porch and started around the side of the house to the broad concrete driveway that went up the side of the home. The hedges bordering the driveway had been carefully cultivated to ensure that the area in front of the attached three car garage could not be seen from the street. Such passive security measures were relatively common and certainly one of the least expensive steps that a home owner could take to conceal if he was not at home. The theory was that anyone coming up the driveway would be seen either form he house or from a neighbors house. He was now relatively sure that there was no one in the house at this time, at least no one alive.

The area in front of the three large garage doors was empty, but by lifting himself up on his tiptoes, Morgan was able to look through the small windows set in the upper portion of each garage door and see that each stall in the garage was filled with an automobile. There was what appeared to be a late model Mercedes, a large American car and an open jeep. Unless the Rosenberg's had a fourth car or someone picked them up, then they should be in the house.

Morgan glanced at Estrada, and motioned toward the end of the house with a jerk of his head. Estrada nodded and slowly began to walk down the length of the garage to go around to the back of the house. Morgan went to the entry door located to his right and tried the door knob, it was locked. This door was ornately carved like the front, but rather than a storm door or a screen door, this entry was covered with a heavy mesh security door. He knocked on the outer security door several times, but received no answer.

Finally, uncertain whether to break into the house or not, he pulled out his cell phone and dialed Captain Jackson's number. The Captain's phone only rang twice before it was answered.

"Jackson!"

"Captain, its Caleb," began the Lieutenant.

"And!" barked the Captain, whose tone of voice showed that he was clearly not in a good mood.

"The Rosenberg house is locked and I can see no movement inside. There are three cars in the garage, a Mercedes, a large American sedan and a Jeep. However, what worries me the most is that it must be a hundred degrees out here and the coolers are not running. It has to be hotter than hell in that house right about now and it is only going to get worse. Unless they all left on a trip and didn't tell anyone, there is something definitely wrong here."

"Hold one!" snapped Jackson. Morgan could hear the Captain's deep voice talking to someone else on his end. In a moment, he was back on the line.

"Lieutenant, I am here with the Mayor and the Chief. The Mayor has just gotten Peter Rosenberg on the line."

There was a pause while the Captain had another conversation with someone in the background.

"Peter Rosenberg has just given his permission, so I am officially authorizing you to gain entry to the Anson Rosenberg home in order to determine whether or not something has happened to the inhabitants. Call me back as soon as you known something."

The connection suddenly ended, but this did not surprise Morgan. Captain Jackson was not a man known for idle small talk. If he had something to say, he said it and if he didn't, then he kept his mouth shut. Snapping the cover of his cell phone shut, Morgan turned his attention back to the security door covering the actual back door. There was certainly no way that they were going to get through this door. Abandoning his examination of that door, he began to walk down the length of the garage toward the back yard.

As he rounded the back corner of the garage, he met his partner coming back in his direction.

"Anything?" asked Morgan, taking care not to step in the well groomed flower beds that lined the side of the garage wall.

Estrada shook his head.

"No, there are a number of windows and two more doors, but everything is locked and nothing appears to be out of place."

He paused for a moment as if looking for the right words.

"But, I just feel that there is something wrong," he finished. "Only don't ask me what it is, because I don't know."

Morgan favored him with a small grin.

"I know what you mean, my friend," he responded, as he continued to walk along the rear of the structure. Estrada fell in with him and they both retraced the path that Estrada had just covered. "But we will soon find out, the Captain just authorized us to gain entry to the house."

Estrada pointed ahead.

"If that's the case, then the best way to enter is through a low set window at the far end of what looks like the kitchen. I can see through those large windows that this first area past the garage is the kitchen and the window I am talking about is just past the kitchen wall. The shades are down over this window, so I can't tell what's in the room, but at least we would be inside the house."

Morgan followed his partner over to the indicated window. It was, like everything else about this house, made to look old. There were six panes of glass in the lower window and six in the upper. He could see that the latch was in the locked position, but that was easily remedied. Covering the window, however, was a security screen made of medium grade mesh.

"That's going to be the problem. Those security screens are a bitch to open from the outside," offered Estrada, sliding his fingers into the openings in the mesh and pulling on the screen. As he had suspected, no matter how hard he pulled, he was unable to budge the screen.

Leaning in close to the wall, Morgan was able to see the inside of the frame of the security screen. The screen was made to open, as there were hinges on the inside of the frame on the left hand side. That meant that the latch would probably be on the right side.

Stepping to his left, he leaned in close to the wall and studied the inside of the security screen on the other side. He was pleased to see that he was right about the location of the latch. It was at the right hand bottom corner of the screen.

"You might ought to back up a few steps," warned Morgan, as he drew his service weapon. Carefully, he knelt out the line of fire of any possible ricochet and lined up his weapon on the location where he judged that the locking mechanism slid into the original wooden window frame. While the security mesh was heavy grade steel, the window frame was wooden and was probably original to the house.

Taking a deep breath and letting it out, Morgan gently pulled the trigger. The crack of the weapon's discharge echoed throughout the neighborhood, but the area of the window frame where the bullet had struck was shattered. The Getting to his feet, Morgan stepped up to the window, grabbed the security screen and lifted up and out. After some initial resistance, the screen finally swung outward, allowing access to the window it had protected for so long. Without any hesitation, Morgan now reversed his weapon and used the butt end to smash the single pain of glass directly in front of the latch. Reholstering his weapon, he, carefully, pushed the latch open with one finger and then raised the window.

He slowly pushed his head through the, now, open window and was immediately aware of two things. It was hot as hell inside that room and the Rosenbergs had not left on an unexpected vacation.

"Aw, Jesus," swore Estrada as he moved up beside his partner and received a face full of the hot air that flowed through the newly opened window. It smelled like a combination of a whore house and a charnel house. There was no doubt in the minds of either of the officers that one or more people were dead inside that very expensive house and that there had been a lot of sex in the immediate vicinity of that open window sometime recently.

Morgan pulled back and took a deep breath of the clean outside air. He did not look forward to going back inside that house.

"Juan, go out to the car and call for backup and crime scene technicians. I'll go through the house and open the front door. By that time I'll know whether or not we need to call the Coroner."

"Better you than me, me friend," remarked Juan as he turned from that open window to hell and walked back along the rear of the house.

After a couple of more deep breaths of fresh air, Morgan pushed his way through that open window. It only took a moment for him to determine that the window opened into a small bedroom, probably for one of the live-in help, he thought to himself. To his left a small reclining chair was placed against one wall and directly across from him was a dresser, topped by a large mirror. He was momentarily amused to see that he looked just like he was mounted on the wall.

He hung there for a long moment, half in and half out of the window, listening intently for any sounds that indicated that someone was in the house. He still heard nothing. Even at this point, he was certain that the house was deserted.

The light in the room was off and since Morgan was filling the only window that opened into that small space, the room was in dark shadows. Pulling himself further through the narrow window, he glanced down and saw that directly beneath the window was a single bed. The bedding was wadded up in the center of the bed as if someone had recently been sleeping there.

Carefully, he lowered his feet, placing them on top of the mound of bedding. From there it would be only a short step to the floor. However, just as he released the window ledge, the mound upon which he was standing twisted and he fell to the floor with a hard thud. The breath was knocked form his lungs and for a moment, he was unable to take a deep breath. The mound of bedding upon which he had been standing was continuing to move wildly and now he could detect faint noises emanating from beneath the untidy mound of bedding. He was not along in the room.

THE HOME OF VIRGINIA TURNER

The killer let the lace curtains in the Turner living room fall back into place and swore. Silently, the killer had watched Juan Estrada come form the backyard and make some calls on the radio in the unmarked patrol car sitting at the curb. It didn't take a genius to figure out that the Spic and his partner had discovered that something was amiss in the Rosenberg home. That meant that in a short time this neighborhood would be crawling with cops and a house to house canvass would begin.

Turning from the window, the killer calmly stared at the now bloody body of the well known socialite that lay face down in the middle of the blood stained Oriental run that covered the center of the well appointed room. There was no doubt that Virginia Turner had one hell of a body and certainly knew how to move her ass. It was too bad that she had to die, but there was no way that the killer could chance leaving anyone alive to give information to the police.

Walking over to the bloody woman, the killer passed for a moment to observe the end result of their question and answer session. Virginia Turner was lying face down on the floor, her arms still bound tightly behind her. Her broad back, interesting thought the killer that most big titted women have broad backs, was crisscrossed with a mass of bloody streaks where the killer had used an electrical cord ripped from an expensive lamp to whip the wealthy woman into submission, forcing her to give up the information that the killer sought.

The killer could have stopped at that point and left, allowing Virginia Turner to live, but the killer enjoyed torturing women. Over the years since the very first time, there had been literally dozens of victims, mostly female. Some were friends of the killer who had somehow offended and had to pay the ultimate price while others were from the ranks of the homeless or tourists who had been at the wrong place at the wrong time.

Virginia Turner had been tied face down over the coffee table while the killer had used the electrical cord to whip her mercilessly. Her generous mouth, that over the years had pleasured many men and not a few women, had been crammed full of her own panties as well as two kitchen towels to muffle her screaming. Periodically, the killer would remove the gag to ask the questions to which answered were needed. It had only taken a short time for Virginia Turner to be reduced to a pathetic mass of pain and answer all of the questions put to her.

However, once the killer had the information needed, the urge was too powerful and it was time for the fun to begin. Leaving the battered woman tied to the table, sobbing in terror and pain, the killer had gone to the kitchen for a large knife and gotten some of the toys always carried in the small black bag sitting just inside the front door.

For the next hour, the killer had tortured the hapless woman to the point that her mind was literally gone. Using the knife, and the sex toys, the bound woman was brought to orgasm after orgasm before the knife was used to inflict unbelievable pain. By the time the killer had finished, Virginia Turner was begging for death.

Finally, overcome by an irresistible urge of sexual desire, the killer had removed the concealing mask, freed Virginia Turner from the table to place her on the floor, where first it had been especially exciting for the killer to run the razor sharp point of the knife around the wide brown nipples of the helpless woman and corkscrew down her breast. Mounting the unresisting woman, the killer had enjoyed dominating the victim until she was unconscious with exhaustion. Then in a final spate of sadistic glee by the killer, Virginia Turner was raped again and again using a number of items.

On the brink of exhaustion from the heavy duty sex, the killer rolled the limp body of Virginia turner onto her back once more. Turner was unconscious, her body covered in sweat and blood from the whippings. The killer's eyes greedily drank in the stupendous breasts that had received so much attention during the afternoon. It was too bad they would not be of little use to anyone. Finally, the killer manhandled the dying woman back over to the coffee table where she was retied face down. Finally, sated, the killer replaced the mask and finished the job by grabbing a handful of Turner's carefully done hair, pulling her head up to expose the throat and with one movement of one hand cut the unconscious woman's throat.

Gathering up the toys and the knife, the killer dropped them into the little black bag and left the house. In the hedge at the far end of the Virginia Turner's yard, the killer changed clothes, changing from the black garb of the vicious killer, now blood covered, to the every day garb of a prominent member of society. With the black clothing now shoved into the small black bag, there was nothing to indicate that the smiling, well known, individual entering the car parked on a nearby street was a cold blooded vicious killer.

THE ROSENBERG HOME

Forcing himself to his knees, still fighting for breath, as if by magic Morgan's Glock appeared in his right hand. He was taking no chances in what he was certain was a house of death. He had no intention of winding up a corpse at his relatively, young age. Slowly, he reached out his left hand to grasp the edge of the pile of bedding that was still moving wildly on the narrow bed. Taking a deep breath, he jerked the bedding from the bed, shoving his weapon forward and froze. Whatever he had been expecting what he saw was certainly not it.

Lying in the center of the wrinkled bed was an older Hispanic woman, her long hair, black with broad streaks of gray, was stringy from sweat. Her face was beet red, her nostrils flaring as her lungs gasped for air. Her nightgown was completely soaked with sweat and had pushed up to the middle of her thick belly; her thick bush was matted from sweat and her own juices, her well muscled legs were covered with a glistening sheen of moisture. Even the mattress beneath her body appeared to be completely soaked with what was probably her own sweat. She also emitted a pungent aroma that was a combination of sweat and sex, similar to that found in some of the flop houses that he had raided from time to time. At a loss for what to say, he sat back on his heels as the woman continued to bounce wildly on the bed, as she emitted deep grunts as if in tremendous pain. It suddenly dawned on him that the woman was not in pain, but she was having one hell of an orgasm.

Even more bizarre, there was a thick gag shoved deeply into her mouth, there was a plastic tie holding her slim ankles together and her hands were behind her back. He had no doubt that her wrists were probably tied together. Running between her thighs, disappearing into the thick hair of her bush was a very slim white electrical cord. As if her bonds were not enough, even her full thighs were held tightly together by a strip of light colored cloth. Someone had gone to a great deal of trouble to make sure that this woman stayed in the bed.

As he watched, the woman's wild bouncing stopped and her deep grunts subsided into low moans. She lay back on the sweat soaked mattress and continued to moan softly to herself. As the room became quiet, Morgan sudden heard a low buzz like a little motor running. He glanced around, trying to find the source of the sound and suddenly realized it was coming from the bound woman on the bed. Looking back at the narrow electrical cord running between her thighs, Morgan suddenly realized what he was hearing; the woman had a vibrator shoved up her vagina.

Taking the white electrical cord in one hand, he used the cord to find the control box for the little vibrator that was hidden in the bedding. He clicked the control from high to off and was rewarded with another low moan from the woman. Slowly and cautiously, he pulled on the white electrical cord until, like magic, a small silver egg shaped device slid from between her tied thighs.

Rising to his feet, Morgan gently rolled the limp woman onto her right side so that he could remove the gag. With the gag untied, he allowed her to roll onto her back so that he could gently remove the thick wad of material from between her teeth. Her only response was to run her tongue over her dried lips. She didn't even open her eyes.

He pulled his pocket knife from his side pocket, and opened the largest blade. Taking hold of her upper arm, Morgan again rolled the woman onto her side so that he could cut the plastic bonds that held her wrists tightly together. Slowly, and gently, he pulled her cramped arms from behind her back to her sides. When the circulation returned he knew that she would be in very excruciating pain. Next he gently cut the strip of blue cloth holding her full thighs tightly together and then the plastic tie that bound her slim ankles.

"Senora?" he asked softly, "can you hear me?"

The only answer he received was another soft moan, a sound halfway between pleasure and pain. There was no way he could determine how long she had been tied this way, but the muscles in her arms and legs had to have been in spasms for sometime. He also had no way to determine if she had any other injuries other than being exhausted. He was actually afraid to help her up until the doctors could check on her. However, there was one thing that he could do for the unfortunate woman.

Rising, he crossed to the door and out into the sitting room. To his right, as he expected was a partially open door and a bathroom. He took a glass sitting on the back of the commode and filled it with water from the sink which he took back to the bound woman. Raising her head, he held the glass to her crusty lips and raised it so that some splashed into her mouth.

"Drink this, senora," he said softly.

He didn't know if she spoke English or the need for water drover her, but she began to avidly suck at the water he held for her. In only a short period of time, she had emptied the glass. He gently lowered her back onto the bed.

"Thank you, senor," she said faintly, her eyes still closed. She laid very still, her eyes still closed as if sleeping.

Not sure if there was anything else he could or should do for her, he quickly found the rumpled sheet and draped it across her naked body.

"Senora, can you tell me what happened?" he asked gently.

"No, senor," she murmured in reply. "I was asleep in my bed and suddenly I found myself the victim of that horrible thing that was in me. I am sorry senor."

"It's O.K.," he soothed her. "Just rest here, I'll get a doctor for you."

His only answer was another faint moan.

Rising to his feet once more, he set out to find the front door so that his partner could come in and help him search this big barn of a house. Though he believed that whoever had done this evil deed was long gone, there could be an army of killers hiding in this place and the two of them might not find them.

He quietly ascended the shot flight of stairs leading to the kitchen and slowly opened the door. He was immediately hit by a wall of heat that caused his shirt to be soaked in sweat in mere minutes. Luckily for the captive woman, the darkened bedroom had been relatively cool or she would have probably died of heat stroke long before now.

His Glock held tightly in his right hand, he looked first to his right and then to his left before leaving the dubious protection of the doorway. As before, there was no indication that anyone else was in the house. However, the odor of decaying flesh was much stronger in the kitchen than in the maid's bedroom. There was no doubt in Morgan's mind that somewhere in the home was at least one dead body and maybe more.

Cautiously, he crossed the kitchen to peer around the doorframe into a short hallway that led to a butler's pantry just off of what seemed to be the dining room. Morgan went through the butler's pantry and peered into the silent dining room. The table was set as if for a party, but no one had come. As with most of the house everything was in place, but there were no people.

Finally, he decided that there was no cause for alarm, at least at this time. Still holding his Glock tightly in his right hand, he walked across the dining room into the front entry way and unlocked the front door. Juan was waiting patiently on the front porch, leaning against the edge of the doorway, his arms folded across his chest.

"Took long enough," he said, joining Morgan inside the house. "Find anything?"

Morgan shook his head, his eyes roaming around, missing nothing.

"Just a maid that was tied up in her room," he responded.

Juan raised one dark eyebrow.

"She see anything?"

"Fraid not," responded Morgan. "Unfortunately, she overcame herself."

"She what?" demanded Juan, his face showing his puzzlement.

"Never mind," responded Morgan, not really wanting to go into what had been done to the poor woman. "She needs a doctor as soon as possible."

"I went ahead and called for the paramedics just in case," answered Estrada, drawing his own weapon and advancing further into the house. He felt as if he had walked into a furnace, the heat inside the house was even worse than outside, additionally, he had now caught the full flavor of decaying flesh that seemed to permeate the house.

"I'll check the rest of the first floor, you take the second," said Morgan, as he entered the hallway that led deeper into the first floor.

Without bothering to answer, Estrada began to mount the carpeted stairs one at a time. He was listening intently for any indication that there was someone on the second floor, but the house was silent as a tomb. When his head was above the level of the second floor, but before entering the landing, he paused once again. With his weapon ready, Estrada both listened intently as well as visually looked for anything out of place. The house still seemed empty.

From what he could see, to the left was a large entry into a short hallway that ended at a set of double doors that seemed to be tightly shut. To the right was another entry that gave way to another hallway. Further complicating the issue, since heat rises, entering the landing was like stepping into a sauna. In fact, it was so hot on the landing that it was actually hard for him to breathe. In just the few minutes that he had been inside the house, his jacket was sweat stained and his shirt was plastered to him. He was sweating so badly that he was afraid that his pistol would slip out of his hand unless he kept a tight grip on it.

Finally, Estrada decided that if he remained on the stairs much longer he would be parboiled himself, so, cautiously he mounted the final steps and entered the landing proper. The silence was complete, not only could he heard nothing on the second floor, but due to the sound proofing in the exterior walls, he could hear neither outside noises nor even Morgan moving about on the first floor. It was eerie.

He guessed that the double doors to his left opened into the master bedroom and decided that he would check in there first. Slowly turning the door knob, he gently pushed the right hand door open. It swung inward on well oiled hinges. The lights were off and the shades were drawn, so at first the room was hidden in deep shadows. However, as his eyes adjusted, he could see that the dominate feature in the room was a large four poster bed against the far wall. To his right was a large dresser. He could not see what was to his left due to the closed left hand door.

Taking a tighter grip on the polymer grip of his pistol, Estrada literally jumped into the room, his weapon up and pointed to the left. The church like silence still prevailed throughout the house. The only sound that Estrada could hear was his own ragged breathing as his lungs struggled for air in the sauna like heat of the house. The room was empty, but the smell of death was even stronger than before.

Further along the left hand wall was a large entertainment cabinet. The cabinet was large enough that someone could actually hide inside. Cautiously, he crossed the thick carpet to jerk the doors open. The only thing inside was a computer and a large television. The screens of both were dark and the touch of a hand revealed that neither one had been activated in some time.

Gently pushing the doors to the entertainment center shut, he turned back toward the bedroom entrance. On the other side of the room was another closed door that Estrada assumed led into the master bath. Weapon ready, he crossed the room as quietly as possible. Reaching the door, he quietly turned the knob and then, dropping to one knee, he flung the door open and raised his weapon. There was no movement in the darkened room.

Rising to his feet, he reached around the doorframe and felt along the wall with his free left hand. As he suspected, he found a panel of light switches a foot or so away from the door. There were a number of switches and rather than waste time experimenting, he swept his open hand across the panel, flipping all of the switches to the on position at the same time. Suddenly, he was almost blinded as the room was flooded with light from four large recessed fluorescent light fixtures set in the ceiling as well as several rows of tract lighting that illuminated the many rows of clothing hung along the far walls.

The bathroom in the Rosenberg home was a combination walk in closet, master bath. The walk in closet was so large, in fact, that a gang of killers could have been hiding in their and still have been difficult to find. Luckily for him, the room was as empty as the rest of the house appeared to be. Where were the people?

He walked the length of the closet area to assure himself that there were no intruders hiding among the hundreds of clothing items displayed on hangars before returning to the bathroom area. The closet had no windows, so the heat in that room was just unbelievable; he could hear himself wheeze as his tortured lungs fought for air. However, it was while he was in the closet that he discovered that the high level of heat in the house was not a natural occurrence, but that the ceiling vents were blowing extremely hot air. No wonder the house felt like a sauna, he thought to himself, the heating system is on.

Estrada returned to the doorway leading back into the master bedroom and paused so that his eyes could once again adjust to the low level of lighting in the bedroom. As he paused, he finally noticed the other occupant in the bedroom. He could see that there was a figure lying in the center of the bed. All he could tell was that the figure was spread eagled and not moving.

His weapon held at the ready, Estrada carefully placed one foot in front of another as he approached the person lying on the bed.

"I am with the El Paso Police Department," he said very distinctly to the shadow covered figure reclining on the bed. "Please identify yourself."

The figure on the bed made no sound and did not move. Reaching the side of the bed the detective actually reeled from the odor of rotting meat. Trying not to breath, Estrada forced himself to concentrate on his job and ignore everything else. He observed that the person on the bed, a woman, was actually tied to the bed and appeared to be asleep, her head resting on top of her arm. Cautiously, he reached out one hand and gently shook the shoulder of the sleeper. In response to the shaking, the figure's head flopped loosely before it rolled off of the flaccid arm onto the edge of the bed and then continued to roll until it fell off the bed to land on Estrada's right shoe.

"Holy Mother of God!" yelled Estrada as he hurriedly backed away, now aware that someone had cut the woman's head off. As the eyes in the victim's severed head seemed to regard him with interest, her partially congealed blood was now oozing over the top of his right loafer and down into his shoe. For the first time in 15 years of homicide work, his stomach rebelled and he barely made it to the toilet.

DOWNSTAIRS AT THE ROSENBERG HOME

Leaving his partner to handle the upstairs, Morgan began to walk slowly down the hallway that led from the entry foyer deeper into the house. The Lieutenant noticed that the heat was even more stifling in the lower hall than it had been in the kitchen and dining room and the smell that he associated with decaying dead bodies was like an overwhelming presence.

Passing a heating vent sat in the upper wall of the hallway, Morgan stood on tip toes to place his hand in front of the vent. He was not surprised to discover that extremely hot air was blowing from the vent. That explained at least some of the stifling heat in the home; the heating system was apparently running full blast. The artificially raised heat level in the house would certainly screw up any possibility of establishing the correct time of death of any bodies found here based on ambient body temperature, he thought sourly.

He came to a closed door on the left side of the hallway and paused. Placing his ear against the hard wood, he listened intently before stepping away and turning the door knob. The door swung inward on well oiled hinges to show only another hallway. At the end of a short hallway, there was another closed door. His weapon at the ready, Morgan silently approached the far door, paused and set his ear against the door. Again, he heard nothing, but the odor of decaying meat was somewhat stronger at this location.

Deciding to chance that there was no one on the other side of the door. Morgan turned the knob and pushed the door open and found himself looking into a small sitting room. The odor of death was so strong in the room that it literally slapped him in the face. Crossing the small room, he cautiously pushed open the door directly across from the hall door. The odor of decaying meat hit him in the fact like a wave. He reeled for a second, before grabbing the doorframe to steady himself. Forcing his eyes open, he found that he was looking into a small, tastefully decorated bedroom and lying on the bed, tied spread eagle to the bed frame, with a wad of cloth stuffed in her mouth and held by a strip of cloth was a very attractive woman. From the intensity of the smell of decaying meat that filled the room, he had found the first victim and she was very, very dead.

The victim's head was facing the wall and her face was partially covered with her long dark hair, her wrists were tied so tightly to the bed posts that her hands were almost white due to the blood circulation to her hands being restricted. She was naked to the waist, but her legs were covered by a starched white sheet. There was no doubt that this young woman was very well endowed, but he could also see that someone had gone to great lengths to abuse her naked breasts. Both of her breasts showed signs of having been physically abused and her nipples appeared to have been burned by something hot. There was no question in his mind that this lovely young woman had been cruelly tortured before she died.

Slowly, he lifted the sheet and saw that her shapely legs, long and deeply tanned, had been pulled so far apart before being tied tightly to the legs of the bed that she must have been in a great deal of pain just from having her leg muscles stretched to such extreme limits at the time she died. Someone hated this young woman very much, he thought to himself. There was no doubt in his mind that this young woman had died very hard indeed.

At that moment, he heard a very uncharacteristic shriek from Juan echo down the hallway and then the sounds of something heavy hitting the floor and then heavy retching, Turning from the dead woman, he literally ran through the sauna like heat toward the front of the house. This was certainly not a routine murder scene, he thought to himself.

THE MASTER BEDROOM

Reaching the front of the house, Morgan took the stairs two at a time, his weapon held out in front of him, ready to fire. He was certain that something had happened to his partner. Everything about this crime scene struck him as wrong, things just did not make sense. He wouldn't be surprised if it was a trap.

The intense heat in the house was sapping his strength, but he reached the doors to the Master bedroom in short order. As he charged in through the double doors of the master suite, he saw his partner come walking slowly out of the bathroom, wiping his face with a paper towel. Estrada looked to be in a bad way.

"Juan, I heard you yell! What's the problem?" demanded Morgan, his eyes searching the dimly lit bedroom for the cause of Estrada's distress. He had not yet gotten a close look at what lay on the bed.

Without answering, his mouth covered by the paper towel that he carried Juan almost staggered across the room and fumbled with the center window until he could get it raised. Then he half hung out of the window, breathing deeply of the outside air. Even though it was hot outside, the air was still cooler then the stagnant air inside the house and did not carry the heavy aroma of rotting meat that so pervaded the interior of the expensive house.

Behind him, Morgan decided that there was no point in continuing to wander around inside a darkened house and flipped on the bedroom lights. He had not wanted to disturb anything until the crime scene techs had arrived, but this was getting ridiculous and he was very concerned about his partner. Using his pen, Morgan flipped all of the switches near the door into the on position. The room was immediately flood with indirect lighting and the two ceiling fans began to rotate. It was then that Morgan got a good look at what lay on the bed and spotted the head lying on the floor, appearing to be staring at him in a quizzical fashion. He now understood Juan's distress.

"Jesus fucking Christ!" he exclaimed emphatically. "What hit this place?"

CHAPTER EIGHTEEN

A DIMLY LIT STUDY

The room oozed wealth and privilege. The desk at which the figure sat was an ornately carved partners' desk made for one of the most prestigious Washington DC law firms. The lamp that threw its light on the top of the desk was by Tiffany and Sons, the fountain pen held in one hand was Mont Blanc, the glass sitting on the corner of the desk that held the twenty year old Scotch was a rare 200 year old Dyatkovo Crystal.

In the center of the pool of light that illuminated the center of the elegant old desk lay a single sheet of paper containing several names. This simple sheet of paper was in fact a death warrant for everyone whose name was written on the paper. The list lay opened on the table and was being intently studied by the individual who sat in the high backed judges' chair. The hit list had originally had thirty names on it; thirty names belonging to some of the most prominent people in El Paso. The killer, now dressed in an expensive dressing gown slowly sipped the twelve year old Scotch and considered the list again for the hundredth time.

God Damn that old man, thought the killer, why did he have to dig up all of that information on that old murder. Even more to the point, why did that bitch Chelsea Mallard have to auction the old man's diaries off to people all over this town. If not for a car wreck, there would have been thirty-one names on the list and all of this death would be unnecessary.

Applying the expensive fountain pen to the page of names, the killer carefully crossed off both Celia Rosenberg's and Virginia Turner's names from the list of those that had purchased items at the Hughes estate sale. Mallard had not remembered, nor made note of, who on the list of those that had attended the exclusive sale had bought which items at the sale, so the killer had to visit each one until the journal that talked about that old murder was found and destroyed.

Those damn books, swore the killer quietly, and that bastard Hughes. If anyone got their hands on those diaries and read what that old fart had written about the past, then the killer, and a number of the killer's close friends would be facing serious charges. For the hundredth time, the killer thought that if the killer had only been able to get to that estate sale, then the books could have been purchased from the estate and quietly destroyed. No one would have ever known anything about the crimes of the past.

Others had purchased what, by rights, should never have existed in the first place. For his silence about the murders all those years ago, Hughes had demanded a number of things from the killer, some of them extremely degrading, but as promised, anything Hughes wanted had been done. Hughes, however, had not kept his end of the bargain. As he grew older, the old Ranger had come to regret many of the things he had done during his years behind the badge and made a record of many of his adventures. Now, people would have to die until the killer found those diaries.

Pausing for a moment, the killer considered the list and then thought about Mallard. That woman was a conniving bitch to be sure, but she was a careful business woman. She must have kept business records, but the damn police had almost taken over her office. Then the answer dawned on the killer – the secretary. That girl was certainly a looker, but she was also the closest person to Mallard. Perhaps the girl knew about records that her boss had lied about. The killer sat quietly for a few minutes and then decided it was high time to make the acquaintance of one Miss Lisa Nettleton.

THE ROSENBERG HOME

Caleb Morgan and Juan Estrada sat patiently at a table in the back yard of the Rosenberg Home. Neither wanted to talk after the grisly discoveries they had found inside that house of death. Though both were hardened homicide investigators, the sheer savagery of the murders had left both pale and shaken. Shortly after the discovery of Celia Rosenberg's body, back up units, EMTs and crime scene technicians had arrived. Both Morgan and Estrada had been very happy to turn the scene over to them and get back out in the fresh air. Due to the prominence of the victims, Captain Jackson had been right behind the crime scene technicians and after he had been briefed on the discoveries the two had made inside the house, he had taken over direction of the crime scene. He now joined the two detectives at the backyard table.

Easing himself down in the comfortable yard chair, Jackson sighed deeply and leaned forward to rest his elbows on the table.

"Man this is one for the books. The mayor is on the verge of having coronary; the Rosenbergs were among his most generous supporters. I reckon that this ended that particular gravy train. That's one of the worst crime scenes I have been at in over thirty years in police work," he said slowly. "I don't know how you guys managed to do as much as you did, the smell inside that house would gag a maggot. At least half of the guys here now have had to step out front and throw up in the bushes. It contaminates the crime scene, but police are only human."

Morgan had let Jackson know that Estrada had lost it after discovering the woman's decapitated body in the master bedroom and this was Jackson's way of letting Estrada know that it was not something that he should worry about. If Jackson had dealt with the matter directly by talking to him, Estrada might have felt insulted, but in this fashion, it was just a general comment. The egos of homicide detectives were sometimes fragile things and one of Jackson's primary jobs was keeping the ego of his men healthy.

"Any other bodies found inside, Captain?" asked Morgan curiously. "As of the time you arrived we had still not found Mr. Rosenberg or one of the maids, but we had not checked all of the rooms in the house."

Jackson took a deep breath and then spit onto the grass near the table.

"Oh, yeah, we found them," he grimaced at the memory. "Mr. Rosenberg appears to have been, uh, entertaining the younger maid in the study. We found both of them there. Mr. Rosenberg was seated behind his desk, naked and it would appear that the maid was servicing him, if you catch my drift. He had been shot squarely between the eyes. The girl was also naked, shot and died on her knees with her head nuzzled into his crotch."

"Well, certainly, an interesting way to go," observed Morgan solemnly.

Jackson glanced at his subordinate with a raised eyebrow. Morgan's comment appeared to interrupt his train of thought and he paused as if to say more, but finally shook his head.

"Whoever did this was a complete animal. Celia Rosenberg was a very lovely woman. I have known her since high school. Who ever did this gutted and skinned her and then left her with her head damn near hacked off her body. There is no question in my mind that the killer is a person filled with a lot of hatred and it was taken out on this family. We've got to find this lunatic before he or she kills again."

At that moment a female police officer came running around the corner of the house and skidded to a stop, almost falling in her haste. Spotting the three sitting at the table, the young woman came pounding across the immaculately kept grass, clearly intent on reaching the three in the shortest possible time.

"Captain Jackson," she gasped out, holding onto the table for support, her face beet red from running in this stifling heat and her breath coming in short spurts. "We've found another one!"

"Another what?" demanded Jackson, taking in the officer's disheveled appearance, "Young lady, sit down before you fall down."

Gratefully, the young officer dropped into another nearby chair and took several deep breaths. Morgan glanced at the young woman's name tag and saw that her name of Dawkins. He remembered hearing that Sheila Dawkins, sister of Detective Pete Dawkins had just been promoted to a patrol unit and he supposed this petite blonde was the kid sister he had heard so much about. At this moment, he had little thought about the attractiveness of the young woman or the way her sweat soaked uniform shirt was sticking to her upper chest as he had a sinking feeling he knew exactly what this young officer was going to say before she said it.

"Sir, we found another body," finally gasped out Patrolwoman Dawkins, resting her elbows on her knees and leaning forward in her chair. The run she had just completed, in this intense heat, was enough to take the starch out of anybody. It was made worse by her upset stomach, caused by the scene that she had just left. "Cut up like the one upstairs."

"Where?" demanded Jackson shooting out of his chair, "in this house?"

"No sir," she responded between gasps, "across the street."

"You what?" he demanded.

Having regained her composure, Patrolwoman Sheila Dawkins was more coherent when she repeated herself. "My partner and I were doing a door to door canvass and when we arrived at the house across the street. No one answered the bell, but while we were there a man that identified himself as the son of the home owner arrived. He was adamant that his mother was home and when he received no answer, he opened the door with his own set of keys and we accompanied him inside. His mother, Virginia Turner was lying in the middle of the living room floor, nude with her throat cut."

"Christ almighty!" exclaimed Jackson. "There will be hell to pay over this one. She owns half the town."

Without waiting to hear more, the three left the table at a run, racing past the officers in front of the Rosenberg home, across the street, now crowded with curious onlookers and reached the front door of the Victorian home sitting directly across from the Rosenberg home. The officer standing just inside the door moved aside to let the three enter the cool, dimly lit interior of the Turner home.

Morgan walked carefully over to the body and squatted, his sharp eyes taking in the crime scene. The victim was nude, on her knees, her head and shoulders were lying face down across the coffee table, the arms outstretched, her still full breasts hanging down below her torso. Her legs were parted; her full upper thighs were tied tightly to the legs of the coffee table closest to the body. Her thighs, back and buttocks were crisscrossed with dozens of bloody marks, making it clear that she had been thoroughly beaten before dying.

Virginia Turner was no longer a young woman, but in her youth, he had heard that she had been considered one of the most beautiful women in town. Morgan was also a witness that even at her age she still had an incredible body. From the ropes on her wrists and the marks on the thick legs of the coffee table it was clear that she had been tied face down over the coffee table while the killer had used the electrical cord, lying beside the body, to whip her mercilessly across her lower back and buttocks.

The victim's face was lying on its right cheek. Kneeling just off of the carpet, Morgan was able to tell that her mouth had been crammed full of, what appeared to be, her own panties as well as two kitchen towels to muffle her screaming. There was no question that she had been sadistically tortured for a long period before having her throat cut. The long red slash that marred her lovely skin made it look like she had two mouths, one crammed full of a gag and a second just below her chin.

There was no question in his mind that there was a maniac on the loose killing the cream of El Paso society. The question that he could not answer was why, what had these women done to set of this killing spree?

Movement behind him announced the arrival of the crime scene investigators, the lab techies who would, hopefully give him some answers to all of his questions. Rising, he moved back so that they could have complete access to the rapidly decomposing body.

After watching a few moments, he left the house, returning to the furnace like heat of the great outdoors. As he crossed the hot dusty street, his cell phone rang.

"Morgan," he responded, narrowing his eyes against the intense glare of the sunlight.

"Lieutenant Morgan, this is Lisa Nettleton," said a very well remembered voice in his ear. "I work, or worked for Ms. Mallard."

"Oh, yes, Ms. Nettleton," responded Morgan, "who could possibly forget you?"

The laughter from the lovely Lisa Nettleton was music to his ears.

"Lieutenant, you do known how to flatter a woman."

"What can I do for you?" he asked, just simply pleased that she had called.

"Well, I've been reading the papers about the murder of Ms. Mallard," she began.

"Yes, it has been a busy time for the coroner," he responded grimly. "The news media has also stayed right on top of the situation."

"Well, I may know something that might help, but then again, it may mean nothing."

"Oh," he responded with interest.

"While, as I told you, there is no complete guest list for those invited to the estate sale for the Hughes Estate, I do have a list of all of those who wrote checks or used credit cards for purchases at the estate sale if that would help. We tracked checks in case any were returned and the credit card receipts are kept automatically."

Morgan froze in the middle of the street, his mind racing, considering all of the possibilities that this information suggested. Finally, he spoke.

"Lisa, I need to ask you a very important question and I want you to promise me that you will not discuss it with anyone."

"Sure Lieutenant, anything you say," she responded quietly.

"Are the names of Celia Rosenberg or Virginia Turner on the list of those who purchased items at the estate sale at the Hughes house?"

He could hear her turning pages; finally she came back on the phone.

"Yes, both are on the list as having written very large checks for purchases at that sale. I do not have a list available of what they purchased, but clearly they made some sizeable purchases as each check is over $1,000.00."

"Lisa, lock the door and stay where you are, I'll be there in a few minutes," he said breaking the connection and moving quickly toward his car. Pausing by the door, he dialed his partner.

"Meet me at the car," he said when his partner answered his cell. "We may have a break in the case."

Dropping the phone back into his pocket, Morgan leaned against the car for a moment and stared down the street. He was well aware that if he could not solve this case that people would begin to panic and resort other ways of feeling safe. Texans have traditionally resorted to their own resources when regular law enforcement has failed to suffice. Heaven help the city if the justice of the old west returned, he thought morosely. There would be blood on the streets in no time.

CHAPTER NINETEEN

When Morgan broke the connection, Lisa Nettleton stared at the phone in almost total disbelief. His direction to lock the door had rattled her more than she wanted to admit. It was one thing to read about the murders in the newspapers, but quite another to become involved and maybe be in danger. Of course, she thought, it would get that handsome detective to come and spend some more time with her.

Dropping the handset back into the phone cradle, Lisa walked quickly across the office to the front door. Just as she reached for the lock the door opened, startling her. Her gasp of surprise made the visitor hesitate.

"Oh, I am so sorry," stammered Lisa. "I didn't see you."

Her visitor smiled graciously and stepped fully into the office, a small box held with both hands.

"Don't worry about it," returned her visitor. "I came to see how you were doing and to see if you had some records that your boss was going to send to me on the lakefront property. I also have some of her things in my car that I need to give to you."

Lisa's eyebrows arched in surprise.

"Things? What things?" she asked.

Her visitor shrugged.

"I'm not sure, I didn't look at them. It is a couple of medium sized boxes full of what look like ledgers and papers. She said that it was some stuff that she didn't want to keep at the Hughes estate and didn't have room for in her car that day. So I offered to let her put them in my trunk. Now I'm going to a trip and need to empty my trunk. Rather than put them in my garage, I thought I'd bring them here."

Lisa was in a quandary as to what to do. She wanted to obey Morgan's instructions, but she also didn't want to displease this particular visitor of all people. Besides, what Morgan wanted might be in those boxes.

"Uh, O.K.," she finally said. "Do you need any help getting them out of the car?"

"It would certainly be a help?" responded her visitor, opening the door and allowing Lisa to precede her out toward the parking lot. "Besides, I think that I pulled a muscle in my back yesterday. If you help, we can make this in one trip. I'll just leave this one on your desk."

Walking over to Lisa's desk, the visitor placed the small box carefully in the center of the cluttered desk. Stepping back to the office door and the visitor allowed Lisa to lead the way to the parking lot. So intent was she on Morgan's warning that Lisa failed to notice the visitor drop a small square object on the thick carpeting near her desk. Not wanting to leave anything to chance, the visitor had left an incendiary device designed to destroy the office and any remaining evidence that might be overlooked in the building.

The two left the building and walked around to the side parking lot where the visitor's car was parked. Using the remote, the car trunk was unlocked by the visitor revealing two medium sized cardboard boxes that partially filled the trunk of the car. Lisa leaned forward to grasp the first one only to find a chloroform soaked cloth suddenly clamped over her mouth. She struggled against her attacker, but the chloroform was too much for her. In seconds she fell limply on top of the empty box.

After a quick glance around the empty parking lot, the visitor quickly bundled Lisa's unconscious body into the trunk, taking the empty boxes that had filled the large trunk and tossing them to the curb. Leaning into the trunk, the visitor quickly removed Lisa's lacy blouse and her mini skirt, leaving the attractive young woman dressed only in her skimpy bra and her bikini panties. Her captor had long ago learned that stripping a woman against her will always instilled a feeling of helplessness in the victim and that would be beneficial in this particular case.

Quickly and professionally, the unconscious woman's wrists were pulled behind her back and secured together with a plastic tie such as was used by the police and her shapely ankles were bound together tightly, leaving her helpless. As a final insurance, a large red ball gag was shoved roughly between Lisa's full lips and cinched tightly around her head. The two items of clothing were quickly stuffed into one of the empty boxes.

Finally, satisfied, the visitor slid behind the wheel of the car and drove calmly from the parking lot just as Morgan's unmarked patrol car slid to the curb outside the building. Morgan had raced across town, siren blaring, sensing that he was onto a lead that might bring this case to a conclusion. He didn't know why he had such a sense of urgency, but he felt that he had to move fast.

As the two officers left their car, Morgan glanced toward the car driving away, but suddenly the front of the building exploded, bricks flying in every direction. As the smoke cleared, flames could be seen shooting out of the lobby.

While Estrada called for emergency services, Morgan pulled his coat over his face and ran into the burning building. As he entered the lobby, he met two bloody women making their way out of the building. A younger woman whose face was covered with soot and her dress was blood splattered, was supporting an older woman toward the door.

"Keep going! Help is just outside" he ordered, "is there anyone else in the building?

Wordlessly, the younger woman nodded; the older woman appeared to be in shock and said nothing. Morgan helped the two women to the exit door before turning to run back into the building. It seemed to him that most of the fire damage was centered around the Mallard office and he just hoped that the secretary was still alive. Bulling his way through the thick smoke, Morgan finally reached the office door, now lying in the hallway and hesitated in the door, trying to see through the flames that now filled the tastefully decorated office.

"Lisa!" he yelled loudly trying to be heard over the crackle of the flames. "Miss Nettleton!"

He heard no answer, but he was afraid she might be trapped in the inner office or in the hidden room behind it. Moving quickly, he ran across the receptionist's office and threw open the closed door to the inner office. The fire that burned inside the private office was not as aggressive as that in the hallway until it was fueled by the sudden influx of air from the door being thrown open. The upsurge of flame was almost an explosion, the force of which threw Morgan back across the outer office, where he slammed against the wall and dropped to the floor where he lay stunned.

The police officer lay motionless on the burning carpet for a short period of time until Estrada stormed in the room, almost tripping over his partner. Grabbing him by the arm, Estrada hoisted Morgan across his broad shoulders into a fireman's carry and staggered out of the office, down the hall and into the parking lot. The smoke was thick and acrid, causing Estrada to stagger as he found that he was unable to draw a full breath. The lighted exit door was his goal as his lungs fought for each breath; no thought of dropping his burden crossed his mind as he staggered his way along the smoke filled hallway.

As he reached the fresh air, he was relieved of his burden by two emergency medical technicians who had just arrived. A fire crew was right behind them and pushed past into the burning building. The two EMTs helped Morgan over to the ambulance which sat nearby. Estrada stumbled along in their wake, coughing to clear his lungs of the thick smoke. A second team of EMTs intercepted him and led him over to another ambulance that had squealed to a stop just after the fire trucks had arrived.

Only a few minutes later, several police cars and the fire marshal's car also entered the somewhat crowded parking lot. The area was a bee hive of activity, but Morgan was not aware of it. His impact with the wall of the office had given him a small concussion and he was still only semi-conscious. The last thing that he remembered of the event was when the door to the ambulance was slammed shut and it pulled out of the parking lot with him stepped to the gurney. He tried to object that he had work to do, but somehow he seemed unable to do more than lift his right arm. Then there was a small pinprick on his arm and his eyes closed of their own accord. Caleb Morgan was going to be out of the fight for a little time.

CHAPTER TWENTY

Anna Ortiz was sleeping soundly, which while a normal enough occurrence for most was unusual for her. From her years of military service, she had become conditions to sleeping very lightly, ready to rouse to full wakefulness in seconds. But not on this night, in fact, she had drowsed since mid-afternoon and had barely roused herself enough to take her medicine when the nurse brought it to her.

Her grandmother, Elena Granado Espinosa, had kept watch over her since her admission to the hospital never leaving her room except for short periods. Now she was present but she slept soundly in the comfortable arm chair that the nurses had gotten for her. The lights in Anna's room were darkened, the curtains were drawn; the room, as well as the entire floor of this normally busy hospital were silent, as if waiting for something important to happen. It was as if a stage had been set, waiting for the actors to arrive.

Suddenly, Anna opened her eyes, she was surprised to see that it was daylight and a nurse was bustling about the room. She was also surprised to see that her grandmother was not in the room, in fact, the recliner that had been moved from the nurses' lounge for her grandmother to use was also gone. She was also aware that her perception of the room was somehow different, as if everything was somehow off.

She raised herself up in the bed to look at the nurse, and was surprised to see that it was the blonde with the little cap on her head that Ana had seen before, the one she was assured did not work here. Before she could say anything to her, the nurse noticed Anna watching her.

"Well, hello, sleepy-head," said the nurse, coming over to help Anna adjust the pillows behind her back so that she could sit up more comfortably. "It's time that you are up and getting ready."

"For what?" asked Anna, in some confusion.

"Why, he is here today," responded the nurse. "You need to get ready to meet him. He is the one and it has taken long enough for the two of you to get together."

"The one what?" stammered Ana, her confusion growing. "What are you talking about?"

"Why the one you need to meet for all of this to come to pass," responded the nurse brightly, as she moved about the room, straightening and cleaning, humming an old 40s tune beneath her breath as she worked.

"Who are you?" asked Anna suddenly.

The nurse stopped for a moment, her attention focused on her task as she spoke.

"Why, I am your nurse," she responded, evasively.

"No, I know that you are a nurse, but what is your name?" asked Anna insistently. "I've not seen you before."

For the first time the smile and cheerful attitude left the young woman as she turned to face Anna.

"My name is Betty Anderson," she responded quietly. "I know that you are puzzled about what is happening to you, but everything will be made clear soon."

Suddenly, the smile returned to her face and the young woman walked over to lay her hand against Ana's forehead.

"You need to sleep, my dear," she said softly. "When you awake, everything will be very clear and you will meet him. Once you do, then everything else that needs to happen will come to pass."

Anna tried to say that she still didn't understand, but suddenly she felt herself slipping back into a deep sleep. The last thing that she saw was the smiling face of Betty Anderson leaning over her as she drifted into darkness.

With a start Anna awoke, the room was silent, darkened. Slowly, Anna raised her head and looked around the room. She smiled to herself as she saw her grandmother lying back in her recliner, sound asleep. So that much of her vision or dream was false, her grandmother was still in the room.

From the lack of sound and the dimness of the light coming from the hallway, Anna was sure that it was night. But is that was true, then she had either slept the clock around, which she did not believe, or the memory of waking up to see the mysterious blonde nurse was a dream. It was hard to know what the truth was; the whole thing was really messing with her mind. It was becoming hard to know what was real and what was not real. Could she be losing her mind?

Fumbling beneath the blanket, Anna found the control to raise and lower the bed. She brought the upper part of the bed to an upright position so that she was sitting comfortably. She had always prided herself in approaching problems in a calm logical fashion. That approach had given her a stellar military career, so she now applied that same approach to her current problem. There were several questions that she was totally unable to answer and none of the answers that she had made any sense. Why was she seeing all of those figures who seemed so real, but could not be here? Was these visions the result of her head injury or were they something else? She ran the various possibilities over in her mind before giving up in frustration. She just did not have enough information to make a decision.

She was interrupted by her grandmother shifting and stretching. Looking over, Anna smiled fondly at the older woman. Her grandmother had been everything to her, mother, father, confessor, and teacher. Now she was spending all of her time caring for Anna just as she had when Anna was a child. Fast asleep, without the worries of her day reflected in the numerous wrinkles of face, her grandmother looked much as she had as a young woman. It was at times like this that she could see her own face in her grandmother. Anna felt a great deal of regret that she was the cause of a new crop of wrinkles on that tired old face.

At that moment, the door opened to admit Dr. Ramey and Dr. Delbert. They were almost moving in lockstep as they approached her bed. The sounds of their entrance also brought her grandmother to full wakefulness and she set up, rubbing her face.

"Good, you are awake," said Ramey, a smile on his face as he pulled a small penlight out of his coat pocket. "We'll see how you are doing today."

Clicking on the light, Ramey point it at Anna's right eye and then switched it to her left eye. He did this several times before clicking off the light and dropping it back into his pocket. For a long moment he studied her before he stepped to the foot of the bed and took her chart from the rack hanging there.

"So, how am I doing, doctor?" Anna asked impatiently. "Are you here to tell me that I have brain damage?"

Ramey wrote rapidly in her medical chart before he dropped it back into the holding rack; turning to face her, his arms crossed across his chest.

"Well, I am still puzzled at the results of your tests, but there is no longer any chance that you have any serious brain damage. Oh, granted there is some damage from your head injuries, but it does not seem to have caused any major problems for you. Your tests show that you have in fact made a major, almost miraculous recovery from what should have been a very deadly injury."

Colonel Delbert moved close to the bed and took Anna's right wrist in his hand as he glanced at his watch. After a moment he placed her arm gently on her chest and shrugged.

"Your pulse is a little rapid, but otherwise there do not seem to be any major problems. All of your vitals from last night's tests were within normal parameters. It is remarkable, almost a miracle."

"You mean she is fine?" asked her grandmother wonderingly. "My granddaughter can go home, she will not die?"

Colonel Delbert gently rested one hand on her grandmother's shoulder in a comforting manner.

"Well, you can't take her home this minute, but if she continues to improve and there are no unexpected problems, then in a week or two, I suspect that she can be released.

As for dying, she probably will in forty or fifty years, however, not anytime soon. But in the meantime we need to watch her carefully for any problems."

He looked back at Anna and smiled.

"Are you still having those headaches?"

She shook her head emphatically.

"Not a single one in several days.

"Do you have any sensitivity to light? Ringing in your ears? How about any unexplained pains?"

Anna pulled herself up higher in the bed, brushing her hair out of her face.

"None, I feel fine. But tell me Doctor, have you figured out what is causing those visions or hallucinations or whatever they are?"

Colonel Delbert shook his head slowly, his face reflecting his concern.

"No we have not, my dear, and that is what is worrying me the most."

"How so?" asked Anna.

"When your helicopter crashed your head took a major blow, in fact your flight helmet was crushed from the impact of your head against the side of the aircraft. Frankly, by all rights you should be dead.

However, for some reason, you are recovering from what should have been a fatal injury. We simply have no explanation for your miraculous recovery."

"So is my injury somehow tied to these visions?" Anna pressed. "Am I going to go slowly insane over time or something like that?

Ramey shrugged and leaned against the wall at the head of her bed.

"Anna, we simply have no idea what is happening, or why you are having these, uh, visions, or whatever they might be," he began. "Your most recent MRI's have given us another puzzle. In most people only 5-10% of the brain is active. However, your tests show that over 90% of your brain is active. Your injuries could have left you a vegetable, but instead it seems to have awakened more of your brains. Of course, we have yet to see if you have more abilities to go with your greater brain capacities."

Ramey paused for a moment as if unsure how to continue, but Anna somehow picked up on what he was about to say.

"But it is possible that I could also have lost some abilities, isn't that true."

Ramey appeared uncertain how to answer and helplessly looked across the bed to Colonel Delbert, who answered for him.

"Anna, when we are dealing with the brain, we literally have no idea what might happen to you as a result of such a serious injury. You could have even more ability in general, or in specific areas or actually no improvement at all."

"The downside?" she pressed. "What problems can I expect?"

"Well it is true that you could have reduced abilities as your brain and body might have to learn how to work together again. As I said, we just have no idea what the long term effects of your brain injuries might be."

They were interrupted by her grandmother.

"But you are sure that my angel is not going to die?" she asked quietly.

Dr. Delbert smiled at the old woman for a moment.

"Madame, one thing we can say at this point in time, is that barring accident or the actions of others, your granddaughter is not going to die of these injuries."

As the two doctors and her grandmother talked, Anna folded her arms and leaned back against her pillows. She was going to live, but what would the future hold? Was she losing her mind, as she half suspected or was she using more of her mind than previously and simply seeing more than most people? Only time would tell.

EMERGENCY ROOM AT BEAUMONT HOSPITAL

Beaumont Army Medical Center has agreements with many local, state and federal agencies regarding offering treatment, especially in the case of burns. So it was that as a result of his own head injuries as well as some fairly serious burns, Lieutenant Caleb Morgan was transported to Beaumont Hospital rather than any of the local hospitals. The ambulance carrying him made good time in rushing to the Emergency Room at Beaumont.

Once the ambulance screeched to a stop, the two Emergency Medical Technicians jerked open the rear doors, pulled the gurney to the ground and wheeled the unconscious Lieutenant into the waiting doors of the Emergency Room. There were two physicians waiting to treat the injured police Lieutenant.

His injuries were serious, but not life threatening, so the treatment did not take a long period of time. Once they had finished, the senior physicians gave orders for Morgan to be taken to a room. However, there was a slight problem with room assignment. The doctors wanted to keep Morgan overnight for observation, so he as assigned a room on the fourth floor. However, another Morgan has been admitted through the emergency room with an injury that required minor surgery and was assigned a room on the surgical floor, in fact the room was just across the hall from that of Anna Ortiz.

However, on this particular day, as the two were being wheeled to their room, the survivors of a major bus wreck were brought into the emergency room and all personnel were called to help triage those arriving. As a result both Morgans were left at the nurses' station, their gurneys pushed up against the wall; each of their charts was laid on the foot of the gurney with the respective patient. At a moment when no one was watching, a blonde nurse wearing an old fashion nurse's uniform walked up to the two gurneys and quickly swapped charts. After that, the two sat for over an hour, waiting to be taken to their rooms.

Finally, the injured were treated and two orderlies came to transport the two patients to their rooms. However, due to the unexpected admissions, everyone was rushed so when Jose Archuleta picked up the first chart he merely glanced at the room assigned, which was for the surgical floor. He glanced at the patient.

"Are you Mr. Morgan?" he asked picking up the chart from the edge of the gurney.

The Morgan that was scheduled for the surgical floor was asleep. Caleb Morgan was just awake enough to respond.

"I'm Morgan," he answered, groggily.

"OK, sir," responded the Orderly as he began to push the gurney toward the elevator. "We are going for a little ride and get you to your room."

Jose never noticed the pretty blonde nurse in the old fashioned uniform watching from the corner of the hallway as he entered the elevator with Lieutenant Morgan. Had he noticed her he might have wondered about her dazzling smile that was directed at the patient. As it was, he paid attention only to his job and stood with arms folded as the elevator began its journey upward.

THE SURGICAL FLOOR

As the elevator doors opened, the orderly exited the car, whistling cheerfully, pushing the gurney containing Lieutenant Morgan down the hall to the nurses' station. Bringing the gurney to a halt in front of the counter, Jose Archuleta handed Morgan's chart to the Charge Nurse, Bertha Campbell.

"Here's another for you, Ms. Campbell," said Archuleta cheerfully.

Bertha Campbell was in the middle of a dozen things at that moment, but took time to cross the floor and take the chart from the orderly, glancing at the label on the front.

"OK, put this gentleman in room 604. I'll be in there in a minute to get him set up," she responded, "I have a few things to finish first."

"Right you are, Madame," responded the orderly, returning the file to the gurney and pushing the semi-conscious Lieutenant a little further down the hall and into an open doorway on the right. Once in the room, he pushed the gurney up beside the bed closest to the door and locked the wheels. "Here you are, Mr. Morgan, your home away from home for a few days."

At that moment a second orderly came into the room. The new comer came to stand at the foot of the gurney while Jose moved to the head of the gurney.

"OK, now Mr. Morgan," began Jose, "on the count of three, we will move you from the gurney to the bed."

He looked at the second orderly and nodded. "OK, now one, two and three." At the count of three, the two orderlies smoothly lifted Morgan and deposited him in the bed. Once the patient was safely in the bed, the two orderlies left and one of the nurses came into the room, an older woman with bleached blonde hair.

"How are we, Mr. Morgan," she asked in a cheerful voice, coming over to check his blood pressure and check his pulse.

"Uh, fine, I guess," he mumbled. "I'm just very tired."

"That's just the sedative you were given in the Emergency Room," she responded. "I'm just going to give you a little bit more so that you will be able to sleep."

Morgan smiled weakly. "I could sleep just fine if everyone would leave me alone."

The nurse laughed a clear tinkling laugh.

"After I give you this shot no one will bother you," she promised as she removed a capped syringe from her pocket. She picked up his arm, holding it close to her side as she expertly found a vein. As gently as possible injected the sedative into Morgan's arm. Almost at once, his eyelids became so heavy that he could no longer keep them open. Finally, he slept. Her job done, the nurse lowered the lights and pulled the door almost closed before returning to the nurses' station. In a few moments, she was busy with the stack of patient files sitting in the middle of her desk.

With a quick glance at the charge nurse busy with her files, a slim figure moved down the hall to pause outside Morgan's door. With a glance in both directions, the lovely blonde nurse wearing an old fashion uniform peeked into the room, checking that Morgan was safely in his bed. Only one more step to the plan of getting the two together.

CHAPTER TWENTY-ONE

Lisa Nettleton slowly opened her eyes and tried to sit up, struggling weakly when she found that she couldn't move. She was also gagged with what felt like a wad of cloth stuck into her mouth. Even so, she did not panic, she was sure that she would be able to escape from whatever, or whoever had put her in this fix. In spite of her fashion model appearance, Lisa had always been something of a Tomboy.

First she was aware that she was lying on a bed, not a comfortable bed, but a bed all the same. Craning her neck, Lisa was able to look above her head to see that her arms were tied to the headboard. She couldn't see her feet, but there was no doubt in her mind that her ankles were tied to the footboard of the rickety old bed. She struggled, trying to free herself, but she only managed to make the knots tighter and tire herself out. Finally, she gave up, her well endowed chest heaving as she fell back against the bed, as she struggled for air.

From what she could see, she was being kept in a small room. In addition to the bed, there was a small dresser and a chair sitting against the wall. Other than these few items, the room was bare; there were not even any pictures on the wall. Finally, she had to face the fact that she had no idea where she was and she was helpless.

There was a sound to her left as a door opened and someone quietly entered the room. She felt a new wave of shock as she recognized the person that entered the room. She tried to shout at the person looming over her, but her gag was tight enough that she could only make unintelligible noises. Finally, Lisa gave up and fell back against the bed once again.

"Aren't we just full of energy," chuckled the intruder. "I hope that your energy level continues to remain high during our little session. However, I would recommend that you should save your energy, because you are in for a long night, my dear."

Turning, the figure took the wooden chair from beside the door and brought it over to sit beside the bed. Sitting carefully in the chair, Lisa's captor pulled a knife from a belt sheath and brought the blade over to lie between Lisa's prominent breasts. The captive girl was still wearing her bra and panties, but nothing else. The blade was brought up to lie beneath the strap connecting the well filled cups and then turned so that the cutting edge was pressing against the lacy material. With a flick of the wrist, the knife severed the material which fell away, leaving Lisa's full breasts bare.

"Now I want to know something about that little estate sale that you helped stage."

Caleb Morgan opened his eyes suddenly, fully alert. From the dimness of the room and the lack of light from the curtained window, it was clear that it was still dark outside. He had only vague memories of his arrival at the hospital, but he knew that he was in unfamiliar surroundings. Slowly, he raised himself onto his right elbow and scanned the dimly lit room. Satisfied that he was alone, Morgan leaned back against the bed, his eyes on the ceiling and then almost jumped out of his skin when a voice spoke from nearby.

"How are you feeling, Lieutenant Morgan?" asked a deep voice from the shadowy area near the door.

"Uh, who's there?" stammered the Lieutenant.

Suddenly a match flared. Morgan saw that the stranger in the shadows was tall, past middle age with long white hair and a bushy white moustache. He appeared to be applying the match to the end of a rather large cigar. After a few seconds, he puffed it to life and only the glowing tip was visible.

"Turn on the lights so that I can see you," asked Morgan, pushing himself up on the bed.

"Oh, that's alright young feller, we don't want to disturb the nurses and I can see you just fine," responded the old man, puffing on his cigar and then blowing streams of smoke from his nostrils. "Besides, we need to talk."

"About what?" asked Morgan, his curiosity aroused.

"Son, you got a killer running around this town," said the old man. "A killer who is heartless, blood thirsty and one that is gonna be very hard to stop."

"What do you know about this killer," asked Morgan sharply.

"Oh, everything, my boy," returned the old man, taking another draw on his stogie. "I know everything about this killer."

"Then tell me who it is!" demanded Morgan, struggling to sit up in the bed.

The initial response of the old man was a hacking laughter.

"You young fellers are always running around and not noticing what's right in front of your nose," observed the old man. "First, it is against the rules for me to tell you the name of this killer, you have to figure this out for yourself. I'm just here to make sure that you keep a close eye on the young lady. I would take it very bad if something happened to her."

"Suppressing evidence is a crime, sir," snapped Morgan. "If you know something about these crimes you have to tell me!"

The old man laughed against as he puffed again on his cigar.

"Boy, I don't have to do anything," the old man said sternly. "However, I hope you are as feisty when you have to defend her. You are her only hope."

Determined to get some answers from the old man, Morgan pushed himself out of his bed at the same moment the door opened and the room was flooded with light.

"Mr. Morgan, what are you doing out of bed!" snapped the voice of the Charge Nurse as she came steaming into the room. "You get right back into that bed this instant. And who are you talking to."

Suddenly she waved her hand in front of her face. "Have you been smoking in here? Young man this is a non-smoking hospital, there will be no smoking in any room of this facility."

Morgan got to his feet and dashed to the door, almost falling in the process. He pushed his way past the nurse, jerked open the door and ran into the hall; there was no sign of any old man in either direction. Realizing that his ass was literally hanging out the back of the hospital gown, Morgan quickly backed into the room and jerked open the bathroom door, to find that the old man had literally vanished into thin air. The only sign he had been there at all was the rapidly fading smell of the big cigar his visitor had been smoking.

"Young man," began the nurse, "I don't know what kind of game you are playing, but I want you back in that bed this instant."

Holding the back of his hospital gown closed with one hand, Morgan swung around to the nurse.

"Didn't you see him?" demanded Morgan, grabbing the nurse's arm with his free hand. "He had to pass you when you came into the room."

"See who?" asked the nurse, jerking away from Morgan and beginning to edge toward the door herself. "Uh, young man, if you will just settle down, I'll get the doctor."

With that, the nurse spun on her heel and almost ran out of the room. Shaking his head in frustration, Morgan took one more look around the hospital room before he finally crawled back into bed and pulled the sheet up to his waist. He was puzzled, he knew that he had talked to an older man in this very room, but when the lights had come on the old man had been gone. It was impossible, but he had experienced it. Morgan was still puzzling over what had happened when the door opened and one of the residents cautiously stuck his head inside the room.

"Uh, Mr. Morgan, are you alright?" he asked hesitantly. "The nurse said that you were having a problem."

Morgan looked at the resident for a moment, before he sighed, crossed his arms and sank down lower in the bed.

"Yes, doctor, I am fine," he sighed, "just a little groggy from the sedatives, I guess."

Seeing that Morgan was now very calm, the resident slowly slipped into the room, though still cautious enough to make sure that the room door stayed open. He probably thinks that I am a nut, thought Morgan.

Suddenly, the resident, Mark Henry, paused and took a deep breath. "Mr. Morgan have you been smoking? No, it is not a question you have been smoking, haven't you?"

Morgan sighed, "No I haven't been smoking; it was the man that I saw in my room who was smoking. He was smoking a cigar, I believe."

Dr. Henry nodded and began edging toward the door.

"Uh, Nurse Rogers mentioned that you thought someone had been in your room. But I can assure you that there was no one here—uh."

Morgan had been looking at the ceiling, but glanced over at the doctor who was looking at the floor. Morgan followed his gaze to see that the doctor was intently staring at a used kitchen match that was lying on the otherwise spotless floor. For a moment, the two just stared at each other as a small curl of smoke came from the head of the burnt match.

The next morning, Morgan awoke to the hustle and bustle of the busy hospital floor as the breakfast trays were being served. Morgan fumbled among the sheets until he found the controls which raised the head of his bed. When he was sitting up to this satisfaction, Morgan reached over for the phone and dialed his office number.

"Homicide, Sergeant Gravenos speaking."

"Jim, this is Caleb Morgan."

"Oh, Lieutenant heard that you were taken to the hospital. How are you doing?"

Morgan snorted, "Frankly I don't know why I was brought here, but I wasn't given much choice in the matter. Anyway, have Estrada get over here and bring me some clean clothes. I have to get out of this loony bin."

Gravenos laughed, "Sure, Lieutenant I'll let him know."

Morgan hung up the phone and leaned back against his pillows. He wanted out of the hospital, but he couldn't run around wearing that silly hospital gown. In the mean time, he might as well keep it too himself, he thought as a nurse's aid came into the room bringing his breakfast tray.

As the aide bustled around Morgan's bed, making sure that he was happy with his breakfast tray a older woman in a gray suit came hesitantly into the room.

"Miss, could I see you a moment?" she asked very softly. She then turned a pair of surprisingly gray eyes toward Morgan.

"I'm sorry young man," said the woman, "but my granddaughter is across the hall and I need to get something for her breakfast tray."

"Quite alright, ma'am," responded Morgan as he distastefully eyed the tray in front of him. He hated hospital food, but this tray was especially bland. "Actually, she can have my tray if she would like."

At that moment, a large black woman wearing a nurse's uniform came bustling in the room having heard Morgan's statement about giving his food tray away.

"Honey child, you need to eat that gourmet meal prepared at great expense by the hospital kitchen. You need to keep up your strength before you have that surgery this afternoon."

"Surgery?" asked Morgan in total confusion. "What surgery?"

"Why the surgery your doctor scheduled you for over two weeks go," the nurse retorted, her hands on her wide hips as her voice raised in pitch. "Why do you think you are here? This is not a vacation home, you know. People come here to be treated for medical problems and you are here for surgery. Now eat your breakfast and quite causing problems."

Morgan threw back the sheet and bounded to his feet, then remembered that his rear was vulnerable and grabbed the open rear of the gown with one hand, falling back against the bed. His antics moved both women to laughter, though that of the nurse was loud and long, like a braying of a donkey.

"Child you ain't got nothing that I ain't seen before so you can quit trying to hide," finally gasped the nurse. "You can run up and down this floor stark naked for all I care, but you are scheduled for surgery. So get your skinny white ass back into that bed and hush up."

While this interplay was going on, the older Hispanic lady tried to suppress a grin while slowly backing out of the room. However, before the she was fully out of the room, the nurse turned to her.

"What can I do for you Miz Espinosa?"

"I'm so sorry to bother you, but my ---"

"Espinosa?" asked Morgan, safely covered by the bed sheet. "Would that be Elena Espinosa?"

Both the nurse as well as Ms. Espinosa looked at Morgan in surprise.

"Why yes," she responded. "My name is Elena Espinosa. Do I know you?"

Morgan smiled at her, "No ma'am, not yet, but if you are the correct Elena Espinosa, have I got some news for you."

UNKNOWN LOCATION

Lisa Nettleton slowly regained consciousness. She was still tied spread eagle to the old bed, but now her last remaining articles of clothing her bra and lacy panties had been cut form her body. Her nude body was crisscrossed with bloody red stripes. Her face was puffy where she had been savagely beaten by her captor. She slowly liked her split lips, her mouth dry.

"Now let's try it one more time," said a voice from above Lisa's head. "I want to know where the diaries are. Who bought them at the estate sale?"

Lisa licked her dry lips once again.

"I don't know," she croaked for the 100th time since her torture had begun. "We didn't keep a list of who bought what. Ms. Mallard was only concerned with how much money she was making."

The masked figure towering over the bed pulled the old wooden chair up close and sat almost primly on the chair. A gloved hand reached out and took a handful of Lisa's long sweaty hair, pulling the captive girl's head up off the pillow.

"I think you know more than you are letting on my dear," said her captor, "and I plan on finding out what you know."

Lisa caught her breath as the blood stained knife was held before her eyes. "Now let's go over all of this again, shall we?"

BEAUMONT HOSPITAL

During the afternoon, Estrada, Morgan's partner arrived and the confusion of the impending surgery was straightened out. Though swearing that the hospital did not make such mistakes, Nurse Deckert, the Charge Nurse for the sixth floor, spent the better part of an hour apologizing for any inconvenience that Lieutenant Morgan may have been caused by the confusion. Morgan was just happy to get a pair of pants back on, though it was after he had to put up with Estrada's amusement of finding Morgan barricaded in his hospital room as two orderlies tried to force the door open in order take him to surgery.

At first Estrada had been confused to find someone else in Morgan's room, but once he discovered that there had been two Morgan's that checked in the night before, he quickly got to the bottom of the matter. The other Morgan who was in Lieutenant Morgan's room was in the hospital for a court ordered sterilization. So when Estrada discovered that Morgan was not in his assigned room, then it was only a matter of a few minutes to discover that someone was in the other Morgan's room on the surgical floor. It only stood to reason that it would be the missing police lieutenant.

A couple of calls to hospital administration had stopped the threatened surgery that Morgan feared, but no one had bothered to tell Morgan or, for that matter, the orderlies who were assigned to take Morgan down to surgery. When Estrada arrived, they were in the process of trying to knock down the room door. After a few minutes of uncontrolled laughter, Estrada showed his badge and sent the orderlies back to work. Then trying to stifle his laughter, Estrada went to the door and knocked.

"Go away!" yelled Morgan. "I am not having any surgery. I am a police officer and I will arrest you if you come through that door."

"Relax, Lieutenant," responded Estrada. "It's safe to open the door now."

In a moment, Estrada heard the sound of furniture being moved and then the door opened slightly. Estrada could see the side of Morgan's face as well as part of what looked like a toga.

"Are you alone?" asked Morgan.

"Sure am, Lieutenant," responded Estrada. "You're safe now, the mistake had been corrected. You are not going to have to have any surgery."

Morgan looked at Estrada suspiciously. "You're sure?"

Estrada worked hard to suppress a smile, as he tossed Morgan his clothes, but failed. "I'm sure Lieutenant, there will be no surgery. It was an error, records were mixed up and you were scheduled for someone else's surgery."

"Humph," snorted Morgan, "it'll be a while before I get over this mess."

He paused a moment and looked at Estrada.

"What do we have on Lisa Nettleton?"

Estrada shook his head and shrugged.

"So far it looks like she just fell off the earth. We found clothes that were identified as what she was wearing earlier in the day, but there has been no sign of her."

With the pending surgery off the table, Morgan's mind turned back to the serial killer case. It seemed odd to him that even while in the hospital he was interacting with this completely bizarre case. He could not shake the feeling that everything that had happened was arranged - from him being taken to the wrong room to Elena Espinosa just happening to walk into his room to talk to the nurse. It was all just too pat, too improbable. But who would be in a position to make sure that all of these things happened? Finally, he shook his head and stepped in front of the mirror while he straightened his tie. Then the thought hit him.

"How would anyone know?" asked Morgan, his eyes still on his tie in the mirror.

"About what?" asked Estrada.

"Miss Nettleton called me about the check list from that estate sale and when we get there she has been abducted. So how would anyone know about that call? She made the call to my cell and I would have to think that she made the call from her office. So unless someone was in her office, then perhaps her office phone was taped. Let's check this out."

Satisfied with his appearance, Morgan turned as Estrada handed him a clear plastic bag with all of his effects inside. After returning his possessions to his pockets, Morgan picked up a folded sheet of paper that proved to be a copy of the handwritten will signed by Hughes.

Morgan looked at the document for a long moment. He was positive that he had returned the document to the case file before answering the call that had ultimately led to his being admitted to the hospital. So how did it wind up among the personal effects collected by the hospital staff when he was admitted? It just did not make any sense. First he winds up in the hospital across the hall from a possible, missing heir to the Hughes estate and then just to make it complete, he just happened to find a copy of Hughes' Last Will and Testament in his pocket.

He paused, tapping the folded document against his chin, deep in thought. None of it made any sense, but he might as well make the best of the situation. He might as well take advantage of the situation to talk to the real heir while he had her.

ANNA ORTIZ'S HOSPITAL ROOM

When Morgan knocked on the door across the hall, the two women were talking quietly. It was Anna's grandmother who got up to answer the door. While her grandmother's back was turned, Anna caught a glimpse of Nurse Anderson standing in the corner of the room smiling at her. Suddenly she mouthed the words, "He's here!" Then before her eyes, the smiling woman slowly faded from sight.

"Who is it?" asked her grandmother, opening the door just a bit.

"Ms. Espinosa, I'm Lieutenant Morgan, with the El Paso police, we met early this morning in my room across the hall." He stepped to the side to allow Estrada to step forward. "And this is my partner Sergeant Estrada."

"Oh, yes, I remember," laughed her grandmother, "you are the young man from across the hall who didn't want surgery."

Morgan smiled ruefully, "Yes ma'am, that true. It seems the hospital had made a mistake and I was never scheduled for surgery. There was another man named Morgan who was supposed to be in that room. It was just a mistake."

"Well I'm glad it all got worked out," responded Anna's grandmother. "What can I do for you two young men?"

"I am sorry for this imposition, but would it be too much of an imposition for us to come in and talk to you?" asked Morgan.

For a moment, Elena Espinosa looked at him in puzzlement before the stepped back and allowed to two policemen to enter the room. She went over to stand beside the bed and took her granddaughter's hand.

"This is my granddaughter, Anna," she said, sitting on the edge of the bed.

Morgan was struck by how lovely the young woman was. Estrada nodded a greeting and went over to the window, glancing through the curtains at the street. He was clearly leaving the meeting up to Morgan.

Morgan came over to the bed and held h is hand out to its occupant.

"Hi, I'm Caleb Morgan, with the El Paso Police Department," he introduced himself, reaching forward to take her hand. Anna leaned forward to take his hand in hers just a moment. Morgan was surprised how soft and delicate her hand felt in his.

"Hi," she responded, "I'm Anna Ortega. I know that I look a sight, but I've been in here a while."

"Sorry to bother you," returned Morgan, "I've read about your injuries in the press. How are you doing?"

"Improving everyday," interjected her grandmother, her eyes sparkling in amusement at the immediate attraction between the handsome policeman and her granddaughter. "But she tires easily. So what was it you wanted to talk to me about?"

"May I?" asked Morgan, pointing to a nearby chair.

"Oh, where are my manners?" exclaimed Elena Espinosa. "Please, have a seat."

Morgan settled himself in the chair and pulled the document from his coat.

"There is no subtle way to do this, I'm afraid, so I am going to just ask you straight out. Ms. Espinosa, how well did you know Ezra Hughes?"

For a moment, the old lady looked at Morgan in total shock and then she pitched forward in a dead faint, to be caught by Morgan before she hit the floor on her face. He quickly pulled her over to the chair that he had just vacated and carefully seated her. Estrada came over with a glass of water from Anna's bedside table and placed it in the old lady's hands. After a few minutes, she was sufficiently recovered to sit up and resume the conversation. In one motion, she downed the entire glass of water Estrada had handed her.

"Grandmother, are you alright?" fretted Anna, her eyes full of concern.

"Of course, child," responded her grandmother, "I am fine. The question just took me by surprise, I guess. I haven't heard that name is many years."

"How do you know him, Ms. Espinosa?" asked Morgan gently. "How do you know Ranger Captain Ezra Hughes?"

She sat quietly for a long time; so long, in fact that Morgan wasn't sure that she was going to answer his question. Finally, she took a deep breath, handed the empty water glass to Estrada, and slowly folded her hands in her lap. Her head was still down as her eyes appeared to be carefully studying her folded hands.

"It was so long ago," she finally whispered, "another time and another world."

She was silent again, Morgan waited as patiently as he could, but finally he felt he had to say something to prod her.

"It really is important, Mrs. Espinosa," urged Morgan. "Could you please tell me how you knew him?"

She took another deep breath and sat up straight in her chair.

"I'm sorry officer, as I said, it has been so many years since I even thought about him ---," she paused a moment and her eyes misted over.

"Actually that's a lie, not a day has passed that I don't think of him. I wish things had been different between us."

She was silent for another few moments before she glanced over at Anna. "I've never told anyone this, my dear. I hope you won't think less of me after you hear this."

"Grandmother there is nothing that you could tell that would have me think less of you," responded Anna. "What is this all about?"

"Oh, very well," she finally gave in quietly. "I was young, nineteen, it was my first job. I was the assistant to the Mayor of Juarez and I loved it. I was in the middle of everything that was going on and it was an exciting time."

She paused for a moment, her eyes staring at her granddaughter, but clearly she was long ago and far away.

"My English was always excellent and I acted as translator for the Mayor, who was a cousin of my father. My family was high born and as was custom, women in my family were sheltered and not allowed to work. However, I was headstrong and knew early how to twist men around my finger. An exception was made for me.

"Oh, I was so proud to be walking beside the Mayor when he went into meetings. It was in a meeting that that I first met Ezra, or as you call him Ranger Hughes. When our eyes met, there was no doubting that we were fated to be together. Oh, he was a man among men. He was muy toro."

For a long moment she sat silent, her mind journeying down the pathways of the past. In her mind, she saw herself as she was at 19 and as her one true love looked all those years ago.

"Wasn't there a large difference in your ages?" asked Morgan curiously.

Elena smiled at him wistfully." Oh, yes, my friend, I was barely 20 and Ezra was probably middle aged. But you have to remember that in Mexico the age differences between a man and a woman is not as big an issue as it is among you gringos. The man my father had promised me to was even older than Ranger Hughes. For a long time the fathers of the noble families of Mexico would arrange marriages for their daughters to older, wiser men."

"So it caused no problems?" he pressed.

"Ah, but it did, young man. It caused a great many problems," replied sadly. "You see, there came a time that I foolishly told my parents that I did not want to marry their choice of husbands, but rather one of my own."

"How did your parents take that?" asked Morgan, curiously.

The old lady sat quietly for a second before she shrugged and shook her head slowly.

"How do you think, sir? I was a properly raised child who saw fit to defy my parents. My father was a descendant of a long line of Spanish nobles and was livid that his daughter had taken up with what he called that "bastard Texas Ranger.""

She paused again.

"You know it is funny, but my mother told me that if it had been fifteen years previously that they would have welcomed him with open arms as Ezra and my father had been the best of friends. But something happened and they became enemies. But even so I was stubborn and my parents loved me, so eventually, I won them over. My father eventually agreed that I could marry Ezra. You see," she paused a moment as if gathering her courage. "I was lonely one evening and slipped across the river to see him. We spent a night of unbelievable passion and, well, I discovered that I was with child."

"So did you marry?" prompted Morgan curiously.

"No, was determined to marry him, but then something happened, I never really knew what it was. It had something to do with Ezra's work, some case he had handled. He only told me that someone had found out about us and that it was too dangerous for me to stay here. My father forced me to leave and go to Mexico City. I had my baby there, but h e and I never got back together. My father told me that Ezra had met someone else and forgot all about me."

She looked at Anna, "it was your mother, child. Your grandfather was Ranger Captain Ezra Hughes. I never told your mother, she thought her father had died before her birth and no one ever told her differently."

Morgan watched the two of them for a moment before pulling the Hughes letter from his pocket.

"Ma'am, Ranger Hughes never forgot about you or his child. You should read this."

With that he handed the old lady the letter signed by Hughes. It would insure that Hughes' estate went where the old man wanted it to go. Her hand was shaking as she took the document and opened it. He had read it so many times that he could almost recite it form memory.

"I have only one living relative that I know and frankly she is a first class bitch who has little love for me. She only comes by to check on me to see if I am dead so that she can sell off what I have spent a

lifetime acquiring. So for this reason, I leave Chelsea Mallard the grand sum of one dollar and that is too damn much.

I have done a lot of things in my life that I have since regretted, but one thing that I do not regret was my affair with Elena Granado Espinosa. When I met her she was working for the Alcalde in Juarez; her father was the Chief of Police across the border and a very proud man of the old school. When I first saw her, I knew that I had to have her and at the first opportunity, I took her. I am not sure that her family ever knew about our relationship, but if not for my own entanglements, I would have certainly married her, propriety be damned. Even though I was more than forty years her senior, I loved her and I know that she loved me. Elena told me that she was going to tell her father and insist that he bless our marriage, however, I never found out if she did.

"The Viper found out about our relationship and I knew that there would be trouble, perhaps very serious trouble. I knew that at this age, I am not much use to anyone and certainly not able to protect Elena from the Viper. Much as it pained me, I gave Elena a large sum of money and pleaded with her to get out of town until I could take care of matters. I never saw her again. I tried to find her, however, her father refused to even talk with me after Elena disappeared. I have heard a rumor that when she left, neither of us knew that she was pregnant. If I am not able to make amends before my death, then by way of showing my feelings for her, I leave her, or if she is dead, her heirs, my entire estate.

"In honoring a promise, and accepting what I knew was a bribe, I never used what I discovered as I should have to bring a criminal to justice. I reckon not being able to live out my last years with Elena is my punishment for turning my back on my duty. However, I was weak, the amount of money offered to me was a fortune even today and in those days things were done a lot different than they are now. I thought that I could watch things and make sure that the Viper killed no more. I was wrong.

I leave it to Elena to do what is right with the information contained in my diaries. Signed Ezra Hughes."

She folded the letter slowly and held it in her lap for a long moment.

"Oh, that poor lonely man," she whispered to herself. "So that was what came between us. I thought that he had forgotten me. I should have known better. We could have been so happy if not for that Viper."

"The Viper," repeated Morgan. "Do you know who this Viper was?"

She shook her head slowly, as tears began to roll down her cheeks.

"No, I only just known learned of this individual. Ezra never told me anything."

Morgan nodded slowly.

"I thank you for your time. When you are ready, I will help you with taking control of the estate."

Elena bowed her head as he granddaughter come over to put her arms around the old lady. Morgan sensed that it was time for he and Estrada to take their leave. His last sight as he gently closed the door was of the two of them, a generation apart bowing their heads together in mutual sadness as Anna comforted her grandmother who was giving way to her grief over missed opportunities and a love lost.

CHAPTER TWENTY-THREE

For once Morgan was glad to get back to his cluttered desk at Police Headquarters. The conversation with Elena Espinosa had given him much to think about. He was now certain that the identity of the killer of all of these people was contained in Hughes' diaries. But he had read a number of them and while they did contain information on his old cases, there had been nothing that remotely dealt with the current time. So that meant either that there was a volume that had not yet been found or the old man had not written the information about the Viper down as he said that he had.

Morgan smiled a slow smile. But from what he knew and had heard about that old man, if he said that he had done something, then he had done it. He was fairly sure that he just hadn't fond the correct diary yet. The question now was where that particular diary might be located. After going through all of Ranger Hughes' diaries that Mallard had stored in her secret room, Morgan was fairly sure that at least one and possibly more of the old Rangers' dairies were missing. He looked up as Estrada entered to drop into his own desk chair.

"What did you find?" demanded Morgan.

"Several of us searched what was left of the Mallard office. Most of the documents on and around Nettleton's desk were either destroyed or severely damaged by the fire. If there was a list of those who wrote large checks on her desk, we were unable to find it."

"Any sign of Miss Nettleton?"

Estrada shook his head.

"Nope, we talked to everyone in the building and in the surrounding vicinity. No one had seen the woman, but one individual did see a large car pull out of the parking lot only a few seconds before the fire. The witness noticed, or rather remembered on the first two digits of the tag number, but did see that the car sported a very distinctive large green and blue decal on the passenger side windshield."

"This witness didn't notice any details of the decal?"

Once again, Estrada shook his head.

"Unfortunately, he only saw the decal, not any details. However, he did say that it was a big car, one of those similar to a limousine."

"Well, if it was a limo that the witness saw, then that certainly cuts down on the number of suspects. Not many crooks that I know drive limos."

"How about that letter?" asked Estrada. "Has the lab confirmed that the handwriting was that of Hughes?"

Morgan nodded; a slight smile on his face.

"Preliminary report shows that the handwriting matches several samples of Hughes' handwriting. So I guess that document will wind up being treated as his last will and testament. That makes Ms. Espinosa a very wealthy lady."

"What's the next step in regard to the Will?"

"After I got the report, I called the DA's office and made them aware of what was going on. One of the Assistants is going to get a copy of the letter to the Probate Judge and help Ms. Espinosa take control of the estate."

UNKNOWN LOCATION

Lisa Nettleton was asleep; her dreams were dark and nightmarish. She jerked awake her naked body covered with sweat, and tried to sit up. To her surprise, she was unable to lower her arms form above her head. It was only after a few seconds of struggle that she realized that she was tied to a bed in a dingy windowless room. Then her memory came flooding back and she remembered the kidnapping. At first she thought that she was alone, but after she quit struggling, she heard movement from nearby. A black gloved hand came into her field of vision and grabbed Lisa's chin.

"So, little one, you are back with us, I see," rasped a voice. "Now we can continue out discussion. Where is the diary?"

THE HUGHES MANSION

The Hughes Mansion had set empty since the death of Chelsea Mallard. Each of the many semi-furnished rooms sat empty, the only sound the popping of the old wood found through the house. A fine layer of dust covered everything. The floors that had been so lovingly cared for by the staff that had looked after the old man were now dull and scuffed. It was as if the house waited – for what no one knew.

Periodically, what sounded like softly speaking voices could be heard echoing throughout the house. Then the sound of heavy footsteps could be heard echoing through the empty rooms. At the sound of a key in the front door lock, the whispering and the footsteps all fell silent. Only the pop of the aged wood could be heard throughout the house as the large front door swung open.

"Here you are Ms. Espinosa," said a man's voice. "The court will treat the letter the police sent over to us as Old man – uh – I mean Mr. Hughes' Last Will and by its terms he left everything to you. So you may as well start taking control of the estate."

Elena Espinosa looked around the sparsely furnished entry hall in surprise. She had gathered that Ezra had become wealthy, but she had no idea how wealthy he had become. She could see that the house alone was worth several hundred thousand dollars even in a down market.

Her companion, Probate Judge Amos Kennedy, led her through the entry hall as if he was a real estate agent. He had known Ranger Hughes well and had hated having to turn the estate over to that gold digger Mallard. Now that it was clear that there had been a grievous miscarriage of justice, he was happy to personally help Mrs. Espinosa claim her inheritance. He was one of those who had heard rumors as a child that Ranger Hughes had a serious romance and now he was able to meet that woman. There was no question in his mind that as a young woman Elena Espinosa had been a truly beautiful woman.

"Uh, Ms. Espinosa, I want you to know that because of the high esteem Ranger Hughes enjoyed in this community, I am taking a special interest in this case. From what Lieutenant Morgan told me and what Ranger Hughes wrote in his holographic will, a miscarriage of justice took place and a false will was filed. I think it only right to move with all speed to correct matters."

He set his briefcase down on a nearby table and opened he latches. From the inside, he removed a large file folder and handed it to Ms. Espinosa.

"Ma'am, in this folder you will find a list of everything that we know was part of the Hughes estate. There are a large number of items in a police warehouse that were recovered in Ms. Mallard's office that we will make sure get delivered back here. There are also a large number of items that we know Chelsea Mallard sold at an Estate Sale that we are in the process of recovering which will also be returned to you."

He took the folder from her for a moment and pulled a bank statement from the back of it.

"Ranger Hughes was a very wealthy man. Miss Mallard was not able to get the financial assets as of yet since the settling of the estate was not final. She was able to get the hard assets only. The money is of course yours under the terms of his Will, here is a copy of the Court Order that gives you control of the estate."

He paused for a moment as if he wanted to say more, but instead, after a moment he handed her a large set of keys.

"Ma'am, here are the keys to your new home. That's all that I can do for you at the moment. But if there is anything else that you need, please don't hesitate to get in touch with me. In that folder you will also find one of my cards with both my office and my cell phone numbers. I am available to you anytime you need anything."

With another look around the entry way of the historic old house, Kennedy suppressed a shiver and then smiled for Elena Espinosa's benefit.

"Now I'll drive you back to the hospital and you can rejoin your granddaughter."

"Thank you for your help, Judge Kennedy," responded Elena as she followed Kennedy back onto the front porch. "You have been so kind to me and I really don't know what to say."

"Think nothing of it ma'am," responded Kennedy over his shoulder as he worked to lock the front door. Once the door was secure, Kennedy offered her his arm and took her to the car.

As they walked down the walk, neither saw the curtain covering the living room window twitch slightly, nor saw the pair of intense eyes staring out at them.

"It is almost time," a whispering voice filled the house. "Soon the time for confrontation will come. Then shall there be a day of reckoning."

BEAUMONT HOSPITAL

Anna was dozing when her grandmother returned to the hospital room. She sat quietly and watched the old woman bustle around the room, placing a ticket package of papers on the bedside table, taking off her coat and slipping into her sweater, as she found he room somewhat cool. Finally, she dropped into her chair, unfolding the newspaper that she had bought in the lobby before she looked at her granddaughter.

"How are you feeling my dear?" asked her grandmother, a smile on her face.

"So what did you find out?" Anna asked impatiently. "What did the judge want to talk to you about?"

"Well child," began Elena, "it seems that Ezra Hughes, my first and really only love, left me his entire estate."

"What was his estate?" demanded Anna.

For the first time, Elena laughed and allowed the wall she had built around her feelings for Hughes to begin to crumble. He had really loved her, she thought to herself. All these years she had believed that he had abandoned her for someone else and he had really been trying to protect her. That sweet, silly old man, all the years together that they had missed. She wiped a single tear that threatened to spill out of her eyes and roll down her wrinkled cheek.

"He – uh –, "she sniffed and wiped another tear from her check, "he left me his house, oh it was a big house, on Montana Street, all of the furnishings as well as a large sum of money in the bank."

Anna's eyes were big as she looked at her grandmother.

"How large a sum of money?" she asked curiously.

"A very, very large sum of money," responded her grandmother.

"Grams," began Anna, "I am curious about one thing."

"And what is that my dear?" asked her grandmother, her attention now turned to the newspaper in her lap.

"Didn't you keep track of this Hughes person?"

Her grandmother raised her eyes from the newspaper and stared off into the distance, her mind winging back over many years. Finally, she breathed a great sigh and looked sadly at her granddaughter.

"That Hughes person was your blood grandfather. AS a result of our relationship I was pregnant with your mother when I was sent away. As for keeping track of him over the years, I did, or tried to. But understand when he gave me money and told me to get out of time I thought he had tired of me and didn't want me any longer.

"My father never told me anything about what was happening here after I left. I know that Ezra talked to my father for the first time in many years. I don't know what they discussed. I was sent to Mexico City where I built a new life and eventually married a good man who gave me and your mother a good life. But I never forgot Ezra. He was a good man, one who acted in my best interest when it was clearly against what he wanted. To know after all of these years that he was actually putting me first by sending me away is the greatest gift that he could have left me."

POLICE HEADQUARTERS

Morgan spent a restless night, tossing and turning until he gave up and went into the office at the ungodly hour of three in the morning. At first he just sat at his desk looking over his notes from the murders. Finally, running out of things to do, he just simply sat for a time, letting it all jell. After a time, he went back to the official reports. Morgan was reading the reports from the Mallard office fire when Estrada walked in carrying two cups of coffee and carefully dropped into his desk chair. He dropped the papers he was carrying on his desk pad and lead over to hand Morgan one of the cups of hot coffee.

Morgan leaned back in his chair, took a sip of the hot coffee and glanced at his watch. It was only 4:00 AM. He savored the taste as he leaned forward to sit the cup on the edge of his desk.

"Anything more on that limo?" he asked his partner.

Estrada pawed through the papers he had just dropped on his desk to find one of them which he handed over to his partner.

"There are eight possibles, including one registered to your friend, Congresswoman Eva Prestridge. It's an older model, but still registered as active."

Morgan sat and thought for a moment. "How many of the eight have the first two digits that match the witness' statement?"

"Three."

"Do we have addresses for those three?"

Estrada nodded, motioning toward the list.

"We have names, addresses and phone numbers for all eight of them."

Morgan took another sip of his coffee before standing up.

"Then let's go."

PRESTRIDGE ESTATE

Congresswoman Prestridge was not a happy camper. Wearing nothing but her bra and panties, she sat in front of her makeup mirror working on attaining just the right look while her brother, Neal, kept harping at her.

"I tell you, the police suspect that you are not what you seem to be," he said for the fifth time since arriving. "I have had to call in several markers to keep you from being drawn into this murder investigation. Several of the area of the investigation point back to you."

"Oh, you worry too much, Neal," she admonished him as she continued to work on her makeup. "If you keep your mouth shut, there is no way that anything can come back to us."

"Eva, I just don't like it," he fretted as he paced the room in his three piece suit. "I would hate for anything to damage the family name. I've worked long and hard to get where I am and don't want to lose it."

She had finally had enough of him and his whining and whirled on him. Eyes flashing, she sprang to her feet to face him, hands on her still shapely hips. It was clear that age had not lessened her physical charms or her ability to exude sex appeal.

"You've worked long and hard?" she demanded, a look of incredulity on her lovely face. "Hell, I damn near worked my self to death in fucking half the wealthy men in this state to get them to back you in your runs for office. You had no idea how to capitalize on the family name, until little sister Eva came along. I'm the one who resolved that pending scandal with those Daniels women and I'm the one who put the police on the wrong trail, me, your little sister. If I had not acted as I did you would have wound up looking like a complete fool and what's worse, you would have involved daddy."

Privately Neal Prestridge had to agree that involving their father in any of the things that they had done in their younger days would have been a disaster. But now some of those things were coming home to roost.

Judge Prestridge shook his head slowly.

"Eva, you've gone too far this time. I mean, I know that these diaries contain information that could hurt the family, but is it worth getting tied up with all of this killing? I mean, there must be some other way to get them, we have money."

He walked over to her and raised her chin with his right forefinger as he slid one of her bra straps off her creamy white skin.

"Rather than get so upset, my dear, who don't we take a time up for some of our little games? It will help you relax."

Eva snorted as she looked her brother up and down and then slapped his hand away.

"Why don't you go home for a nooner with that proper little wife of yours that father picked out," she retorted.

Neal moved a step closer and smiled what he thought was a seductive smile.

"Well, while she does look great naked, she's not as athletic or as enthusiastic as you are," he said to her in a soothing voice. "You know you have always been my favorite. Besides we have people who can take care of any problems. We don't need to -. "

She shook her head slowly.

"You fool, you have no idea how far this has gone, do you?" she asked curiously. "You really have no idea?"

He stopped his pacing and looked at her in puzzlement.

"What do you mean 'how far this has gone'?" he demanded. "I trust you have acted with the proper decorum."

She looked at him in complete and total disgust.

"You idiot, who do you think has been working to tidy up all of the scandals that you and our brother have created over the years?" she demanded. "Proper decorum, indeed, I'm the one who has removed those who would cause us problems brother. Me – your little sister."

He looked at her in total confusion.

"You! You killed those people?" he asked, his face turning white. "I mean – uh, how could you? Killing is so undignified."

"Neal you are so stupid it amazes me," snapped Eva, "I find it difficult to believe that you can be so uncaring about information that can result in all of us going to prison or perhaps being executed."

"What?" he gasped. "Are you serious?"

"Just this, my dear brother, while the two of you have been strutting before the world, I have been cleaning up your messes, beginning with your college bimbo who was going to tell the world that you were impotent."

He looked at her in total disbelief.

"That woman and her mother, the Daniels women, you killed them?" he demanded. "But someone else was said to have killed them. That man who kidnapped you, our old foreman, I know that father told me that he killed them."

Eva shook her head slowly.

"Neal, first our old foreman, as you call him, did not kidnap me, I went with him willingly to try and escape from the sexual demands that both of my darling brothers required of me as well as my, oh so self righteous, father required."

Neal Prestridge's mouth dropped open as he looked at his sister in total disbelief.

"Our father?" he gasped. "But you never said ---."

"What, you thought that I told you everything that ever happened to me?" she demanded, her anger beginning to grow. "Our father took me to bed when I was ten. Two years before you and our darling brother got the chance to get at me."

"But I thought you enjoyed what we did," sputtered the flustered Judge. "I never had any clue that you didn't want to, uh."

"You mean fuck?" she asked sweetly. "Let's call it what it was, my dear brother. It's not like I had any choice in the matter."

Now it was Eva who started to pace the floor, her anger growing by the moment. The stress of her worry about the missing diary and her potential exposure as a cold blooded killer was pushing her closer and closer to the edge of madness.

"All three of you treated me like a piece of meat, as if I had no feelings of my own. I was just there for your sexual pleasure and our darling mother either didn't know or didn't care what was happening to me. The was too busy running the social life of this backwards burg."

Judge Prestridge watched his sister become more and more enraged as she worked herself up.

"I was just a sex toy to our father, and then he gave me to that old fossil Hughes. Did you know that Hughes had figured out what had happened and blackmailed our father? It would have been fine if he had just wanted money, but no, money was not enough. What he wanted was me. So now I had to service that old fart whenever he wanted me.

"But I showed our father that I was just as smart as you two. I showed him; in fact I showed both our parents that I wasn't just a pretty face. I was smart enough to kill them both and no one suspected."

Prestridge looked at her in growing horror.

"You killed our parents?" he demanded. "But the State Patrol said that it was a car accident. The brakes failed."

"Of course it was me," she snapped. "My darling father had gotten me pregnant. Rather than let me have my child I was sent for an abortion. Remember that month I was supposed to have spent touring Europe, actually I was in a Swiss Hospital having an abortion. I was forced to kill my child, Neal. It was painful and I was emotionally shattered. But when I got home, our darling mother treated me like nothing had happened. It seemed that she blamed me for the little problem, as she called it."

"She knew?" gasped her brother.

"Oh, yes, brother dear," she responded, "she knew. She had to know after I became pregnant. In fact, she told me that it was a relief for her not to have to give into father's crude demands. So she let him have me. That truly showed a loving mother don't you think?"

Prestridge looked at his sister in total confusion.

"So you killed our parents?" he asked again as if to reassure himself of what she had said. "It wasn't just an accident?"

"Then there was our brother," she continued as if she had never hard him. "He seemed content to concentrate all of his attention on me. He expected me to service him every night and then there were the times when he insisted that I join him and his current girlfriend in a three way. I hated it, but he gave me no choice.

"He became very demanding and started treating me like he owned me. So, having killed already to protect your secret, it was nothing for me to kill our brother in that 'hunting accident', you might say that I solved another family problem.

"You hadn't gone on that particular hunting trip. Our brother called me to come up to the cabin for some 'fun' as he called it. I didn't want to go, but he demanded and I gave in. When I got there he starting talking about me being the party favor for some of his friends he had called to come up to the cabin. I finally had enough, so I picked up his shotgun and gave him both barrels. Then I staged the scene so that it looked as if it had been an accident and returned to town."

"Eva, you're sick, you have to turn yourself in," said Prestridge, his sensibilities outraged at what he was hearing. "Let me get help for you. I'll call Dr. McKay and he can get someone who can help you, we'll get you into a good hospital and I'll personally handle your defense."

Eva stopped pacing at looked at her brother, her eyes cold. She seemed to exude anger from every core.

"Help me? Turn myself in?" she asked, in a flat voice devoid of any emotion. "You would handle my defense yourself?"

"Yes, Eva, you know me," he soothed. "I'm your brother; I wouldn't let anything happen to you. I'll pull every string I can; I'll get you the best help available."

Silently, Eva Prestridge walked to her dressing table and resumed her seat. Picking up her hair brush with her right hand she began to slowly brush out her long hair. As she brushed, her left hand was searching in the drawer to her left. Prestridge walked up behind her and gingerly put his hands on her bare shoulders.

"Eva, just let me handle everything," he said firmly. "I'll get you out of this."

"Neal, you have no idea, how happy that makes me feel," she said, rising to turn and put her arms around her brother.

Suddenly Judge Prestridge gasped and pushed his sister away. Slowly he raised his left hand, pulled his coat back and looked down to see that the left side of his shit was stained red. He looked up at his sister, who had backed away until she was pressed back against the front of her dressing table. In her right hand she held a bloody knife; the knife that she had just pushed into his side.

Judge Prestridge looked at his sister in total confusion.

"Eva, why?" he demanded in a pain filled voice.

"You're just like all the others, you bastard. You wanted my body but you don't want me. I am trying to save this family from scandal and you want me to turn myself in. Those people I killed were trash, they threatened to harm the Prestridge name and I needed the name to stay untarnished and I succeeded. Look at me, I'm a Congresswoman, one of the most influential people in the state and you want me to give it all up?"

She gave a short laugh.

"I've seen how you help people," she sneered. "Before you became the judge, when you were the District Attorney in this town you knowingly sent more than one innocent person to prison to raise your conviction record so that you could run for judge on he law and order ticket. Yes, I'm sure that you would help me right into a padded cell some place."

As she watched her brother, his eyes rolled back in his head and he fell to his knees and then onto his side. Cautiously, she edged around her brother and opened the bedroom door.

"Eric!" she yelled down the hall.

In a moment a large bearded man came up the steps and halted at the bedroom door. Not worrying about modesty, Eva Prestridge swung open the door and motioned the bid man into the room.

"Get rid of the body," she ordered. "Make sure that no one will ever find him."

Dismissing the issue from her mind, Eva went back to her dressing table and went back to work changing her appearance. She paid no attention as the bearded man picked up her brother's cooling body. She was now the sole heir to the Prestridge fortune that was still in trust.

It was late in the afternoon before the two finished tracking down seven of the limo style Mercedes. None of them sported the green sticker that the witness had described. After checking the two at the top of the list with tags that matched the first two digits remembered by the witness, Morgan decided to be thorough and check the rest of the list. After checking the last of the first seven, Morgan got back into his patrol car and took a deep breath. He picked up the list of the eight limos and studied it once again.

"Well, we've exhausted the list. None of the seven we have checked have the green sticker on the windshield and each of them have an alibi for that afternoon. So where are we at? We've run out of suspects."

"Well, there is one more on the list, Lieutenant," observed Estrada.

Morgan glanced at the list and then looked at his partner in totally disbelief.

"You think that Congresswoman Prestridge might have been involved in kidnapping Lisa Nettleton? Are you out of your mind?" he demanded. "She is one of the wealthiest women in the country and a powerful Congresswoman. Why possible motive could she have had to kidnap a real estate secretary?"

Estrada shrugged and looked out of the windshield at the street.

"What I think, Lieutenant is that her car is one of the possible vehicles that fit the description that was given by a witness. The first two digits of the tag reported by the witness match the tag issued to her car and that we are not being thorough if we do not check out her car. When I swore to uphold the law, I agreed that there would be no favorites."

He paused for a moment.

"Don't think with your little head, Caleb," said Estrada softly. "I know that she impressed you, in fact she came on to you, but this is a kidnapping investigation and a murder investigation."

Morgan looked at the list once more and than slammed the car in gear.

"If she was hot over me talking to Reynaldo, she'll have a coronary when she finds out that she is a suspect."

Estrada smiled for a moment while considering the thought.

"Weren't you the one that told me that no one is above the law?"

Silently the two drove west toward the Prestridge Estate. The house was huge; it covered almost an acre. In addition to the main house, there were a number of out buildings. As Morgan drove out Interstate 10 toward the Prestridge Estate, he began to remember what his father had told him about the area. Where the Prestridge Estate now sat was once a number of small farms. In fact he remembered hearing stories that the Congresswoman had been quite insistent about having that particular property and had actually paid a premium for the land at a time the property wasn't worth what she paid for it.

Exiting the Interstate, the two drove along the country road until they came to the entrance to the estate. The gates stood open and there didn't seem to be anyone around. Entering, Morgan drove slowly up to the front of the house. Exiting the car, Morgan went to the front door while Estrada began to walk toward the garage area of the house. Morgan first rang the doorbell. After several tries, it was clear that no one was going answer, which meant that either no one was home or that they were not going to answer the door. Finally he gave up and walked out toward his car. Leaning back against the driver's side of the car, he folded his arms and stared off into the distance. He didn't feel good about being here; Congresswoman Prestridge had too much power to antagonize her with an unauthorized search. There were too many possible problems associated with screwing around with this type of people.

Impatiently, he looked around for his partner but didn't see him anywhere. Finally, he pushed away from the car and began to walk toward the end of the house where the garages were located. He was almost to the corner of the house when he heard voices.

"I said lay your weapon on the ground cop!" rasped a deep voice.

"And I said that you are under arrest on suspicion of murder," shot back Estrada.

"I ain't giving my gun to no Spic cop!" snapped the deep voice. "I bet you ain't no cop, in fact, it's my guess that you're probably here to steal something."

Slowly and silently, Morgan drew his own weapon and raised it in front of his face. Side stepping silently, he drew even with the end of the house. Then several things happened at once, there was a very loud gunshot, then a second just as Morgan stepped around the corner and raised his own weapon. Estrada was on the ground clutching his side while a large bearded man in black clothes towered over him, holding a double barrel shotgun.

"Drop it!" snapped Morgan.

Rather than dropping his weapon, the big man raised the barrel toward Morgan. Without hesitation Morgan fired two rounds, both of which hit the dark clad figure in the chest. However, rather than falling, the big man staggered backward and then ran through a side door of the garage. Morgan moved toward Estrada who weakly raised up on one arm.

"Go after him. I'm O.K."

Not needing any other urging Morgan took off running after the shooter. As he exited the side door of the garage, Morgan saw his target running toward one of the out buildings. As if aware he had been spotted, the big man swung around and triggered his weapon at Morgan. Hearing the slug whip past his head, Morgan dropped to one knee and fired, causing the big man to stagger to the side, his left leg sagging.

"Drop your weapon, or I'll drop you where you stand!" yelled Morgan, drawing a bead on the center of the big man's chest.

Rather than complying, the big man staggered through an open door in one of the out buildings. Morgan reached the building braced his back against the wall immediately beside the door. He listened intently, but heard no sound. Ducking low, he dodged through the door and dropped behind a low bookcase. He still heard no sounds. Cautiously, he raised his head to steal a glance around the room. He saw no movement, heard no sounds. The room was dark, the shadows were deep, there were plenty of places that the guy could be hiding. There was a large draped object across the room, certainly big enough to conceal his target.

Rising to his feet, Morgan slow began to make a circuit of the room, his senses alert for the tiniest sound. Foot by tense foot, he moved slowly along each wall, his Glock held at the ready. The darkened room was gloomy but there were only so many places that a man that big could hide in the one room structure. Just as he moved to the final wall, he heard a slight sound behind him. Spinning, he saw a figure just seem to rise up from the floor. It was the shooter, his shotgun held in his hands. Morgan dropped to the floor and fired two shots directly into the shooters' face. The big man froze, a look approaching shock on his swarthy face. He looked down at the holes in his chest for a moment before he fell limply to his knees, then forward onto his face. The shotgun dropped from his limp hands as he fell.

Uncertain if his opponent was actually dead, Morgan slowly came to his feet and left his position. His Glock still trained on the man lying on the floor, Morgan slowly approached the still form. Using his foot, Morgan pushed the shotgun well out of reach should the man on the floor be playing possum. Slowly he knelt beside the perp and placed the first two fingers of his left hand on the stranger's throat, he felt only a faint pulse. In one move he rose to his feet and stepped back away from the man on the floor. A sound at the door caused him to swing around. Estrada leaned against the door frame, one hand pressed tightly against his side. His other hand held his own Glock, cocked and locked.

"Thought you might need some help," said Estrada, somewhat weakly. "But I see you were selfish as usual and didn't save anything for me."

Morgan grinned, "I do wish that you would remember to wear your Kevlar vest, it saves a lot of time patching you up."

Estrada made a face, "the slug caught me at the lower edge of my vest. I'm leaking, but my skin I still fairly in one piece. It just hurts like a son of a bitch."

"Did you call this in?" asked Morgan, his eyes still on the still figure.

Estrada nodded, "We should have both backup and medical help here in short order."

He motioned toward the figure lying on the floor.

"Is he dead or just sleeping?"

Morgan slid his Glock back into his belt holster and walked over to help his partner over to an old chair sitting just inside the door.

"He's not dead, but he is out of it." Morgan paused for a moment until his partner was settled in the chair. "What did you do to set him off?"

Estrada shook his head.

"The garage door was open and I stepped inside to look at the car when this guy came in the side door with that shotgun. I identified myself as a police office, but it didn't seem to matter to him. In fact, it seemed to me that he was more determined than ever to use that gun after knowing I was a police office."

Estrada grinned up at Morgan.

"I checked the car in the garage when I finally got back to my feet. It was a Mercedes, but there was no green sticker."

Morgan shook his head slowly.

"Well there is going to be hell to pay when the Congresswoman get word about this, especially if sleeping beauty over there is someone she likes. You did enter the garage without probable cause so she could say that he was just defending her property from an illegal search."

"Oh, I don't think she'll say much."

"Why not?"

"Judge Prestridge's dead body is in the trunk."

Estrada didn't say much as Morgan began to walk restlessly around the room. Since one wall was a sliding door, and there was a lowered area in the center of the floor similar to what is found at an oil change facility, there was no doubt in his mind that this room was for automotive repair. But more importantly in his mind, he knew that he and Estrada were up shit creek unless they found something to justify being here.

He walked over to a canvas covered thing that what was obviously a car, sitting against the wall. He grabbed the front and lifted the cover, pulling it back until he had uncovered the windshield. He breathed a great sigh of relief when there clear as could be was a large green and blue decal on the passenger side windshield just as the witness had described. He had found the car he suspected had been used to kidnap Lisa Nettleton. There would still be hell to pay, but now he at least had a chance to justify their presence at the Prestridge estate.

He pulled his cell phone and dialed headquarters.

"Captain Jackson, please."

"Jackson," said a voice.

"It's Morgan," said Morgan staring down at the man on the floor.

"And?" prompted Jackson.

"We've got an officer involved shooting and I also believe that we have a lead on the kidnapper of Lisa Nettleton."

"So who was shot?"

"The man shot is an unknown white male. He tried to kill Estrada."

"So what's the big deal? Why are you calling me?"

"The scene is the Prestridge estate," responded Morgan.

"Oh, shit!" groaned Jackson.

"Oh there's more," continued Morgan.

"What could be worse than a dead man at the Prestridge estate?" demanded Jackson.

"We also fond the dead body of Judge Prestridge."

CHAPTER TWENTY-FOUR

BEAUMONT HOSPITAL

Anna Ortega was dozing in her bed; her grandmother was nodding in the chair near the bed. The afternoon was a slow drowsy one; the air was still and slightly warm, even in the hospital room. It was just another day in the hospital for the two of them. However the day would end very differently from what they expected.

Both were disturbed by a soft knock on the door. Before either could react, the door swung open and a nurse came in to the room.

"Time for our medication," chirped the nurse, coming over to the bed and handing a small cup to the young woman lying in the bed. Anna was already drowsy, so she opened her eyes long enough to take the pill she was given and then drifted off to sleep.

Anna jerked awake as if answering a summons. For a moment, she had no idea where she was. She was also alone, but what concerned her was that her grandmother's sweater was lying on the floor. Her grandmother was compulsively neat.

Pulling herself up in the bed, Anna reached for the nurse call, but stopped when someone spoke to her.

"I'm afraid that the nurse really can't help you, my dear," rumbled a deep voice to her left side. "You grandmother has been taken by a very dangerous killer.

She snapped her head to the side to see who spoke to her. She saw a big man, well past middle age, with somewhat long silver hair. He had a full moustache, and wore a western cut suit with a string tie. He was also wearing what looked to be a single action .45 strapped low on his right hip. On the left front of his jacket was the star of a Texas Ranger.

"Who are you?" she demanded. "What are you doing in my room?"

For the moment he looked at her with what she could only describe as a fond smile.

"Just someone who wishes you well," he said as he pushed away from where he leaned against the wall. Carefully, he placed his big white Stetson on his head and headed for the door. Just as he was ready to go out the door, he paused and looked back at her. "Oh, you might tell your young man that he had better get a move on or your grandmother will be in serious danger. Tell him to get over to my place on Montana."

He turned to leave and then paused again.

"Oh, and tell him to be sure to shoot straight. He will only get one chance."

With that final statement, the Ranger walked out the door. Anna watched it close slowly, not really sure what to say. She fumbled beneath the sheets until she found the nurses' call. Almost frantically she pressed the button several times, hoping that the nurse could answer her questions. She was so intent on the closed door that she never noticed someone walk up on her right side. As it was she was startled when someone spoke. She jerked around the see the blonde nurse that no one else seemed to know.

"We're coming down to the wire, sweetie. Your grandmother has been taken by the Viper. Her only hope is your young man, he can save her, but only if he gets a move on."

Anna was so rattled that she really didn't know what to say. Who was this woman who kept coming and going without anyone seeing her or knowing who she was? What was this "young man" she and the old Ranger kept talking about? She had no young man, she had not dated much and none of those she had dated were even in the country, they were all military officers and most were either dead or stationed in Iraq. It made no sense.

"Who are you?" she finally demanded, throwing back the cover and swinging her legs over the side of the bed. "You are dressed like a nurse, but no one seems to know who you are. People seem to pop into and out of this room like an airport waiting room and I want to know what the hell is going on and I want to know now!"

The young woman smiled a small smile.

"There is no doubt that you are his granddaughter. I see much of his fire and determination in you."

Anna was getting madder by the moment, and she was developing a massive headache.

"Who's granddaughter?" she demanded. "Miss whoever you are, what the flying fuck are you talking about? I want to see the doctor, someone has to know who are you and I want to know now! Where is my grandmother? What have you done to her?"

The blonde nurse took a step or two closer to the distraught young woman, though she was careful not to touch Anna. She moved into a position to block Anna from getting to her feet.

"Anna, you must be calm and think this through," soothed the blonde woman. "If you fly off the handle, you will waste too much time and the one that will pay will be your grandmother. You must keep calm and use your tactical abilities."

At that moment, the room door opened and Anna glance over to see her doctor, Dr. Edmund Ramey, come bustling in the door. She turned back to the nurse and was shocked to see she was gone. There was no one else in the room and no other way out of the room. Anna fainted.

The next thing Anna knew, she realized that she was lying across her bed and her doctor was leaning over her gently slapping her face. Two nurses were also bustling around straightening the bed and preparing a syringe.

"Anna, Miss Ortega, can you hear me?" asked her doctor, his face showing medium concern. Seeing that she was now conscious, he took hold of her wrist to check her pulse.

"Wha -?" she finally muttered. "What is happening to me?"

"What do you mean?" he asked, anxiously. "What's happening? Do you hurt?"

Anna pushed herself up in bed shrugging off all of the well meaning hands that tried to help her.

"That nurse, the blonde one that we discussed, she was here," burst out Anna. "She told me that my grandmother was in danger and that I needed to get in touch with someone to help. She was talking to me when you came through the door; I looked at you but when I looked back she was just gone."

"Gone?" asked Ramer in some confusion. "Who was gone?"

"Her - that blonde nurse," snapped Anna, her temper beginning to ignite. It was clear that the doctor didn't believe her. "I think she said her name was Anderson."

"Anderson!" exclaimed one of the nurses standing beside her bed, an older woman with short gray hair. "Not Betty Anderson? That's absolutely impossible."

Anna's head sapped around toward the speaker.

"Yes, that was the name she used," responded Anna, grabbing the woman by the forearm. "Do you know her?"

The woman looked quickly at the doctor and then gently removed Anna's hand that was gripping her arm. She opened her mouth twice, but closed it without saying anything. Finally, at a quick nod from Dr. Ramey, she finally answered.

"Betty was a nurse who worked here when I first was hired almost twenty years ago. I had been working here, oh, maybe two years when she was found dead in the parking lot, the victim of a hit and run. The perpetrator was never discovered. I went to her funeral."

The nurse paused a moment as if searching for the correct words.

"So you see dear, she couldn't possibly have been here. She's been dead almost twenty years."

Anna opened her mouth and then closed it without speaking. Sudden a thought hit her and she looked around wildly.

"Where's my grandmother?" she demanded.

Dr. Ramey looked at the other nurse.

"See if you can find her grandmother."

Wordlessly, the second nurse left the room.

Turning back to Anna, Dr. Ramey searched for the proper words.

"Anna, you've just heard that this nurse, Betty Anderson, died almost two decades ago, so she couldn't possibly have been in your room just a few minutes ago."

Anna fixed the doctor with a glare.

"I assure you I am not crazy, Doctor!" she snapped. "I was talking to that woman when you entered this room. She was as real as you and I."

At that moment, the second nurse came back into the room.

"Dr. Ramey, Ms. Espinosa I s not on the floor and I called down to the cafeteria. She not there either and no one remembered seeing her since last night."

Anna once again tried to throw the cover back and get to her feet, fighting against Dr. Ramey's attempts to keep her in the bed.

"Miss Ortega – Anna -," he soothed. "You need to stay in the bed, I am sure that your grandmother is fine. We will find her."

She finally succeeded in pushing the Doctor away, and pushed to her feet.

"I have to call someone," she said, going over to the bedside table and pawing through the papers on top of the table. Not finding what she wanted, she pulled open the top draw and searched until she held a business card in her hand. Turning she grabbed the phone and, placing the card where she could see it, she dialed the number written on the back of the card. She listened as the phone rang on the other end until someone answered.

"Lieutenant Morgan, this is Anna Ortega," she began. "I need your help. My grandmother is missing."

THE PRESTRIDGE ESTATE

The brass had arrived with an hour of the shooting, but Congresswoman Prestridge cold not be found. Her office staff had no idea where she might be. Wanting to make sure that there were no gaps in their case, the Department applied for a search warrant, but there was no judge in town that would issue one for the Prestridge home. They did manage to get one for the out buildings. Crime scene technicians had swarmed all over the buildings for most of the night.

The biggest pain in the rear was the Chief of Police's insistence of knowing everything that was going on. He called Morgan at least every fifteen minutes. In fact Morgan spent more time talking to the Chief that actually investigating the scene.

It was about five in the morning when Morgan snapped his cell phone shut after talking to the chief of Police for the third time that hour. The fact that there was a police presence at the Prestridge estate had everyone in an uproar. The mayor was going out of tiny little mind trying to contact the Congresswoman. So far, no one had been able to find her.

Morgan turned to speak to Estrada when his foot bumped a partially full oil can causing it to fall into the oil changing recess in the middle of the floor of the out building they were searching.

"Well, crap," breathed Morgan as he pulled his flashlight from his pocket, knelt down and shone the light down into the pit. He expected to see the oil pooling on the floor, instead he was surprised to see that the oil was seeping beneath a hidden door set into the side of the pit. He got to his feet and called for assistance.

"What's up, sir?" asked one of the investigators who had been searching the far end of the building. His coverall was covered with dust and his face was streaked.

Morgan stepped away from the steps that led to the bottom of the recess. He motioned to the darkened recess in the floor.

"There's something strange about this oil changing station," he said. "How about going down there and seeing if there's not a hidden doorway down there. I spilled some oil down there by accident and it seems to be seeping beneath the edge of the concrete rather than pooling."

The investigator slowly went down the steps and knelt at the bottom. He used his own more powerful flashlight to minutely examine the area along the edge of the wall. Slowly he raised his light, studying the wall itself, stopping periodically to given special attention to certain areas. Finally, he lowered his light, placing it on the floor and began to exert pressure against a small area. At first there was no reaction, but then suddenly, as if a catch had been released. A section of the concrete wall, the size of a narrow door rolled back on well oiled hinges to reveal the entrance to a tunnel.

"Got something down here you need to see, Lieutenant," said the investigator as he picked up his light and flashed it into the dark entrance. "This thing appears to go some distance underground."

Drawing his weapon, Morgan quickly descended the steps and pushed past the investigator into the dark tunnel.

"Call Estrada and ask him to join me," Morgan called over his shoulder as he descended three steps to enter the main tunnel. Once inside the tunnel Morgan could see that from where he stood the tunnel ran in three different directions. The tunnel appeared to run beneath the entire estate, Morgan figured that it connected each building that made up the estate. This was getting stranger and stranger. A noise behind him caused Morgan to turn to see Estrada descending the few steps.

"So what have you found, Lieutenant?" asked Estrada as he joined Morgan in the tunnel.

"It looks like this tunnel connects all of the buildings on the estate. So let's see what we can find," said Morgan as he led the way through the tunnel.

For several minutes the two officers walked slowly through the silent tunnel. The only sounds being their footsteps. After a few minutes, Morgan saw the first of the doors. Set into the upper part of the door was a small window that allowed someone in the tunnel to see into the room on the other side without being seen. At the first one, Morgan looked through the window to see that the room contained only a chest of drawers, a bed and a chair; otherwise the room was empty.

The second door also opened into an empty room. However, at the third door, Morgan and Estrada struck gold. Morgan looked through the observation window to see that someone, clearly a woman, was tied to the bed. Quickly he unlocked the door and, after checking that no one was hiding in the room, crossed over to the bed. The woman tied to the bed was naked and her face was covered by her long dark hair. He smoothed it back from her face to see that it was Lisa Nettleton and she had been worked over severely. Her face was bruised and bloody and her naked body showed that she had also been beaten extensively.

"Call for medical attention," snapped Morgan as he gently untied the roped holding the woman to the rickety bed. "Lisa?" he said softly. "Can you hear me?"

The young woman moaned softly and threw her head from side to side.

"No more," she moaned, "please no more."

"Lisa," said Morgan again. "It's me, Caleb Morgan. You are O.K. now. We've found you, you are safe now."

She opened her eyes with a start, looking at Morgan in wonder. "You've found me. I knew that you would come," she whispered.

"Who did this?" asked Morgan softly. "Who did this to you?"

For a moment, she was silent, her eyes closed. Just as he thought she wasn't going to answer, she muttered a name very softly. Morgan was shocked; he sure that he had misunderstood her.

"Are you sure?" he demanded.

Weakly she nodded, "I am sure."

Morgan stood and backed up to allow the EMTs entering the room to get to the injured woman. He was somewhat stunned by what Lisa had told him. He found it hard to believe, but it made sense. He finally made a decision and motioned to Estrada to join him.

"We need to go see the chief," he told his partner. "She just handed me a bombshell."

At that moment, his cell phone rang. He glanced at the caller ID and didn't recognize the number. For a moment he considered not answering, but finally he decided to see who was calling.

"Morgan," he said into the phone.

"Lieutenant," he heard.

"Yes."

"It's Anna Ortega, my grandmother has disappeared," she blurted. "Please help me."

"Calm down," soothed Morgan. "We'll find her. In fact, my partner and I will come by the hospital to see if we can help. In the meantime, ask hospital security to look for her."

He snapped his cell phone shut and dropped it in his pocket. He took a deep breath and rubbed his eyes with the heel of his hands. This was turning into a very bad day, but at least they had been able to rescue Lisa Nettleton. After a moment, he turned to Estrada.

"We need to get over to the hospital to talk to Ana Ortega. It seems that her grandmother has vanished. Something tells me that all of this is connected." He paused for a moment before continuing. "I don't know how or why, but I feel that it is connected."

Estrada shrugged and glanced at the two EMTs and the stretcher that they carried out of the secret chamber.

"When are you going to tell the powers that be what she told you?" he asked with a small smile. "I want advance warning so that I can be at a safe distance before the fallout from this particular bombshell hits."

Estrada followed Morgan back along the tunnel until they reached the exit into the maintenance building. Neither spoke until they were inside the car. Morgan was not looking forward to his next communication with his superiors. What he would say would open an unbelievably large can of worms that would stretch all the way back to Washington DC. Finally, unable to stall any longer, he picked up the microphone to his car radio and started to contact headquarters; however, at the last moment he dropped it back onto the car seat and took out his cell phone.

He keyed in the speed dial for Police headquarters. When the switchboard answered he asked for the office of the Chief. It seemed to take only seconds before he heard the cheerful voice of Della Morgan, the Chief's secretary.

"Chief's Office," she chirped.

"Della, Caleb Morgan," he responded. "I need to talk to the Chief."

Normally, the Chief would either be in a meeting or in conference, but today of all days, he came on the line almost immediately.

"Chief Amos," said a deep voice. "Is that you Morgan?"

"Yes, sir," responded Morgan.

"Something wrong with your radio?" the Chief asked. "Or are you trying to avoid me? I am on the way to take personal charge of the crime scene. It's not every day that a Judge is found dead in the trunk of the car."

"Sir, you need to be sitting down for what I have to say to you," said Morgan as he started the car and pulled out of the Prestridge driveway. "We know who the killer is, but you are not going to believe who it is."

BEAUMONT HOSPITAL

Anna was almost beside herself with worry. The hospital had been searched from top to bottom and her grandmother was gone. She knew that her grandmother would never leave her willingly so that only left kidnapping, though she had no idea who would want to kidnap her grandmother. She was determined to for search for the missing woman, but the doctor was equally determined that she was going to stay in the bed. So it became a battle of wills between the two. The doctor was still struggling to keep her in the bed when Morgan walked into the room.

"Lieutenant Morgan, did you find my grandmother?" she demanded.

Morgan shook his head.

"I'm sorry, Miss Ortega." He responded. "There's no sign of her. My partner is looking at security tape now."

"Well, this man will not let me out of here, so please help me," she begged. "They won't let me out of here and I need to search for my grandmother."

Before Morgan could say a word, the doctor interrupted.

"Lieutenant, she needs to stay here," protested the doctor. "Her injuries are too severe to let her out of the hospital. If she leaves, I can't be responsible."

"I'll sign myself out," offered Anna, struggling to put her blouse on beneath the hospital gown. "I'm leaving if I have to break out of here."

Dr. Ramey finally threw up his hands in disgust.

"Young lady, if you leave here you may die," he yelled at her. "You suffered massive brain trauma. You need to stay here so that we can study your injuries."

"Study my ass," snapped Ortega. "You can say here and study everyone else, but I'm going after my grandmother."

Finally, she tossed the hospital gown to the floor and rose to her feet. Her grandmother had been so sure that her granddaughter was going to get out of the hospital that she had brought a suitcase of Anna's clothes. Anna had dumped the contents of the suitcase on her bed and found that while clothes were some of her older ones, they were still a relatively decent fit. Her grandmother had even included a paid of her cowboy boots which still fit her. So now she stood in the middle of the floor fully dressed and ready to go kick some ass. For just a moment she felt a touch of dizziness but it ended quickly.

Morgan watched the byplay until the doctor left in disgust. Ortega grabbed a hair brush from her bedside table and went into the bathroom. He glanced inside and she was angrily brushing her hair, which was much longer than he had noticed, except for the area where they had shaved her head to open her skull at the tie of her original injury. From the way she was almost tearing at her hair, there was no doubt in his mind that she had a temper.

"Miss Ortega, we will find your grandmother," he offered. "She couldn't have gotten far."

There was no answer, just the sound of the brush pulling through her somewhat tangled hair. He could almost feel the anger and the fear emanating from the bathroom. He hoped that she would get her temper under control soon, as there was nothing more disturbing to him than an angry woman.

However, it was just as well that she was taking some time to get ready, since he was waiting for Estrada's report on what the security cameras had recorded. Besides, once that initial anger and frustration and, to be frank, fear, was out of her system then perhaps she could actually be of some assistance in the search. He looked up as Estrada came in the door.

"What'd you find out?" he asked, getting to his feet.

Estrada glanced at the open door to the bathroom before answering.

"Security footage showed Ms. Espinosa doing out the emergency room exit with someone dressed as a nurse about five thirty this morning. Unfortunately, the camera was not able to show where they went or what kind of car they may have used to leave the parking lot."

Morgan glanced at his watch; it was a little bit after seven thirty in the morning. He had been up over twenty-four hours.

"Could it have been one of the nurses taking her somewhere on a legitimate errand?" asked Morgan wanting to exhaust all possibilities.

Estrada shook his head once again.

"No, we thought about that, but all of the nurses that came on duty at five o'clock are accounted for. Whoever that was leaving with Ms. Espinosa was not a nurse, or at least, not a nurse working here."

At that moment, Anna Ortega came out of the bathroom, her hair looking somewhat better and a pensive look on her face.

"Lieutenant, something strange happened this morning," she began.

He looked at her expectantly.

"Well," she paused. "It sounds strange now, but at the time, it seemed very real."

"So what happened?" he asked, dropping back into the chair.

Estrada leaned against the wall beside the door and watched the young woman as she began to pace the room.

"I woke up early this morning to find a strange man in my room. He was a big man and he was dressed western style, with a white Stetson. He had somewhat long scraggly hair and a bushy white moustache. He was also wearing what looked to be a single action .45 strapped low on his right hip. On the left front of his jacket was the star of a Texas Ranger."

"A Texas Ranger badge?" asked Morgan in surprise. "Are you sure?"

She nodded emphatically.

"Did he give you his name?" asked Estrada, straightening up from his position by the door.

Anna shook her head.

"I asked him his name and he just smiled and said he was just someone who wished me well."

"Did he say anything else?" asked Morgan. The hair on his arms was starting to stand up. A cold chill ran up his spine.

Anna hesitated for a second and actually seemed to blush before looking directly at Morgan.

"Well, he did say something else. As he was going out the door, he said you might tell your young man that he had better get a move on or my grandmother would be in serious danger. He said to tell him to get over to his place on Montana. He also said to tell him to be sure to shoot straight. He would only get one chance."

"His place on Montana," murmured Morgan. He paused and glanced at Estrada. "Is it possible?"

Estrada gave his usually shrug and pursed his lips.

"My old grandmother would certainly believe it. She thought he could do anything."

"He who?" demanded Anna Ortega.

Morgan looked at her and grinned.

"You just described Ranger Ezra Hughes," said Morgan, leaning back and staring at the ceiling. "Yes sir, you described the old Ranger himself."

CHAPTER TWENTY-FIVE

THE HUGHES MANSION

Elena Espinosa was totally disoriented. She also discovered that her wrists were tied and she was blindfolded. She struggled for a moment, but found that she could not get loose. She had been kidnapped from the hospital by someone pretending to be one her daughter's nurses. With a gun in her back, she had been taken out of the hospital through the Emergency Room and stuffed into the trunk of a car sitting in the parking lot.

First she had been driven around for a time until she thought she would go out of her mind. Finally she felt the car pull into what was obviously a driveway and brake to a stop. She heard the engine shut off and the door open. Then she heard the door shut and the sound of footsteps approaching the trunk. Then the trunk was popped and she was looking at up the dawn's early light. Then her vision was blocked by the face of her kidnapper, eyes covered with dark sunglasses and a pert little nurse's cap. Two arms came down and grabbed her upper arms.

"Upsay daisy, my dear," said her kidnapper cheerfully. "You can come willingly or I will drag you."

As best she could Elena tried to get her legs underneath herself to push out of the trunk, but she wound up almost falling at her kidnapper's feet. The blonde woman pulled her to her feet and pushed her toward the nearby house.

"Keep walking deary," directed her captor, sticking the barrel of a gun in her back again. "We have a lot of work to do before we are finished."

Espinosa didn't have any idea where she, the area around the car was dark. She could only see the outline of a huge house, which appeared to be completely dark as if no one was home. Her captor was moving as if she was sure of not being seen. There was no doubt that she knew the layout of the place in the dark because she directed Elena to an almost hidden side door partially sheltered by a large hedge.

Her captor reached around her and inserted a key into the dead bolt lock. In seconds they were inside the dark house. Though it dawn was breaking outside, the inside of the house was still dark since all of the windows were covered by heavy drapes. Elena expected a light to be turned on, but instead her captor pushed along a darkened hallway until they came to a set of double doors. The phony nurse pushed one of the doors to the side and shoved Elena through the opening.

"Don't move," ordered her captor in a somewhat flat voice.

Elena froze, afraid to move since the room was just dark enough that she was unable to see anything more than shapes. Suddenly the room was flooded with light as her captor flipped on a light. The room was almost bare; there was a desk, a chair and a table lamp sitting on the desk.

Elena was pushed into the chair and with a click loop of duct tape she was secured to the chair. Once that was done, the nurse walked over to the desk and removed her nurse's cap, which she dropped on the desk top. The cap was followed by the sunglasses. Then the woman turned and sat one shapely hip on the desk top.

"Now, we are going to have a nice talk you are going to tell me what I want to know," said the phony nurse in a flat voice.

MORGAN'S POLICE UNIT

Morgan was driving while Estrada was on the radio calling for backup. In the backseat was Anna Ortega, fretting over her missing grandmother.

"But are you sure?" she demanded of Morgan for the fifth time since they had left the hospital.

Patiently, Morgan explained it again.

"You said the Ranger said his place on Montana, correct?"

"Uh, yes, that's what he said," responded Anna. "I'm sure, he said Montana."

"Hughes' home is a big place in the historic part of Montana. If that was Hughes then he was telling us that your grandmother is at his house."

Anna was silent for a moment before she voiced her real concern.

"But you said that this Hughes guy is dead," she ventured.

"That's right," said Morgan, his eyes meeting those of Anna in the rearview mirror. "He died a short time ago of a broken neck, in his house."

"But this is crazy," she burst out, sitting forward on the seat so that she was only inches from the back of Morgan's head. "How can a dead man come to my hospital room? How can he know what's going to happen? I mean, none of this makes any sense!"

Morgan took a deep breath.

"I don't know, Miss Ortega," be finally said. "There is a lot in this world that we don't understand. If anyone could come back form the dead, it would be Ranger Hughes. He was a determined man who spent a lifetime enforcing the law. If he covered up a crime, and it sounds like he may have from what he said in his will, then I doubt that his spirit would rest easy. Maybe he came back to make things right."

At that moment Morgan pulled up to the curb outside the Morgan Mansion. It looked especially imposing in the early light of morning. From the car, they could see that the windows were covered and there appeared to be no activity whatsoever.

"How long till backup gets here?" Morgan asked Estrada, never taking his eyes off of the front of the house.

"At least ten to fifteen minutes," responded Estrada, leaning back in his seat. "Most of the available units are out near the Prestridge Estate. A judge finally issued a warrant to search the entire estate. They flushed a couple of the Congresswoman's aides hiding in the main house who tried to shoot it out. Now the Chief has assigned every available man to look for the Congresswoman. He is sure that one or more of her aides has kidnapped her."

"Jesus," moaned Morgan, "Congressional aides shooting it out with police. How much weirder can things get?

'This is El Paso," offered Estrada.

"What if they are already inside," asked Anna from the backseat. Morgan glanced at her. He sympathized with her concerns and noticed how she was picking at the material along the top of the seat. "My grandmother could already be inside that house being tortured by that madman."

Morgan thought about it long and hard before he opened his door and exited the car. He turned to speak to Estrada only to find that Anna Ortega was standing close behind him, having exited the back seat as soon as he had opened his door.

"Miss Ortega, having you in the car is one thing," he began, "but I can't take you into that house. You could be killed, if they are inside."

"Oh, no, Lieutenant," she responded heatedly, "I will not wait here. That is my grandmother who may be inside this house. If I can fly helicopters in a war zone, then I can certainly go into a house where my grandmother may be held captive."

Tiring of the argument, she walked around Morgan and started up the driveway. He caught up to her in a few steps and grabbed her arm.

"Miss Ortega, I can't let you go into that house –," he began.

"Look," she pointed, pulling away from him. "There's a car parked by the garage. Could that be the kidnapper's car?"

Without waiting for a response, she ran lightly up the driveway.

"Damn it!" muttered Morgan, looking over at Estrada who just grinned at him. Morgan hesitated a moment, but knew that he had no choice but to follow her. When he reached her, Anna was looking through the window into the empty car. She moved around the car to pop the trunk, dreading what she might find. To her relief, the trunk was empty.

Morgan moved to the front of the car and laid his hand on the hood, it was warm, very warm. The car had arrived there only a short time before. Walking around to the rear he checked out the license number and pulled his radio out.

"Hey, Estrada," he said softly into the radio.

"Go," came back his partner.

"Check out a tag, DMZ498," responded Morgan.

He turned to check on Anna Ortega and found she was gone.

"Shit!"

Hearing a sound, he turned and finally saw her at the back door. Before he could get to her, she had turned the knob and pushed the door open.

"It's open," she whispered to him as he joined her.

Left with no choice, Morgan pulled his sidearm and put a hand on her arm.

"Wait here," he said as forcefully as he could.

Leaving her at the door, Morgan slid quietly into the dimly lit house, moving to his left. Just enough light was entering through the heavy curtains to let him be able to make out his surroundings. He had entered in what looked like a small ante-room. To the left, which would be toward the rear of the house was what looked like a kitchen. Morgan slowly glanced into the kitchen to see that it was empty, the counters were bare.

Turning he retraced his steps, passing by the doorway, reassured when he saw Anna still just outside. She was actually following his instructions, he was pleasantly surprised. Raising his free hand to place a finger over his lips to caution her to be silent, Morgan began to move cautiously and slowly along the hall leading to the front of the house.

Partway along the hallway, there was a set of double doors. One side of the double doors was slid open; however, what was the most interesting thing was that a faint light emanated from the doorway. He heard no sounds but there was no doubt that there was a light coming from that particular room.

Slowly he made his way along the hallway, pausing every few steps to listen intently for any sounds. So far he could hear nothing from the room, but he knew that didn't mean the room was empty. He paused just outside the entrance to the room and listened once again, still he heard nothing. Finally, he moved through the doorway, his Glock held out in front of him.

From his position in the hallway, he could see that the room as sparsely furnished. A huge desk took up most of the room that he could see. On the wall to his left, over a large empty fireplace was a large portrait of Ranger Hughes sitting comfortably behind the same desk that filled most of that end of the room. Lying on top of the desk in the picture was his famous ivory handed .45 single action Colt. From his position, Morgan could neither see nor hear anything.

As he slowly slid into the room the first thing he saw was Elena Espinosa lying on the floor in the shadow of the desk. Instinctively, he moved forward, almost lowering his gun. Concentrating on the prostrate woman, he almost failed to notice the movement to his right. Realizing what it meant, he swung to his right, but was too late. He heard the discharge of a weapon and felt a sledgehammer blow to his chest. He was knocked backward across the room; his weapon flew from his hand.

Morgan was out for a few moments, and when he awoke his entire world was red tinted with pain. He was flat on his back, struggling to draw a breath. He tried to get to his feet, but was unable to really move. All he could do was raise his head to see Anna Ortega and a woman in a nurse's uniform. Fighting was the operative word for those two. Both appeared to be expert at martial arts. The punches and kicks that the two threw at each other would have probably killed anyone else. As it was, the two were literally flying around the room, ducking and dodging each others' blows. Statistically, unfortunately, one of them would be bound to make a mistake and take a hit. It was just unfortunate that the first one to make a mistake was Anna, who stumbled over her grandmother's outstretched legs.

In spite of herself, Anna glanced down for a split second, which was all it took for her opponent to snap a kick to her head than laid her out on the floor. Her opponent pulled an automatic pistol from a pocket and came to stand over the groggy Anna. At that moment, Morgan felt something heavy impact on his chest. He looked down to clearly see Hughes' .45 lying on his chest. Slowly, he raised his right hand to grip the worn grips of the antique weapon.

Slowly, too slowly, he thumbed back the hammer and raised the heavy weapon to point it at the phony nurse.

"Drop your weapon or I'll shoot," he croaked.

The nurse spun, bringing her weapon to bear on Morgan. At that moment, he heard a deep voice.

"Drop the weapon, bitch!" thundered the new voice.

For a moment, the nurse hesitated, her weapon wavering between Morgan and a spot over his head. From his position on the floor, Morgan could see that her eyes widened almost in shock.

"You!" gasped the phony nurse. "That can't be! You're dead!"

She raised her weapon to fire at the newcomer and Morgan took that moment to drop the hammer on the nurse. The old single action sounded like a cannon going off in the room and heavy .45 round impacted almost center of the phony nurse's chest. Her body flew across the room to slam into the desk with a nerve shattering crack. She dropped to the floor like a marionette with its strings cut.

At that moment Estrada came crashing through the back door.

"Morgan!" he yelled.

"In here," croaked Morgan, his attempt to talk ending in a coughing jag.

His partner came through the door, his gun drawn, quickly taking in the scene. He holstered his weapon and dropped to one knee beside Morgan. From outside came the sound of sirens, cars screeching to a halt and car doors slamming shutting.

"Are you alright?" Estrada asked as he took the heavy .45 from his partner's hand and laid it on the floor beside him. He opened Morgan's jack and unbuttoned his shirt to reveal the Kevlar vest that covered his chest. There gleaming in the weak light was a bullet. It had hit him almost dead center. Had he not been wearing the vest, the bullet would almost certainly have killed him.

"Who was the other man who was here?" he asked weakly. "Was he hit?"

Estrada glanced around for a moment, but saw no one.

"Are you sure that you are not seriously injured?" he asked. "There was no one else here, my friend. Certainly there was no other man."

At that moment, the sounds of a number of footsteps were heard coming in the back door.

"Help me up," he asked of his partner, reaching over to take a firm grip on the old .45.

With Estrada holding tightly to his arm in support, Morgan crossed the room to where Anna Ortega was working to untie her grandmother. From the look of Elena Espinosa, she had been ill used in the time she had been held hostage. Anna looked up at Morgan.

"She's still breathing," she told him. "But she needs a doctor."

Estrada pulled Morgan to the side to allow two EMTs to push past. Anna crawled slowly to the side, waving away treatment for herself.

"Help my grandmother," she begged. "Don't worry about me."

Morgan moved slowly and painfully over to where the phone nurse lay crumpled on her side. With Estrada's help, he got down on one knee beside the still figure. Reaching out one hand he rolled her over onto her back. Her face was covered with her long blonde hair. Morgan pushed her hair to the side and uncovered her face. He looked at her still face for a moment and then took a handful of the long hair and pulled. The blonde wig held for a moment before coming away in his hand. Now with her disguise gone, it was clear, the phony nurse had been Congresswoman Prestridge.

Morgan pulled himself into a seated position beside the body. None of this made any sense to him. Why would an extremely wealthy woman like the Congresswoman commit murder and kidnapping? What could she possibly hope to gain? At that moment, he noticed that a potion of the desk top was askew. He pulled himself to his knees and closely examined the area of the desktop that had attracted his attention. He saw that it would open like the top of a small drawer. Inside the recess was another of the diaries written by Ranger Captain Hughes.

He dropped back into a sitting position against the front of the desk and pulled the book into his lap. He opened the cover and turned to the first page. It was as if a voice read the words aloud that he read.

"As I reach my eightieth year, I find that there is much that I regret. Much of my reputation that I have enjoyed these last years since leaving the Texas Rangers came from having covered up a crime. I also misused my position to gain a future that I thought would be truly wonderful. Instead it turned to dust in my mouth. Therein lays the tale."

As the EMTs readied Elena Espinosa and Ana Ortega for transport to the hospital, Morgan sat reading a dead man's diary. As was his personality, Hughes pulled no punches, he told the story, letting the chips fall where they may. He did a wrong, but it was a sin of omission, not commission. Leaving this diary and the tale that it told was his way to trying to make it better. Perhaps he saw it was a way for him to make up for the harm that his silence had caused.

Finally, it was Morgan's turn to be helped from the room. Estrada helped him to his feet and started to help him to the door. Then Morgan paused, as if he had forgotten something. He turned to look at the portrait of the old Ranger hanging over the fireplace. He noticed that now the desk top in the portrait was empty, where before there had been the twin to the gun Morgan now gripped in his hand. Suddenly he understood; he knew who else had been in the room with them. He knew who had distracted the crazed Congresswoman at just the right moment.

Pushing away from Estrada, Morgan walked slowly over to the desk and carefully laid the historic old .45 on the smooth wood. He stood there a moment before turning to leave. It was as he left the room that he heard or thought he heard the voice.

"You take care of her, boy. You take very good care of her."

Morgan turned back for a second to see that the old Colt he had laid on the desk was gone. He looked up the portrait to see it was back where it had started, lying on the desk in the portrait. The old man looked at stern as ever, but now he seemed to have a twinkle in his eye. It was as if he knew a joke and the rest of the world id not.

Morgan nodded his thanks to the old man in the portrait and it seemed to him as if he old man nodded back. Then Morgan was out of the room being helped to the door. No longer was there a secret in the dead man's diary. Now the truth would be known.

www.ingramcontent.com/pod-product-compliance
Lightning Source LLC
Chambersburg PA
CBHW051301210726
48287CB00002B/612